FRONTIER
THUNDER
AT DAWN

FRONTIER
THUNDER
AT DAWN

S. K. SALZER

PINNACLE BOOKS
Kensington Publishing Corp.
www.kensingtonbooks.com

PINNACLE BOOKS are published by

Kensington Publishing Corp.
119 West 40th Street
New York, NY 10018

All Kensington titles, imprints, and distributed lines are available at special quantity discounts for bulk purchases for sales promotions, premi-
ums, fund-raising, educational, or institutional use. Special book
excerpts or customized printings can also be created to fit specific
needs. For details, write or phone the office of the Kensington sales
manager: Kensington Publishing Corp., 119 West 40th Street, New York,
NY 10018, attn: Sales Department; phone 1-800-221-2647.

PINNACLE BOOKS and the Pinnacle logo are Reg. U.S. Pat. & TM
Off.

ISBN-13: 978-0-7860-3627-1
ISBN-10: 0-7860-3627-3

First printing: June 2015

10 9 8 7 6 5 4 3 2

Printed in the United States of America

First electronic edition: June 2015

ISBN-13: 978-0-7860-3628-8
ISBN-10: 0-7860-3628-1

For the four beauties:
John France, Hallie France, Max France, and Lily Salzer.
You guys mean the world to me, and always will.

Chapter One

Fort Phil Kearny, Dakota Territory
December 21, 1866

The laudanum began to take effect. He turned, trying to find comfort, and was just drifting toward a fevered sleep when a shadow darkened the doorway.

"Who is it?" he said. "Dr. Horton, is that you?" Getting no answer, he reached for the eyeglasses on the bedside table. The shadow sharpened to the silhouette of a man, outlined against the flickering red light from the heating stove in the room behind him. "Sam," he said, "did you forget something?"

The man in the door came forward. "Lieutenant Mark Reynolds?"

"Yes, of course. What is this?"

"Do you know me?"

"I can't see you," Reynolds said, impatiently motioning to the coal lamp smoking in its glass chimney on the table. "Come closer, I can't see your face."

The visitor stepped into the dim circle of light.

He was of middling height, with short hair and sunburned skin. He wore civilian clothing, the clothes of a range rider.

"You're Gregory, the scout," Reynolds said. "We met at Fort Sedgwick. What's this about?"

Jack Gregory had been hunting Mark Reynolds for three years, but now that the end had come, it was not as he pictured. The wasted, one-armed wretch on the bed was just a shadow of the proud officer Gregory's sister pointed out to him that day in Kansas City as the murderer of their father. That man rode by in a fine carriage, high and handsome as the pharaoh of Egypt. This fellow was so low he was mostly dead already. Gregory knew this from the room's queer rooty smell, an aroma he knew only too well. Nonetheless, he would do what he came for. He raised his revolver and leveled it at Reynolds's left eye.

"I am Jack Gregory, of Cass County, Missouri," he said, speaking words he had rehearsed many times. "On the ninth of September, eighteen sixty-three, you killed my father. You and the Kansas trash you rode with burned John Jordan Gregory alive, with his wife and daughters looking on. After that, you burned our home to cinders, putting my mother and sisters out in the hedges. Now, in my family's name, I have come to put you through. If you have anything to say, Reynolds, now is the time. Hell is about to gain a new devil."

Reynold's eyes glittered in the weak light. "I don't know what you're talking about, Gregory. Like I said, you're the scout I met at Sedgwick.

Other than that, I don't know you, or your pa, from Adam's left-off ox."

In Gregory's imagining of this moment, Reynolds quaked in his boots when confronted with his gun and pleaded for his life in a womanish voice high as a bat squeak. But Reynolds did not tremble. He was cool as an April morning.

"You are a lying son of a bitch," Gregory said, "but I will tell you, like you don't know. You and your Jayhawker assassins came to our farm, looking for the guerilla Quantrill. You thought my pa knew where he and his boys were hiding, so you hung him by the neck from the apple tree beside our kitchen, cut him down and hung him again, and when still Pa wouldn't give you what you wanted, you threw him in the barn, barred the door, and put the torch to it. You and your goddamn Jayhawkers burned or stole everything us Gregorys owned—our house, animals, crop, the whole shebang. And now you will die for it."

Reynolds closed his eyes and wrinkled his brow. "Cass County, you say? I do recall it now, September of sixty-three, that would've been right after the Lawrence business. Feelings were high then, very high. My orders were to find William Quantrill and his Missouri ruffians and bring them to justice for the murder of two hundred men and boys. Yes, we thought the old man—your father, apparently—knew Quantrill's whereabouts, maybe he didn't. Who knows? John Jordan Gregory? To tell you the truth, I don't believe I ever knew his name, or if

I did, I didn't remember. Why would I? There was nothing personal in it."

"Nothing personal in it?" At first Gregory thought Reynolds was mocking him, then he realized he was simply stating a truth, the way another man might say, "I believe we'll have snow tonight."

Reynolds shrugged his bony shoulders, wincing with the pain even that simple movement caused him. He was meaty as a skeleton and shirtless under a thin army blanket, even though the dark room was bitterly cold. If he were another man, Gregory would have felt pity.

"It was war, Gregory," Reynolds said. "I should think someone like you would understand that. Sometimes a man must distance himself from his actions. Sometimes, in the fulfillment of his duty, a man must do things he would otherwise find distasteful. Surely, you have found yourself in this position."

Gregory felt hatred, black and bilious, rise inside him. "Don't talk to me about duty. We were a Union family, goddamn you. We stood proudly for abolition, from well before the war started, despite the trouble it brought us from our slaver neighbors. On the day you came, I was soldiering in Mr. Lincoln's army, and see how the Federal government rewarded our allegiance! You are the reason I deserted to throw in with Quantrill in the Sni Hills. You are the reason I rode under the black flag. I would not have done it otherwise."

Reynolds sighed. "Oh, well, I suppose we had bad information from your neighbors. That happened often." He smiled. "You Missouri pukes were always eager to sell each other out."

Gregory stepped closer to the bed. Reynolds's wife, Rose, might return to the cabin at any moment. The time had come, but still, despite Reynolds's lack of remorse, Gregory sensed killing him may not bring full satisfaction. Though no stranger to death, he had never ended a man who was not actively trying to do the same to him, or one who appeared so helpless. His gun hand wavered.

"Having second thoughts?" Reynolds said, still smiling. "I would if I were you. After all, the Indians and U.S. Army medicine have already finished me." He raised his stained, bandaged stump. "This will put me in the grave soon enough, and if you don't believe me, just ask Sam Horton—he'll tell you. Or take a deep breath, that says it all. Why risk your immortal soul when I'll be dead in forty-eight hours anyway?"

"Saint Peter won't turn me away on your account, Reynolds."

Reynolds smiled. "But are you sure of that?" His remaining arm moved under the blanket and, quick as a rattlesnake, Gregory found a navy revolver pointed at his chest. Had the man been in full health, Gregory would have perished there and then, but Reynolds was unequal to the pistol's weight. His hand shook and he was too weak to pull the trigger. Without hesitation, Gregory sent a bullet into Reynolds's forehead. The officer died with his eyes open, an expression of surprise on his face, as if a trusted friend had betrayed him.

Gregory crossed the room in two long strides,

raised the window and climbed out into the icy darkness. Already he heard shouts and the sound of men running toward Reynolds's cabin. Gregory made for the sally gate behind officers' row, hoping to find it unguarded. He did not want to kill an innocent man, but he would if he had to. This night was ordained to be Lieutenant Mark Reynolds's last on earth. It would not be Jack Gregory's.

Chapter Two

The alley behind officers' row was dimly lit by lamplight from the cabin windows. Gregory dropped to the ground, concealing himself in the shadows at the base of a cabin. There was a guard at the sally wicket but, as Gregory hoped and expected on this night when the world had been turned upside down, the young soldier was frightened and distracted. After a few minutes of indecision, he fled his post to join the rush to Reynolds's quarters, passing within inches of Gregory's hiding place.

Fear was a living presence at Fort Phil Kearny that arctic night. Just hours before, hundreds of Sioux and Cheyenne warriors, led by the Lakota chief Red Cloud and the warrior Crazy Horse, had killed and butchered Captain William Judd Fetterman and each of the eighty men who rode with him. Earlier that day, Gregory had been a member of the recovery party sent out to bring back the soldiers' remains, and never in his long experience of war had he seen such a display of hatred. The faces of Fetterman's men were unrecognizable, smashed by heavy war clubs to a meaty, half-jelled mix of brains, bone, and hair. The ground was slippery with frozen entrails. In some cases, guts encircled the necks of the dead like the devil's twine. As Gregory and the others went about their grim task, eyeballs watched them from atop a rock where they had been positioned beside a severed nose. Some of the bodies had been sliced open from thorax to pubis, the empty cavities stuffed with dry grass and set aflame. The soldiers stacked the bodies of their friends and comrades head to heels, like cordwood, in open wagons and carried them back to the post.

Now, hours later, the remaining soldiers along with the women and children waited in terror, expecting the Indians to come for them too. Even as he hid in the darkness of officers' row, Gregory knew Sioux and Cheyenne warriors might well be gathering on the far side of Lodge Trail Ridge, preparing for first light when they would ride down on the walled soldier town to finish off the last of the hated Long Knives.

Gregory slid the bar from its bracket, pushed open the gate, and slipped out, closing the gate behind him. He flattened himself against the stockade wall, knowing the sentries on the banquette above couldn't see him. He'd wait there until the guard changed, then make his way to the dry ravine by the main gate where he would find a cluster of abandoned dugouts, once homes to the civilian employees of the post quartermaster. He wouldn't have to wait long. Because of the desperate cold, commanding officer Colonel Henry Beebe Carrington had ordered the sentries be changed every twenty minutes. Still, the wait would hurt. It was the coldest, meanest night Jack Gregory had ever known, and the iron wind had teeth. His hands felt wooden inside his wolf-hide mittens and the bones of his legs fragile and snappable as dry twigs. Even so, he knew his leathers were warmer than the clothes the soldiers wore. He pitied them. When would the Quartermaster's Department stop fussing over frog buttons and black silk braid and give its fighting men something better than the poor, worsted wool that the wind penetrated like water through cheesecloth? Yes, it was bad luck to make a run on a night like this, but then luck had never been kind to Jack Gregory. At least he knew better than to expect it.

Finally the replacements arrived. He heard their voices above him on the banquette.

"So what was that shot?" a man said. "We heard a shot."

"Someone killed Lieutenant Reynolds," said another. "At first they thought he did himself in, there was a gun in his hand, but it hadn't been fired. So someone else did it. Shot him in his bed and went out the window."

"The hell. Maybe his wife? Wouldn't nobody blame her."

Gregory heard laughter as he crept on his stomach toward the steep ravine that lay between the main gate and Big Piney Creek. He was undiscovered. He climbed into one of the cave-like holes dug into the ravine's sides. These had been deserted in late summer when all civilians fled Fort Phil Kearny for the safety of Fort Reno some sixty miles to the south. Gregory used to pity the cave dwellers, not understanding how a man could live in a hole in the ground like an animal. Now he thanked God for those hardy souls and their dens. He would lay low for an hour or so, warm up and collect himself before pressing on to the ridge where his fortune was buried. Then, a rich man, he would turn his back on this godforsaken country and never look back.

He lay still, hardly breathing, listening. The cave was surprisingly warm. It felt good to be out of the wind. He closed his eyes and imagined himself in a tub of hot, steaming water, so deep he could immerse himself all the way to his chin. He felt gooseflesh raise on his skin as the heat penetrated. Gradually, his breathing slowed and the knotted muscles of his back begin to soften and relax. This was a device, a trick, he had learned, the ability to lie to his brain so convincingly his body believed it. It was a talent he discovered at an early age, the power to transport himself beyond an unpleasant circumstance, and it had comforted him often during a lonely childhood when his affliction had been a torment. Because of the cleft in his palate and upper lip, his speech was peculiar and a source of amusement. Other children, the few he encountered on trips to nearby Harrisonville, laughed when the milk he tried to drink sometimes ran from his nose and refused to be his friends. He was solitary and ashamed until he found his trick. He told himself he could talk just as well as anyone else and gradually this became true, though because of the attention it required, his manner of speaking was slower and more formal than most. He told himself he was handsome, that he could eat and drink in public with the best of them, and that one day girls would be pleased to dance with him. These imaginings also came to pass, though they might not have if not for the ministrations of an itinerant surgeon, who saw six-year-old Jack on the street in Harrisonville and told his mother he would correct the fissure in return for a home-cooked meal of fried chicken, mashed potatoes, and apple pie with cream. His mother agreed. On the day of the operation, Jack was alarmed when he detected the smell of whiskey on the surgeon's breath, but despite this he did a fine job. Jack healed quickly and without complications, and he was deeply grateful to the physician though he never saw him again after that day. By the time he was old enough to grow a mustache, the scar was hardly visible.

What was that? He tensed. Then it came again, a noise, a scratching, the sound of something stirring. Gregory was not alone in his hole. He felt his skin tighten as he crawled toward the rear. He squinted into the darkness, but saw nothing other than shadows in the silvery moonlight filtering from the cave's entrance.

"Show yourself!" Gregory said, drawing his pistol. There was no response. He crept deeper, feeling cloth beneath his hands. He struck a match and saw the floor was covered in feed sacks, pegged down at the corners. In the rear of the cave he saw a pile of dirty blankets, heaped next to a cracker box that must have served the former resident as a table. As the match burned down, he saw the blankets move.

Something was in there, something small. Gregory kneeled by the pile, struck a second match and threw the stinking blankets aside. He found a cluster of pups, all cold and still but for one who raised its face to the match. Gregory returned his pistol to his belt and took up the pup with his gun hand. The animal was shaking and made a small mewling sound.

Gregory carried the pup back to the mouth of the cave to examine in the moonlight. It was a male, black with white spots and floppy ears. One of the ears was bloody, as if it had been nibbled on. Maybe a rat, Gregory thought, or one of his dying siblings, trying to stave off starvation. He poured a small amount of water from his canteen into his cupped hand and held it under the pup's nose. He went greedily to work with his pink tongue. Gregory opened his kit, broke off a bit of hard cracker, and offered this to the pup also, but he didn't have the teeth for it, so Gregory chewed the cracker for him and offered it again. This time he had no trouble getting it down. After giving him another bit of chewed cracker, Gregory tucked the pup into his coat, leaving only his face exposed, and they sat together in the cold moonlight. The little animal curled in close, taking Gregory's warmth.

They had a hard night ahead. Somehow, Gregory had to get to the old Indian fort on top of the mountain without being spotted by the Indians or the soldiers. Either way, discovery meant death. And he'd have to do it on foot. His horse, General Jo Shelby, was in the stables back at Phil Kearny. It pained Gregory to leave him, but he had no choice.

There was no way he could have made an escape on the back of the Appaloosa stallion, one of only two strong and healthy animals left at the post. The rest, those not killed along with Fetterman and his men, had been reduced to bone racks by overwork and starvation. General Jo may prove a lifesaving gift for the survivors, though Gregory doubted Carrington would thank him for it. One thing was certain: someone would have to ride for help. That was their only hope for survival. The rider, whoever he was, would have to go all the way to Horseshoe Station, nearly 200 miles distant, or maybe even Fort Laramie, a journey of nearly 240 miles. General Jo and the colonel's thoroughbred were the only horses that stood even a remote chance of making it. It pained Gregory to see how the animals suffered. Horses and mules were eating bark off the stable walls, eating even their harness and tack. It was Carrington's fault. He was not up to the job of commanding officer and everyone was paying for his incompetence, even the animals. Gregory was soft on four-leggeds. Most animals would treat you right if you did the same for them. They were better than people in many ways and this was one.

He looked down at the pup curled up inside his coat. That ear looked bad. It must pain him something terrible. If he left the brave, uncomplaining pup, the rats or foxes would finish him off. He gave him another round of cracker and water. No, Gregory would not leave the pup. He would feel bad about himself if he did.

He did not feel bad about shooting Mark Reynolds,

though it bothered him some that he had made Rose a widow. This country was hard on a woman without a man, even if that man was a snake, like Reynolds. But it comforted Gregory to know Rose wouldn't be alone for long, not with eyes that shade of blue. She had a nice shape too, if a bit on the skinny side. Gregory was pretty sure she and the doctor, Daniel Dixon, would hook up and that was all right. He, Jack Gregory, would like to have a woman like Rose himself, but if that couldn't be, he had no complaint with the doctor. If any man was good enough for Rose, it was Dixon.

The time had come to leave the cave. The moon was behind the clouds and it was starting to snow. Gregory took the pup out of his coat and set him down to pee, which he promptly did. After checking the sky, he buttoned the pup back up in his coat, leaving a space undone for his head.

"How can something little as you stink so bad?" he said, wrinkling his nose. Together, they crept out of the cave and into the bitter night.

Chapter Three

Sounds carried well in the cold, thin air, especially at night, and Gregory was still close enough to Phil Kearny to hear voices. It seemed two riders would try for Horseshoe Station. Gregory hoped they weren't going to double up on General Jo. Strong as he was, he could not bear that.

"The colonel's going to let them take his horse, Dandy," a man said. "That foreigner, Phillips, will ride him and Dr. Dixon will ride the Appaloosa."

Gregory was surprised for two reasons. First, Carrington's thoroughbred wasn't made for work like that. He probably wouldn't survive the trip. Second, he didn't expect Dixon to be a rider. He wasn't surprised that he would volunteer, but that Carrington would allow it. A skilled physician was worth his weight in gold to a frontier regiment.

Gregory continued on hands and knees, staying low in the ravine, heading south toward Little Piney Creek. He would follow the frozen stream to the old Indian trail and follow that up the mountain to the ruin. He'd been there once before, about five months earlier, when he and Ignacio buried the money they'd taken from the paymaster. Thirty thousand dollars in greenbacks was a fortune, even after they split it two ways. He'd take his share back to Missouri and give it—most of it—to his mother and sisters, America Alice and Sarah. It would set them up well, and Jack's father had always told him a man had no greater responsibility than to keep his women safe.

It made him happy to think of the money and all the good that would come from it. The Gregory women were entitled to some comfort after all the misery they had endured these last five years. Most of their misfortune had come from living in Missouri during the war. Missouri was the worst place on God's green earth during this time, a place steeped and ripened in its own corruption. And at the end of it all, the land he grew up on had been taken over by Yankees and Jayhawkers. It was land he and his pa farmed hemp on, and made a good living selling to the ropewalks along the river where it was turned into baling twine for cotton. But then the war put an end to the cotton business in the South and no one needed hemp any longer. They planned to switch to tobacco, and would have made a go of it too, but the devils killed pa and the Jayhawkers took their land. They were a murderous lot, Jayhawkers, sneaky and cowardly, who kept to the woods and shadowed the Federals, feeding off their leavings like a snarling band of jackals. Everywhere a man turned in west Missouri, there was some freebooter waiting for a chance to cut him down and take what was his. Now was Jack Gregory's time to get even. Pa was gone, but there was still mother and the girls, Sarah and America Alice. Fifteen thousand greenbacks would go far to see to their happiness.

Once he reached the Little Piney he was out of earshot and eyesight of the post. He stood, feeling the tight and frozen muscles of his back complain. Snow was coming harder and the cold nigh to unbearable. Gregory looked up at the stars, the few he could see between the clouds and falling flakes, and asked for their help in finding the Indian trail. The only other time he'd used it was in the summer, and then it was easy to follow, twisting like a scar through meadows of wild wheat and oats, then through a dark forest of pine, balsam, and hemlock. When he emerged from that forest he'd be halfway up the mountain, halfway home. On top of the ridge was an ancient Indian fort, hidden by wind-blasted trees, and in the center of those crumbling stone walls, he and Ignacio had buried the money. God willing, the Mexican was waiting for him there even now, with blankets, food, and a horse or a mule.

The cold had penetrated every part of him, taking root deep in his stomach. Every breath was painful, hitting the back of his throat like a knife thrust. The pup must be suffering too and now he had the hiccups. Gregory tried to warm him by putting his hand around the cold head sticking out from his coat. All the while he kept moving along the bed of the ravine, knowing if he didn't find the trail, he was dead. He had imagined his own end many times, but freezing to death with a stinking pup inside his coat was a new one.

The snow stopped and clouds blew off, exposing the moon and a sky spangled with stars. Together the stars and moon threw a light that showed landmarks in stark relief, like black paper cutouts. This was helpful. Also, he was becoming less worried about meeting up with Indians. They would be wrapped in furs and warm inside their lodges. Only a fool would be out on a night like this.

He kept walking. Their plan called for Ignacio to wait for him through the night of December 21. If Gregory did not show up by morning, the Mexican would take his share of the money and move on. That was their arrangement and there was no turning back. Gregory had to find that trail.

Finally he saw it, a depression on both sides of the ravine cut by the unshod hoofs of countless ponies for countless years. The narrow ribbon of worn earth ran through the meadow and into the forest. Gregory ran for the trees. If he was going to be spotted by Indians, this was the time. The distance was about one-half mile and he covered it in less than five minutes, suffering agonies with each stabbing breath, but knowing he would find safety in the trees and some protection from the heartless wind.

When at last he made it, he sank to the needle-covered forest floor and leaned against a tree, breathing hard from his run. Shafts of moonlight penetrated the trees like bars of silver. He was not so far removed from his higher soul that he failed to see the natural beauty around him. He uncorked his canteen and poured water into his palm for the pup. They shared a piece of elk jerky before resuming the march uphill. After about two hours of walking they cleared the trees and Gregory could see the summit above him. Another ninety minutes, he thought, and they'd be home. Maybe Ignacio would have a fire going. Maybe he'd greet him with a mug of hot coffee.

He continued climbing. Soon he saw a dark shape on the trail ahead, motionless on the ground. With a heavy sense of dread, he approached. It was the remains of a man with clumps of long, black hair clinging to the fractured skull. The remnants of jeans and a red plaid shirt dressed the bones and two arrows penetrated the rib cage. Gregory recognized the shirt, and his worst fears were realized. He was looking at Ignacio, or what was left of him.

Chapter Four

The rest of the night unfolded like a dream. The Mexican had been dead for some time, probably since that August day when he and Gregory buried the treasure. He remembered his friend as he resumed his climb. Ignacio was a one-eyed Mexican with a bad hand and a temper to match, but he was a man of his word, someone Gregory trusted with his life. They had been in high spirits that hot afternoon, pleased with themselves for having skunked the paymaster for the Department of the Platte, the gasbag Major Ranald Henry. They considered themselves something other than common criminals, for had they not, despite considerable risk, ridden to Fort Reno to tell them of the disaster unfolding to the south, at Reno Redoubt? No telling what the Sioux and Cheyenne would have done to those people had Gregory and Ignacio simply made off with the money and abandoned them to their fate. To his credit, the Mexican never argued for this, even though the white soldiers seldom treated him with the respect he deserved.

After planting the canvas bags of money in the ruin, they split up, with Gregory headed north to seek work in Bozeman City. Ignacio said he would go south, to sign on as a teamster with one of the freight lines. The two shook hands, solemnly, and resolved to reunite on the evening of December 21 to divide the spoils. They had no way of knowing their prearranged date would be the bloodiest in the frontier army's history of Indian warfare, and one of the coldest too.

Gregory crested the ridge. The wind was deadly and, despite the danger, he knew he would have to build a fire. He couldn't survive without one. He piled branches against one of the decaying rock walls, fashioning a kind of lean-to, and built a small fire inside, piling rocks and dried brush around it on three sides to direct the heat and also conceal the flames' glow. The wind was his enemy as he struggled to coax forth a blaze, but then, after the fire was going, became his friend as it immediately dispersed the smoke. He and the pup feasted on hard cracker, elk jerky, and water before dozing beside the fire. Once he woke to find the pup licking his face.

As soon as there was sufficient light, Gregory took a small spade from his pack and began to dig. They had marked the place with a pile of stones, which had not been disturbed. Not once had he doubted the money would be there, and he was right to trust for there it was, just where he and Ignacio left it five months before. The greenbacks were in two canvas bags and Gregory took them both, imagining his mother's face when he put the money in her hands. He had disappointed her many times in his life, and this, he hoped, would make up for those. He was smiling when he returned to the fire, but that smile disappeared when he discovered the pup had died. He lay on his side, in a puddle of urine, his eyes at half-mast. His chewed ear lifted in the wind.

"Pup," Gregory said, a stone in his throat. He thought the little dog was getting stronger, that they would keep each other company on the long trip ahead. That little pup was a sweet thing. Now he was alone again. *Would it always be this way?* he wondered. Living things seemed not to thrive in his company. Was he born under a solitary star?

He dropped the pup in the money hole and filled it with dirt. Then he shouldered his pack, heavier now, and began the journey down the mountain and back to Missouri.

Chapter Five

Custis Lee was dead. The finest, most loyal horse that ever lived was rotting on the Kansas plain, food for the wolves and carrion birds, all because of her husband's stupidity. She read his letter again, her hand trembling. It was dated April 20, 1867, and posted from Fort Hays.

> *And now I am called upon to relate a most unfortunate occurrence, and one too that you will deeply regret. That noble animal, Custis Lee, is no more. I killed him last Tuesday while buffalo hunting.*

She skipped to the part where he described the moment of dear Lee's death.

> *I drew up my pistol, intending to use both hands in controlling the horse, when just as my hand was raised to the reins, my finger accidentally and in the excitement of the moment pressed the trigger and*

discharged the weapon, the ball entering Lee's neck
near the top of his head and penetrating his brain.

Elizabeth crumpled the paper and threw it in the fire. She had heard rumors of Lee's death days before—the Delaware scouts spoke of it, smiling behind their hands—but she had tried to convince herself they weren't true. After all, Armstrong was not well-liked, this was obvious to her, and it was not uncommon to hear unflattering gossip about him. Of course, most of his troubles were of his own making. If only he weren't so excitable. She was beginning to wonder if he would ever learn to master his emotions. In the early days of their courtship, she found his boyish energy and spontaneity attractive, but now, after three years of marriage, he seemed merely childish and tiresome. Worst of all, his career was suffering because of it. If she had to spend the rest of her life as a military wife, she did not plan to spend it tethered to a mere lieutenant colonel.

Elizabeth set her jaw and went to her desk to write a letter of her own. She would invite her friend Kate to come from Michigan. She preferred Kate's company to that of Anna Darrah, her current companion, but Kate was less adventurous than Anna and Elizabeth had to be careful about the things she wrote of life on the Kansas frontier. In the same letter from Fort Hays, Armstrong told her of finding the burned bodies of three stage station keepers, killed by Indians. Their blackened corpses had been partially eaten by wolves and the remains, he said, were "one of the most horrible sights imaginable." This, of course, Elizabeth would not mention to Kate though such sordid reports of Indian depredations here in Kansas eventually made their way into the Eastern newspapers. No, Elizabeth would describe the handsome, unmarried officers who were keen for the company of a pretty, cultured, and available young woman. And Kate was kind, something Elizabeth could not say of Anna.

She signed the letter and put down her pen. How alone she was! Ever since her father's death the year before, she had felt increasingly isolated. Only he, dear Judge Daniel S. Bacon, knew her true heart, though even he had seemed to abandon her at the end. Only to him had she confessed her mounting fear that she had erred, grievously, in marrying Armstrong. Only to him did she speak of her need to make a change, despite the scandal it would bring, and she thought she would have the judge's support. After all, had it not been he who cautioned her against Armstrong when he first began paying court? Was it not he who said the young, impetuous officer from a poor and undistinguished family was not worthy of his beautiful and intelligent child, he who called the brash young man "not remotely good enough" for his once-chubby daughter who had grown into a slim but shapely beauty, who graduated from the Young Ladies' Seminary and Collegiate Institute as valedictorian? No, the judge had nourished other plans for his cherished Elizabeth, his only surviving child.

Eventually, of course, Armstrong won them over. After all, how many men could say their daughter was being courted by the Union Army's youngest general? As Armstrong's star ascended, so he grew in her father's estimation. But always, always, she believed the judge would support her if it should turn out her happiness was imperiled. How shocked she had been when, on his deathbed, the judge betrayed her. When she told him of her unhappiness, he said, "No man could wish for a son-in-law more highly thought of than General George Armstrong Custer." He admonished her to "ignore self" and, as a true woman should, subordinate herself to her husband's needs and illustrious career. Armstrong's career, she reminded him, was not so illustrious as it once was, and he was no longer a general. She reminded her father too of her need to be a mother. The only one of her three siblings to live to adulthood, Elizabeth had always dreamed of a houseful of children; strong, raucous boys and pretty, spirited girls. But Armstrong, it seemed, had no interest in fatherhood, despite what he had told her before their marriage.

"Do you understand what I'm telling you, Father?" she said. "I am not happy. Armstrong is not the man I—we—thought he was. I shouldn't have married him. I made a mistake." The judge only shook his head. "Remember your vows," he said. Perhaps he was not thinking clearly, because of the apoplexy. To be sure, his illness had diminished him. But no matter now. Her father, and greatest champion, was gone. She would have to decide on her own.

She walked to the window, which was partly open to admit the spring breeze. The white, gauzy curtains she made herself—she had to make everything herself out here!—billowed in the wind. Soldiers were drilling on the parade ground. Drill, drill, drill. It seemed that was all they did, drill for hour after hour, back and forth, day after day after day. How dreary! How tedious this place is! Could any spot on God's green earth be less lovely than Fort Riley, Kansas? It was nothing more than a collection of squat limestone buildings, none more a story and a half high, all arranged around an unlovely, brown parade ground. There were no trees, no vegetation of any kind, other than the poor buffalo grass, its green blades curling in the pitiless sun. How her eyes ached for a bit of color, just one window box of red geraniums to sooth her female soul. Was that too much to ask?

She sighed. Armstrong had expected to be posted to Fort Garland, by all accounts a fine and well-maintained post, nestled in the foothills of the snow-covered Rocky Mountains. They had talked about it, the two of them, about how he would spend his free time hunting and fishing and she would ride Custis Lee—another dream dashed—through the green meadows and learn to paint landscapes in watercolor. They would teach themselves Spanish. That was a life she could imagine, but instead, the Indians, the army, and the railroad magnates had conspired to send them here. Fort Riley, Kansas.

As she stood at the window her eyes fell upon a man sitting in a chair under the shaded veranda of the sutler's store. He was someone she had not seen before. His skin was dark and his black hair was straight and long, and she thought it unusual that an Indian or a Mexican would be lounging so insouciantly in a public place. In fact, he appeared to be asleep, with his hat pulled down over his eyes and his chair on two legs, tilted back against the stucco wall. As she watched, a Mexican boy stumbled through the store's open door, pushed by an angry-looking man who followed him onto the boardwalk. She recognized him as Louis Cheney, a civilian working for the quartermaster, memorable because of his penchant for quoting scripture and because of the large purple birthmark that covered the lower half of his face. Cheney was a head taller than the Mexican boy and at least sixty pounds heavier.

"Stinking greaser!" Cheney said. "You stole my money." He balled his fist and struck the boy in the face, knocking him to the ground. "It's time you filthy Mexicans learned how to behave." He took another step toward the fallen boy. "I'm about to teach you a lesson and it will be a harsh one, but no more than you deserve. Like the Bible says, 'The way of transgressors is hard.'"

At once the sleeping man was out of his chair, helping the boy to his feet. Elizabeth saw this man was young also, not much older than the Mexican. They spoke briefly in Spanish, then the young man placed himself between Cheney and the lad.

"Stay out of this, Mendoza," Cheney said. "I wasn't referencing you with those greaser remarks. I regard you as a white man—or mostly anyhow. Step aside."

Mendoza did not move.

"I said step aside. What's this Mex to you anyway? He ain't worth it, man."

"I know him," Mendoza said. "His name is Yadier

Cruz and he wouldn't take your money. You lost it some other way."

"No, it was in my pocket when I went in there," Cheney said, nodding toward the door, "and when I reached back for it, it was gone. Wasn't nobody else around." He pointed to Cruz. "I'm a say it one more time, Mendoza. Step aside so I can teach the greaser a lesson."

By now a crowd had gathered. When Mendoza failed to move Cheney lunged toward him with his fists raised. Before he could land a blow, Mendoza struck him in the jaw with such speed and force Cheney's head snapped back as if he'd been hit with a bag full of coins. He staggered and fell off the boardwalk, losing his hat and landing on his back in the street where he lay, stunned. A full minute passed before he slowly got to his feet. Blood ran from his fleshy nose.

"You'll be sorry you did that, Mendoza," he said, wiping the blood from his face with the back of his hand. "You and your greaser friend. 'Vengeance is mine; I will repay, saith the Lord.'"

"The Lord?" Mendoza said. "Funny, all I see is a Bible-spouting gringo with blood on his face." This drew snickers from the crowd.

"All right, but we'll see who has the last laugh," Cheney said. "We'll see." He bent to pick up his hat and walked away, rubbing his jaw. The heel of his right boot left a mark, the sign of a cross, in the dirt.

Elizabeth, watching from the window, laughed.

"What's funny?"

Startled, she turned to find Anna behind her. Anna walked on cat's paws, a trait Elizabeth found annoying.

"That vile Cheney fellow just learned a lesson in humility," she said. "That one was his teacher." She pointed to Mendoza, who had returned to his chair.

"Oh, yes," Anna said. "That's Mendoza, a scout. I'm surprised you don't know him. Romeo, they call him. Very handsome, don't you agree?"

Elizabeth shrugged. "I didn't notice." In fact, she had. Even from a distance she could see that his features were regular and well formed, with cheekbones high and sharp as a red Indian's. His range clothes were worn but neat and clean and they fit him nicely, almost as if they had been tailored to suit his trim, well-muscled frame. "How do you know him, Anna?" she said.

"Tom mentioned him in his last letter," Anna said. "Romeo is going to be part of our escort to Fort Harker. I'm surprised Armstrong hasn't said anything to you. It was Armstrong's new man, his new scout, who asked for him, or so Tom said."

This was news to Elizabeth though she did know her husband had written to Captain Myles Keogh at Fort Wallace requesting the loan of that post's head scout, Joe Grover. She did not know any of Grover's particulars, but if he was a man like Romeo Mendoza, things might be looking up. So far, Custer's attempt to find and punish the Indians had met with nothing but failure.

"They skedaddle, they spread out, they vanish into thin air!" Custer complained in letters to his wife.

These were growing increasingly petulant. "How can I punish the red devils if I can't find them!" Nonetheless, that was what was expected of him. Generals Sherman and Sheridan had been clear in their charge to General Winfield Scott Hancock, and Hancock, in turn, had been firm with Custer: find the Sioux and Cheyenne and deal with them, for they were interfering with the Union Pacific Eastern Division railroad's westerly progress. Custer was to use the Seventh Cavalry as a mobile, fast-acting strike force. "Find the Indians, Custer," Hancock said, "and if they refuse to retreat to their agencies, pitch into them—smite them in their lodges if you must! Show no quarter!" It was an assignment Armstrong had accepted with relish, for his career had languished since the war ended. The Boy General with Golden Curls had become the Lieutenant Colonel with Receding Hairline, though he was still addressed, as a courtesy, by his brevet rank of general. The bloom was off the rose, Elizabeth thought, in every regard. She was hoping a glorious victory against the Indians would restore Custer's career and, as a consequence, their romance as well. So far, things were not looking promising.

"Oh, speaking of Tom," Anna said, "have you written to Armstrong about his drinking? I truly think it's getting worse." Anna was keeping company with Armstrong's younger brother, Captain Tom Custer, also a regimental officer. "I'm quite weary of it. He acts the fool when he's in his cups. He can be quite boorish."

Elizabeth had witnessed this herself, more than once. She shook her head. "Not yet. I will, though I doubt it will do any good. This is something Tom must resolve on his own." She knew this to be true. So many of the officers were slaves to John Barleycorn and nothing, no amount of hectoring by wives or friends, could convince a man to break the chains unless he chose to do so himself. Armstrong did not drink alcohol, not even a glass of wine with a meal. He had foresworn it and blaspheming to please her—and Judge Bacon—during the early days of their courtship, although he did not keep this latter pledge as assiduously as the first. In truth, Elizabeth didn't mind the swearing so much, abstaining from liquor was far more important in her mind. All too often she had seen a promising officer's career derailed by dependence on drink. In fact, Elizabeth had come to think of chronic drunkenness as an occupational hazard, brought on by the crushing monotony of army life, and, in her heart of hearts, she was not entirely unsympathetic. One could hardly blame these poor souls for seeking comfort in the bottle. A person has to find peace and happiness somewhere, and certainly these were in short supply on the flat, lifeless plains of Kansas.

Chapter Six

Fort Wallace, Kansas
April 1867

The orderly found Jack Gregory in the stables, saddling his horse, Jeff, a chestnut gelding. "Captain Keogh wants to see you in his office, Grover," he said. When Gregory gave no sign of hearing—he was still unaccustomed to his assumed name—the corporal said, "Now." Gregory removed the saddle and followed the orderly to Keogh's office.

The captain sat at his desk with an open letter before him. "Sit down, Joe," he said. "I've got a job for you." Everyone at Wallace knew Gregory as Joe Grover. He didn't know if he was wanted for the murder of Mark Reynolds, or the payroll theft, but even so Gregory chose to conceal his identity. Experience had taught him always to expect the worst. He pulled up a chair.

"General George Custer, now campaigning with General Hancock, has requested your services," Keogh said. A native of Ireland, he still spoke with a slight lilt. "And of course I've agreed. Make a list of any supplies you think you'll need and give it to the quartermaster. Your first stop will be Fort Harker. From there you're to meet up with Custer in the field. My last communication from him"—he raised the letter on his desk—"was from a camp on Big Creek, near Fort Hays. They'll have more information for you when you get to Harker."

Gregory rubbed his jaw. "You said I could have time off, captain, to work on my place. You said I could have a week."

Gregory had used some of the thirty thousand to buy Rose Creek Ranch, a hay ranch eight miles south of Fort Wallace, just to the south of Eagle Creek stage station. Because his meadows were practically the only source of forage in the area, he made good money selling hay to the post, but the house he'd acquired along with the property was in sore need of repairs. As chief scout at Fort Wallace, the westernmost and most Indian-plagued of Kansas's Smoky Hills posts, Gregory had spent most of the winter and spring recovering stolen livestock and chasing down rumors of Indian trouble. He'd had little time to tend his fields, and he knew he'd ultimately make more money selling hay to the army than scouting for it.

"I know I did, Grover, and I'm sorry to do this to you, but Custer asked for you. He ranks me. I can't say no. And he needs you, man. So far this campaign of Hancock's has been a complete fizzle. The Sioux and Cheyenne are giving them the devil, just running circles around them. Custer's hot to turn things around." Keogh chuckled, enjoying the boss's misfortune. "And there's more. Custer wants his wife with him. You'll meet her at Fort Harker—she has a friend along, I believe—and escort them both on to Custer's camp. It's about eighty miles."

Gregory thought he had misheard. "His wife and her friend?"

"That's right."

"General Sherman allows this?" Gregory remembered the problems women and children caused—not by their actions but by their very presence—during Carrington's ill-fated Powder River campaign the winter before. A man can't do his job if he's worried about his wife and child. Would the army never learn from its mistakes?

Keogh shrugged his shoulders. A great favorite with the women, Keogh was a handsome and devout Catholic whose colorful past included service abroad as a Zouave with the Papal Army of Pope Pius IX. The pope personally had awarded Keogh a medal, the *Medaglia di Pro Petri Sede*, which he wore around his neck at all times, usually under his shirt, but now it gleamed against his jacket. "What Custer wants, Custer gets," he said, "as long as he's got Phil Sheridan around to see to it. But don't worry about Mrs. Custer, Grover. You'll like her, I promise you that." He grinned knowingly. "She's a good-looking woman and she's got spirit. She won't give you trouble—not much anyhow."

Of course she would give him trouble, Gregory

thought. Women brought trouble in different ways—
to be fair, not always intentionally—but they always
brought it. The only woman he knew who was no
trouble was Maggie, the Sioux who kept his house,
cooked his food, and took care of him every way a
man needs to be taken care of. She worked hard,
didn't talk much, and wasn't bad to look at, other
than the scar. No, Maggie was no trouble.

"I don't suppose I have a choice," he said, getting
to his feet. "When do I leave?"

"Now," Keogh said. "You leave now."

Gregory did not protest. A year ago, he would
have, but no longer. Once a man escapes death as
Jack Gregory had done, once a man feels death's
grave-cold hand poised above his shoulder, very few
things seem worth complaining about.

He had nearly died that bitter December night
and again, in the days that followed, but the cold that
nearly killed him also worked in his favor. The soldiers at Fort Phil Kearny, immobilized by the weather
and their fear of the Indians who had massacred Fetterman and his eighty men just hours before, did not
pursue him. The Indians, however, retreated to their
warm robes and lodges. Not even their hatred of the
trespassing Long Knives was sufficient to drive them
out. Slowly, painstakingly, Gregory made his way to
Horseshoe Station, following the traces left by the
two rescue riders Carrington dispatched that bloody
night. Gregory was beginning to fail, to lose heart,
when he found an army mule, perhaps a refugee

from the battle earlier that evening, sheltering in a ravine. He would never know how he came to be there, but that animal saved his life. For the second time in his twenty-five years, Jack Gregory raised his eyes to the stars and gave thanks to God.

He and the mule traveled for days, existing on crackers, tree bark, and snow, hiding during the daylight hours and moving at night, arriving at Horseshoe Station just a few hours after Daniel Dixon and the foreigner, Portugee Phillips. There, Gregory acquired a horse, a chestnut gelding consigned to the dead herd.

"His name's Jeff," the telegraph operator, John Friend, said, "and can't nobody ride him. He won't take the bit." Gregory examined his mouth. "Give me a hackamore," he said, "and I'll take him."

Jeff never gave him a moment's trouble. Some animals are soft-mouthed and don't cotton to a piece of cold metal in their mouths, banging up against their teeth, and the chestnut was one of them. Gregory and Jeff came quickly to trust each other.

Once in Kansas City, Gregory was unsure where to find his mother and sisters. He had not seen or heard from them for more than three years, but, again, he was fortunate. The day he rode into town, Gregory encountered an old friend who told him where the widow Gregory and her daughters were living.

"They're in Harlem," he said. "Your ma's got a place on Woodland Avenue. I guess you know she's taking in boarders?" The man was about the same age as Gregory, tall and thin with a long face and ears that

winged away from his head like handles on a sugar
bowl. Gregory knew the neighborhood of Harlem, a
fishing and ferryboat community on the north bank
of the Missouri River. He was disturbed to learn she
had been reduced to taking in strangers to put food
on the table. "One of the boys, Frank Gregg, is staying there. Funny how things turn out, isn't it?"

"*Funny* is not a word I would use," Gregory said.

"No, I suppose not. How long you in town for?"

"Just long enough to make things right with
mother and the girls. Then I'm going back out west.
There's nothing for me in Missouri."

The tall man blew on his hands to warm them.
"Say, Jack, it's colder than a witch's kiss out here." He
nodded toward a tavern. "Let's go in there and sit a
spell. I might have something to interest you."

They entered the smoky tavern and sat at a round
table, its surface marked with cigar and cigarette
burns. The dark room smelled like sour beer and
pickled herring and was mostly empty. The tall man
removed his hat and called to the bartender, ordering two beers. Gregory would have preferred a hot
cup of coffee, but he would drink the beer.

"Jack, you say there's nothing for you in Missouri,
but could be you're wrong on that score," the tall
man said after the drinks were delivered. "There is
something here. There's banks, is what, and they're
run by Northern men mostly, who are tight with their
holdings, especially when it comes to dealings with
sesesh like us." He and Gregory eyed each other

across the table. "Me and the boys are working on a plan you might want part of."

"Which boys are you talking about?" Gregory suspected he knew the answer.

"You know, the old gang. Cole Younger, Ol' Shepherd and George, Bud Pence, all them, and we have had some success already. Last February we got sixty thousand dollars in bonds, paper, and coin from the Clay County Savings Association in Liberty. Maybe you heard about that?" Gregory had heard of it, including the fact that they'd killed a civilian, an innocent passerby, in the harvest. The tall man continued, "Archie Clement was with us until they killed him, last December in Lexington. You know, Jack, Little Archie died fine, just like you'd expect. I wasn't there, but they tell me that even after he was shot through the back, and couldn't use his hands no more, he died trying to cock his pistol with his teeth." He shook his head in admiration. "Anyhow, we got a dozen men lined up. You should join us."

Gregory sipped his beer. Cole Younger was all right, the Shepherd cousins too, they made up in enthusiasm and loyalty what they lacked in brain power. Though he would not say so, he was not sorry to hear of Archie Clement's demise. The man was four feet eleven inches of pure meanness. "What is your plan?" he said.

"Right now we're looking at a bank in Ray County. The Hugh and Wasson in Richmond and it does appear ripe for the picking. Anyhow, they owe us in Richmond, ever since they tied Bill Anderson's body to a board and propped him like a circus attraction for people to make photographs of and piss on. We been studying it, me and the boys, we know how many men will be there when we go in, we know pretty much what they got. We'd be honored to have you ride with us, Jack. Me, I'd really like to have you with us."

Gregory nodded. He could use the money. He planned to give most of the payroll treasure to his mother and the girls, so he'd need something to get by on. On the other hand, the job would be dangerous and with companions like these, there'd be a good chance things would go wrong.

"What about your brother?" Gregory said. "Is he in on this?"

"He will be eventually. You know, Jack, Dingus is still bad from that chest wound he got back in sixty-four. He's not riding much yet."

In Gregory's estimation, the kid brother was even more ruthless than Little Archie.

"I'll give it thought," he said. "When do you move?"

"It'll be awhile, sometime in the spring. But let me know quick as you can. I won't say nothing to the boys till I know if you're in or out."

"All right." Gregory stood and put on his hat. The two men shook hands.

"Good-bye, Jack," the tall man said. "When you see Mrs. Gregory and the girls, tell them Frank James sends regards."

Chapter Seven

In the end, Gregory decided not to take James up on his invitation. He had no need to reunite with the men he rode with during the war, those particular men at any rate, and he did not countenance the casual killing of innocents. He reckoned Frank and the boys might enjoy success for a time, but eventually their enterprise would end badly for all concerned. Of this he had no doubt, especially if Frank's blue-eyed brother, Jesse, got involved.

He found his mother at the Harlem address James had given him. The house was a two-story, white frame structure that needed a fresh coat of paint. Even from the street, it was obvious to him a man's presence was needed. In addition to the chipping paint, a window shutter was hanging askew and he saw popped nails on the stairs as he climbed to the door. His sister America Alice responded to his knock, but several heartbeats passed before she recognized him.

"Jack!" She jumped and threw her arms around him. "Oh, Jack! I feared we'd never see you again."

His mother entered the dark, candlelit hallway and froze at the sight of her eldest daughter beaming in the arms of a rough-looking stranger. "America Alice," she said, "what in God's name—"

His sister stepped out of Gregory's embrace. "Mother, look! It's Jack! Our Jack's come home to us!"

The old woman covered her mouth with a gnarled, arthritic hand. Jack went to her and put his arms around her. She seemed much smaller than he remembered.

"Hello, Ma." He bent to kiss her cheek and she began to cry. "Please don't, Ma," he said, patting her on the back. "Please don't cry." She rarely wept and when she did her tears distressed him beyond all reason. "Come, let's go to the parlor. Let's sit down." He took her arm and guided her to a chair in the front room. It was clean, sparsely furnished and, like the entryway, dimly lit. Gregory glanced around, recognizing nothing. Everything the family owned had been destroyed the day Mark Reynolds and his Jayhawkers burned their farm.

"I'll make tea," his sister said, pausing at the door. "Just wait until Sarah gets home—won't she be surprised!"

Gregory pulled up a chair and sat close to his mother. "I'm sorry it's been so long," he said. "How are you, Ma? Are you and the girls all right? Do you have all you need?"

"I do, now that you're here." She touched his cheek. "Jack, we haven't heard from you since that letter. A woman named Rose sent it, she said you were very brave, that you risked your life to save her and some other people, soldiers, who were surrounded by Indians at a place called Reno Redoubt. Then those government men came, and said you and a Mexican stole a lot of money and asked us all these questions. They thought we knew something about it. Of course, we told them we didn't, but I don't think they believed us. They watched the house, they frightened me, Jack." She started crying again. The tears ran down her wrinkled cheek. "It's been terrible—I didn't know what to think. Why didn't you write—you should have written."

Gregory took his mother's hands. "Yes, mother, you're right. I should have, I'm sorry. Those government men, Ma, what did they look like? What exactly did they say? Can you remember?"

She pulled her hands from his. "Oh, yes, I remember all right, all too well. I wish I could forget. One was big, he did all the talking, and he bore the mark of the devil on his face." She traced a circle around her mouth and up one cheek. "The skin was purple and raised, bumpy. I've seen it before, it means the devil had truck with his mother when he was a child in the womb." She shook her head. "It's a sorry thing, when a little child is punished for a mother's shame."

"And the other man? What did he look like?"

"Also tall, but skinny, with sharp, narrow features. His face came to a point, like a human rat."

"Did they wear uniforms, Ma? Did they say which part of the government they were from?"

The old woman shook her head. "No, no uniforms, just with the government. That's what they said. They kept asking where you were and what happened to the money you stole. I couldn't tell them anything, but they kept coming back. I'd see them standing across the street, just standing there, watching. I shouldn't be telling you this, Jack. It's making you angry. I can see by your hands."

Gregory looked down at his balled fists. He relaxed and forced a smile. "I'm sorry, Ma, but it upsets me to see you and the girls threatened. And I believe those men were a threat to you. Have you seen them recently? Have any other government men come looking for me?"

"No, just the two. They came in the fall, before Christmas."

Good, Gregory thought. That meant no one had come seeking him as the killer of Mark Reynolds. "Enough of this," he said. "Did you get the money from Lieutenant Bell at Fort Sedgwick?"

She waved her hand, as if shooing a fly. "Yes, yes, I wrote and he sent it," she said. "Money, money, money—that's all anyone talks about nowadays. I don't care about money. It's you I care for, and your immortal soul. I'm worried by the things I've heard. I'm frightened about what my son has become." She looked as if she would start crying again.

Gregory searched for words, for some way to make her understand the code he lived by was not so different from the one she'd taught him. Yes, he stole, and yes, he killed, but not wantonly. Yes, he had violated the commandments, but only to punish those who had done harm to his family. But he did not say these things. Instead, he leaned down, reached into his kit, and pulled out a package, wrapped in brown paper and tied with string. In his kit were five other packages just like it.

"This is for you, mother. You, America Alice, and Sarah. It is money, Ma, a lot of it. I know you don't care about that, but I want you to have it. It will be enough for you to stop taking lodgers. I want you to stop doing that, Mother. It is not fitting. Pa would not want that for you and neither do I."

His mother regarded the bundle in her hands, then raised her eyes to his face. "Where did this come from, Jack? Is this the money those government men were looking for? Is this the fruit of your shame? If it is, I don't want it!" She thrust the bundle back at him.

"No, Ma, listen to me. Those two men were not from the government. They were thieves, they were after this money, which is ours. Yes, I took it, but it is due us—this and more—because of what the Yankee officer and his Jayhawkers did to Pa that day, what they did to all of us. You and the girls must have it. It's justice! And not only that, Ma, I want you to know I found that Yankee bastard, I found him and I put him through, just like I told you I would. He rots in hell."

The old woman's tears stopped and her faded eyes took on a flinty gleam. Gregory almost smiled. For all her talk of immortal souls, his mother had plenty of steel in her and he was seeing it now. "You found him?" she said. "You killed that Yankee devil?"

"I did. He was up in Dakota Territory, at an army fort. His name was Lieutenant Mark Reynolds. America Alice pointed him out to me one day in Kansas City, he was riding in a parade. Anyhow, I told him who I was and why I was there before I put a bullet in his head. He was a devil, but he was an officer and the army may be looking for me, though I think they believe me dead. Even so, I cannot stay. Here with you and the girls is the place I'm most likely to be recognized and killed. I'll move on to Kansas and go back to scouting. Scouts come and go as they please and no one asks them questions. I'll be calling myself Joe Grover."

His mother nodded. "All right," she said. He could see the name meant nothing to her.

America Alice entered the room carrying a tea tray and a plate of buttered bread. As Gregory took it from her and set it on the table, his eyes fell on the sugar bowl and he thought of Frank James.

"Ma, do you have a lodger from Clay County?" he said. "A man of about my age?"

America Alice answered with a blush. "Yes, that sounds like Mr. Gregg. Mr. Frank Gregg." Her blush deepened. "He's a fine man."

Gregory suspected his tall, awkward sister knew precious little of men and their ways. The Frank Gregg he knew was many things, but *fine* was not one of them. "Stay away from him, America Alice," he said. "He's not right for you. He's has had his hand up more skirts than a dressmaker."

"Jack, please," his mother said. "Don't be vulgar." America Alice said nothing, but her hand shook as she poured tea.

"Put him out, Mother," Gregory said. "You don't need his money now." If Gregg was one of Frank James's boys, as he suspected, authorities may be drawn to the house. He didn't want anyone noticing the Widow Gregory's newfound prosperity. "Give him one week to find other lodgings, and don't say anything about me. And don't be splashy with the money I have given you."

"Money?" America Alice said. "What money?"

Before he could explain, his younger sister, Sarah, came through the front door with her arms full of packages. Unlike America Alice, she recognized her brother immediately. She dropped her bundles and ran to him, jumping into his arms and kissing his stubbled cheek.

"Jacky!" she said. "Is it really you? Where have you been? I've missed you!" At nineteen, Sarah was three years younger than America Alice and far prettier, with curling hair the color of corn silk and lively blue eyes. Gregory returned her kiss.

"I have missed you too, Sari." He had not spoken her childhood nickname in years and, again, he was almost overcome. "I have missed all of you, more than you know."

"And soon you'll be leaving us again," his mother said.

"No!" Sarah said, striking him on the shoulder. "You just returned to us. You can't leave."

"We can't hold him," the widow said. "It's been the same, ever since he was sixteen years old when he went out to Nebraska to truck with the Indians. I didn't understand him then, and I don't now, but he's just like his father, always chasing some star. He always had his own notion of the eternal fitness of things and it won't do to tell him different. Your pa was nigh on to forty by the time he settled. I reckon our Jack will be the same. He's going to call himself by a new name—Joe something? I forget."

"Joe Grover."

Sarah's face brightened. "Oh, yes, I remember him! He was the surgeon who fixed your lip all those years ago."

Gregory smiled. "That's right." Sarah was only a child then, but she remembered her brother's savior while his own mother did not.

"Well, at least stay for supper," Sarah said. "You can do that, Jacky, can't you?"

Gregory smiled. "Yes, Sari, I can do that."

Chapter Eight

Elizabeth stood on the platform, waiting to board the train. The sun was a blister in the cloudless sky. She pulled a handkerchief from her sleeve and touched it to her brow and upper lip, feeling a drop of sweat roll between her breasts.

"Are you sure this is a good idea?" Anna said. She was perspiring heavily in her navy riding suit, with stains growing under her arms. Elizabeth had tried to warn her friend that light-colored and looser clothing was more comfortable in the Kansas heat, but Anna thought the fitted suit most flattering to her figure. *Maybe she would listen next time*, Elizabeth thought.

"Armstrong and Tom want us with them," she said, "and there's certainly nothing to keep us in this hole. If I don't get out of here, I'll lose my mind! I've never seen Fort Hays, but it's got to be better than this."

Elizabeth looked about the platform, but did not see the familiar face she sought. General William Tecumseh Sherman was taking the train also, as far as Fort Harker, but Elizabeth had not shared this information with Anna. Her friend was a compulsive, competitive flirt and this was becoming a source of tension between the two women. Though Anna was attractive and accomplished at working her womanly wiles, it was Elizabeth who usually drew a man's attention. This was a talent, or gift, she had recognized in herself as a young woman and carefully cultivated since. It had proved useful many times and she hoped it was about to once again.

She sat by the window reading *The Galaxy* magazine while Anna, lulled by the rhythmic clack of the wheels on the rails, dozed beside her in the upholstered seat. A shadow fell across the page and Elizabeth looked up into Sherman's dark, weather-beaten face.

"May I join you, Mrs. Custer?"

"Of course," she said, though the general was already taking his seat.

"Do you mind if I smoke?" His hand was already in the inner pocket of his coat.

"Please do." Elizabeth despised the smell of a cigar, but she was not about to deprive the Commander of the Division of the Missouri, and her husband's superior officer, the pleasure of his tobacco. To escape the smoke, she turned her head to the window. It was early May and the prairie was at its best, green and dotted with purple and yellow wildflowers. For perhaps the first time, Elizabeth found Kansas beautiful.

"Armstrong says this is fine country," she said. "All it needs is more water and good society."

"That's all hell needs," Sherman said with a short laugh.

She looked at him, eyebrows raised in mock surprise. "Why, General Sherman, you surprise me. Who was it who once told me the Kansas plains were intoxicating, that the very air was like champagne?"

He laughed. "You remember, do you? Yes, I suppose I did say that, and it's true—or would be but for this Indian problem. They are a pestilence and it's only going to get worse now that we're into their swarming season. I'll tell you frankly, Elizabeth—may I call you Elizabeth?—this campaign of General Hancock's is not starting well. In fact, so far it's been a fizzle. I didn't give him fourteen hundred men to host peace talks with the chiefs—pure twaddle!—and burn empty villages. I'm turning that husband of yours loose on them. He's never been one to run from a fight."

She smiled. This was the conversation she had hoped for. "No, sir, you need have no fear on that score."

Sherman drew on his cigar, then exhaled a cloud of blue smoke. "Yes, Phil Sheridan and General Grant speak very highly of him, Little Phil especially. Brave even to rashness, I gather. I'm not being critical, mind you. God knows I need a cavalry officer who'll do more than just ride around the country and stir the bucks up."

She nodded, sensing no words from her were necessary. Sherman was getting at something, but what?

"Yes, there's only one answer here," he said, "and I don't give a damn what the Indian-lovers of the

Interior Department say, sooner or later, Lo, the noble red man, will have to go under. No amount of sentiment can save him. We can't let a few thieving, ragged Indians stop the progress of the railroads. We'll have to make them stay where they're put or wipe them out. This will be an inglorious war, Elizabeth, not one to add much to an officer's personal fame or comfort."

She felt him studying her through a haze of smoke. "Yes, general. I'm sure Armstrong understands that. Fame and comfort are of no concern to him." *If God punished liars,* she thought, *I'd be a smoking lump of charcoal.*

Sherman crossed his long legs. He famously refused to wear boots and his shoes were worn and unpolished. "I don't want to offend you, Elizabeth," he said, "but I feel I must speak frankly. Your husband is having some difficulty. I don't know if you're aware of this, but his men don't like him, not like his Michigan boys during the war. It's not entirely his fault, of course, conditions in the frontier army are far from ideal, but desertion is becoming a significant problem. There's a lot of grumbling in the Seventh Cavalry, and I'm speaking of his officers too. I have received letters—please don't ask from whom, I can't say—complaining of his treatment of the men. They say he's a tyrant. Even I am beginning to question his judgment. What was it I heard a few weeks back—something about him bolting the column to chase an antelope or buffalo? Shot his own horse, didn't he, had to walk back? A stunt like that doesn't inspire much confidence, does it? And I don't like the way he plays up to the pygmies of the press. What is he, political?"

Elizabeth felt her face redden. This was unexpected. It was most unusual for an officer of Sherman's stature to discuss such things with the wife of a subordinate. This was dangerous territory, to be sure. She would have to tread carefully. "I don't know about political things, General Sherman. Armstrong does not discuss these things with me. But I do know my husband and his devotion to the United States Army. You can rely on him, sir. Surely he proved his worth during the war."

His pale gray eyes met hers, glinting like a flick-knife. "Your husband is a very lucky man," he said. "Do you remember that night last October, the night you and he first arrived at Fort Riley?"

"Very clearly," she said, smiling. "It was the twelfth, a Tuesday. Our quarters weren't available so we stayed with Major Gibbs, as you were. Your brother John was there too. Mrs. Gibbs served a lovely meal." She continued, relieved to take the conversation in a more manageable direction, "Chicken salad, a very nice turkey galantine—"

"I did not sleep that night," he said. "I could not rest for thinking of you just a few feet away. Do you know that still, when I close my eyes, often I see your lovely face, your hair, your smile. Did you have any idea you had done this to me?"

How he looked at her! Elizabeth's heart hammered behind her ribs. His eyes did not waver and he was not smiling. She was quite sure of herself when managing, or deflecting, a casual flirtation, but this was not one of those. This powerful man held her husband's future in the palm of her hand, and therefore her future as well. She was afraid, but at the same time exhilarated. What woman wouldn't be thrilled to hear such words from one of the most important men in the country, one whose place in history was guaranteed? She searched for words, but none came.

"You know," he said, "I sometimes think the Mormons have it right. A man should be allowed to change his wife if he wants to." He rubbed his eyes. Unlike her husband's, Sherman's hand was calloused and ungroomed, with fingers thick as sausages. "I am weary. Very weary."

If he were someone else, a lesser officer, she would reach out, touch his arm, offer soothing words of comfort. But he was not a man to trifle with, and what he asked of her—if she understood him correctly—was simply too dangerous.

"I am sorry for your unhappiness," she said. "You deserve more. I don't know what else to say."

He smiled and nodded. "I suppose I'd have been disappointed if you'd responded any other way. But just know this, Elizabeth, if that husband of yours should ever disappoint you, if you ever find yourself alone, remember what this shabby old soldier said to you today. You can be sure he will."

He stood, inclined his head, and left the car. When he was gone, Anna opened her eyes and smiled. Not for the first time, Elizabeth noticed that Anna showed too much gum when she smiled. She looked predatory, rapacious.

"My God, Liz," she said. "What a feather in your cap! What will you do with this? Will you tell Armstrong?"

Elizabeth turned her head to the window. She felt no sense of triumph. Instead, she was sobered and saddened by the loneliness she had seen in the aging warrior's gray eyes. She pitied him, though this, she was certain, was the last thing he wanted from her.

"I am not going to mention this to Armstrong, I am not going to speak of this to anyone." She looked directly into Anna's eyes. "And neither will you." She picked up her discarded copy of *The Galaxy* and pretended to read.

Chapter Nine

"That must be Grover," Elizabeth said to Anna, pointing to the man wearing a faded black hat, standing slightly apart from the others on the platform. He was well built, of middling height, with light, closely cropped hair and the look of a horseman, she thought. The train had barely stopped when Romeo jumped off to greet him.

"Mrs. Custer, Miss Darrah, this is Joe Grover," Romeo said when the ladies were disembarked. "Chief scout at Fort Wallace, best scout on the plains, best guide, best tracker—I tell you, ladies, Joe Grover could track a wood tick over solid rock. Joe saved my bacon when I first came out here, I tell you that. Why if it weren't for him, those fellas at Monument Station would have killed me. I'd be—"

"The ladies don't want to hear all that." Grover inclined his head and removed his hat. His face was dark as an Indian's and his green eyes were pale, as if faded by years of prairie sunlight. He wore a heavy mustache which almost, but did not, conceal a thick scar on his upper lip. Elizabeth took his hand and found it rough as sandpaper.

"So good to meet you, Mr. Grover," she said. "Why, that's quite a recommendation our friend Romeo gave you, and I hear fine things about you from my husband too." As she looked into his pale eyes, she saw a light in them, a glint of recognition. *I remind him of someone,* she thought. He held her hand a beat longer than was custom.

He guided the women to an ambulance drawn by four well-fleshed mules. Soldiers were already loading their trunks and bags. "We could stay here at Harker tonight," Gregory said, "or we could get started right off. Either is fine with me, but if we stay here you ladies might not be real comfortable. The best accommodations go to General Sherman's party."

"Yes, Mr. Grover, I know how the army works." Elizabeth sighed as she surveyed the fort from the train platform. If anything, it was even less lovely than Fort Riley; gravel streets surrounding a sun-scorched parade, squat frame buildings and a few of red sandstone, the whole expanse treeless other than a brave, transplanted few struggling to survive along each side of the parade.

"We'll start now," she said. It was mid-afternoon and she was tired, but she hoped to avoid another meeting with General Sherman. It would be awkward, she thought, for both of them.

"There's a stage station about ten miles down the

road," Gregory said. "We could stay there tonight. Meanwhile, you and Miss Darrah should be comfortable in here." He opened the ambulance door and offered his hand as they climbed in. It had been refitted from its original purpose to accommodate civilian passengers. One interior bench had been removed to make room for two padded chairs, secured with nails to the floor, and the canvas on the sides had been rolled up to block the sun while still allowing a breeze. Two deep, leather pockets hung from hooks on either side of the door. One of these held two neatly folded army blankets and the other, Elizabeth was annoyed to discover, several issues of *Godey's Ladies Book*. Apparently their scout thought women were interested in nothing but Butterick dress patterns and housekeeping advice.

Romeo drove the team and Gregory rode his chestnut gelding alongside. As they pulled away from Harker, Elizabeth noticed a series of cave-like holes in the sloping banks of Spring Creek, about half a mile from the post. Some had chimneys and timbered doorways large enough to admit a horse. She had not seen anything like these outside of forts Riley or Leavenworth.

"Mr. Grover," she called from under the roll of canvas. "What are those holes? What are they for?"

"Those are dugouts, ma'am," he said. "Men live in them."

She wrinkled her nose in distaste. "What kind of man would live in a hole in the ground?"

"Teamsters, hay cutters, civilians who work for the quartermaster, general workers who move around a lot. Granted, they don't look like much, but I can tell you that under the right circumstances, one of those holes, as you call them, can appear mighty welcoming."

Elizabeth tried to imagine the circumstances that could render such a place welcoming. An Indian attack, she supposed, or perhaps a blizzard. She closed her eyes and drifted off, dreaming of red Indians in war paint riding toward her through a driving snowstorm. She woke as the ambulance jerked to a stop. It was dusk.

"This must be the stage station," Anna said, peering under the canvas. "We should've stayed at Fort Harker."

The station house was made of stone. Yellow lamplight shone from two windows on either side of the heavy plank door. The windows were equipped with shutters, made of the same heavy wood as the door, with loopholes for shooting through when closed. Nearby was a stable made of rough-hewn timber and an enclosed corral with stone walls no higher than a tall man's waist. About two hundred yards from the house there appeared to be a creek, lined with scrubby cottonwoods.

A big man stepped out of the door. He had a headful of unruly red hair and massive shoulders with arms and hands to match. Next to him was a boy of about sixteen, with the same red hair, but of the short stature, sloping eyes and distinctive features peculiar to the form of idiocy called mongolism.

"Evening," the man said. "Will you folks be staying the night?"

"We mean to," Gregory said, dismounting. "We've

got two ladies in the ambulance who would appreciate a bed and a meal. A washup too, I imagine."

Not likely, Elizabeth thought. Just the mention of bathing in such a place made her skin crawl.

"Two ladies?" the boy said, craning his head to get a look under the rolled canvas.

"Never mind, June. They're no concern of yours. You just get busy with the mules and horses." The big man offered Gregory his hand. "Benjamin Wilkins is my name and that there's my boy, Junior. We call him June. He's simple, but a good worker. He loves the ladies, but he won't bother them none. Anyhow, you folks are welcome here. My wife's inside, she's just getting food on the table. A bed for the night is one dollar and meals are seventy-five cents—each."

June, unhitching the mules, froze and stared at the women as they climbed down from the ambulance. Elizabeth felt his eyes on her as she followed his father into the house.

A foul smell met her as she stepped through the door. Mildew? Instinctively, she pulled a handkerchief from her sleeve, thinking to cover her nose, but Gregory caught her eye and checked her with a firm shake of his head. He was right, of course, it wouldn't do to be rude, even to people rough as these. Still, she tried to identify the smell. No, it wasn't mildew, there wasn't enough moisture in the air for that. Cabbage? Soured grease? Maybe it was just the perfume of unwashed bodies and slovenly housekeeping.

The house was divided into two rooms. The one in which they stood was dark, with candles burning in soot-blacked tin sconces affixed to the stone walls. It was furnished with a grimy oven, a short table for food preparation, a longer dining table and chairs, and shelves thinly stocked with dry goods for purchase. She saw bottles labeled whiskey (no doubt some kind of high wine mixed with water and flavorings, she thought), gin, and rye (she doubted that the liquid in those bottles ever made the acquaintance of a juniper berry or a grain of rye), jars of nutmeg and cinnamon, clay pipes, navy tobacco, tin cups, a few cans of fruit, and items of clothing. The floor was of packed earth.

The second room was set apart with a blanket hanging in the doorway. When Mrs. Wilkins exited, Elizabeth got a glimpse of the room's dark interior. She saw a number of beds. Some appeared to be occupied, and, in a corner behind a dingy sheet, a tin bathtub. *No*, she thought, *I will not be bathing tonight. Neither will I go anywhere near one of those vermin-infested beds.*

"I'll put supper on," the woman said. She was short and thickset and her calico dress could use a good scrubbing. Elizabeth and Anna exchanged glances as she brushed by them on her way to the stove, where a large covered pot was bubbling.

"Come, Anna," Elizabeth said, "let's wait outside." The women walked out into the red dusk. The evening breeze had come up and the air was beginning to cool. On the side of the house they found a pine bench and two cane-back chairs. Romeo joined them.

"May I keep you company?" he said with a slow smile that warmed her like a prairie sunrise. Elizabeth noticed not for the first time how straight and white his teeth were and she wondered if he, like Armstrong, carried a toothbrush and brushing salts in his shirt pocket at all times. Clearly, Romeo was a young man who took care of himself. He kept his clothes neat and clean and his person too. Elizabeth found cleanliness an attractive quality in a man, and a rare one on the Kansas frontier.

"Please," Elizabeth said. "Romeo, I've been wondering, what is your real first name? I assume it's not Romeo."

"Milo," he said. "My parents called me Milo, but no one's called me that for a long time. Well, Grover does, but he's the only one. You and Miss Darrah can use it if you want to."

She smiled. "No, I think Romeo suits you better. Do you think we'll reach my husband's camp tomorrow, Romeo?"

"No, ma'am. Day after, I'd say. But today wasn't too hard on you ladies, was it? I mean, you're comfortable in the wagon?"

"Oh, yes, so comfortable, in fact, I believe I'll spend the night in there instead of the house. We can fold the bench down to make a bed. I've seen it done."

Jack Gregory approached from the stables, followed by June Wilkins. "That's not a good idea, Mrs. Custer," he said. "You'd be safer inside." June stopped to smile bashfully at her and Anna, then ran inside.

"Nonsense," Elizabeth said. "Anna will stay with me."

"No offense, Miss Darrah," Gregory said with a smile, "but I don't think you'd be much help if Indians or a party of road agents pay us a visit."

Elizabeth tossed her head. "Well, pull the wagon right up to the house," she said. "You and Romeo will be right there, and I don't think we'll have any visitors anyhow." She lowered her voice. "Mr. Grover, I will not spend a night in that, that place—and there's an end to it." She got to her feet just as June Wilkins appeared to say dinner was ready.

Inside, the table was set with plates of bacon, boiled cabbage—so it was cabbage, Elizabeth thought—canned peaches in a bowl, two pots of hot coffee, a cup of sugar and a can of condensed milk. Benjamin Wilkins and three men, Elizabeth supposed those she had seen in the beds earlier, were already eating. Two were twins, with ghostly pale skin and long white-blond hair that hung to their shoulders. Both wore goggles with thick lenses of green glass. This strange pair stood when the women entered, but the third man, the tallest of the three, kept his eyes on his plate and continued to eat. With black hair and swarthy skin, he was as dark as the others were pale.

Elizabeth and the others served their own plates. After a few minutes of silence, Romeo asked the three men what line of work they were in. The tall man gave no sign of hearing, but one of the white twins answered. "We ride for the U.S. Express Company— or we did. Our route got shut down on account of the Indians. Now we're heading north, up to the Gallatin Valley. There's work up there, so we hear." The table went quiet again, but the tall man stopped eating and looked up when Romeo asked Mrs. Custer to pass the sugar.

"Mrs. Custer?" he said. "Would that be any kin to the general?" His face was long and narrow, like a hatchet, and his eyes were like slits in a mask. Elizabeth hesitated before answering. Her husband inspired strong feeling in others, and this fellow looked unpleasant.

"Armstrong Custer is my husband," she said. "I'm on my way to join him at Fort Hays."

The dark man laughed. "Armstrong? That's what you call him? We had a different name for him back where I come from."

"And where might that be?" Gregory asked the question even though he knew the answer.

The dark man fixed his eyes on Gregory. "Jackson County, Missouri, God's country. And how about you, friend? Where you call home?"

"Texas."

"That so? Whereabouts in Texas?"

"You wouldn't know it."

Elizabeth felt tension rising at the table. No one was eating.

"What's your name, friend?" the dark man said. "You look familiar."

"Joe Grover."

The tall man shook his head. "You surely do feature a man I used to know back in Missouri. Jack

Gregory, his name was, and that son of a bitch looked just like you, maybe a little smaller, but same harelip and everything. I did not care for him. Pass me the peaches, friend."

Gregory handed him the bowl of peaches. "I choose my friends," he said.

Though he had not seen him for almost four years, Gregory recognized Cave Gillespie the moment he sat down at the table. Gillespie rode with Quantrill for the raid on Lawrence and for a short time afterward, until Quantrill demanded he leave the company for abusing black women. Gillespie called for a vote and Gregory, then Quantrill's top lieutenant, supported Gillespie's exile. His vote turned the tide; all who followed cast theirs the same way. Though his time and Gillespie's overlapped only briefly, it was long enough for Gregory to know what manner of man Cave Gillespie was.

"All right, all right." Gillespie gave Gregory a yellow smile. "No need to get your pants in a bunch, mister. Just because you feature that bastard don't mean you're the same kind of trash as him. Sure do feature him though. You surely do."

In the darkest corner of the room, Junior Wilkins rocked back and forth on his feet, wringing his hands. His mother left the stove and went to him, speaking softly and stroking his arm. The boy was simply responding to the mounting pressure in the room. Elizabeth stood and dropped her napkin on her plate.

"Thank you for the meal, Mrs. Wilkins," she said. "It was very nice. But now it's late and I'm tired.

Come, Anna, let's prepare for bed." Gregory and Romeo pushed back their chairs and followed the women out the door. As before, the twins rose. Gillespie remained seated, watching them with a smile on his thin lips.

"What happened in there?" Elizabeth said to Gregory once they were out of earshot. "Do you know that awful man? Have you seen him before?"

"If I have, he's not anyone I'd care to remember."

She looked directly into his eyes. "Are you really from Texas?"

"No."

"Is your name Joe Grover?"

"No."

They stood face-to-face in the gathering darkness while Anna and Romeo rearranged the ambulance interior for the evening.

"I don't know what's going on here, Mr. Grover," Elizabeth said, "but whatever it is, we can't stay here tonight. Hitch up the mules and let's go."

Gregory shook his head. "We don't want to be crossing the prairie on our lonesome at night. Besides, the animals need a rest. No, we'll stay. Don't worry about Cave Gillespie, Mrs. Custer. I can handle him. Tweedledee and Tweedledum too."

Elizabeth studied his face, half lit by the light from the window. "Cave Gillespie? He never said his name."

Gregory smiled. "Not much gets by you, does it?"

"Please tell me what's going on, Mr. Grover or Gregory or whatever your name is. I'm not sure I should trust you."

"I will, Mrs. Custer. I'll tell you my story, but not now. Not tonight. For now I'm asking you to count on me to get you and Miss Darrah to Fort Hays safely. Will you do that?"

Elizabeth considered. What choice did she have? "Yes, I suppose I'll have to. But I'm not comfortable with this. I expect answers."

"And you shall have them."

Elizabeth lay awake in the ambulance. Her bed was the lowered bench while Anna had a straw-tick mattress on the floor. The night had gone cold and a light rain pattered on the canvas roof. Gregory and Romeo had placed their bedrolls under the wagon. *Who was this Grover or Gregory fellow, and why had he changed his name?* Elizabeth wondered. *Was he running from something or someone?* Her instincts told her he was worthy of trust, but she had been wrong before. And Kansas was full of lawless, desperate men.

"Liz, are you awake?" Elizabeth thought her friend was asleep.

"Yes."

"I can't sleep either. I'm too upset. I keep thinking about that man. I get the feeling he wants to hurt us. What time is it, do you think? How much longer till we leave? I can't wait to get away from here."

Elizabeth threw off the blankets and peered out the small window in the ambulance door. The rain had stopped, but there was no moon and no stars. The night was black as Egypt. "Two o'clock or so," she said, "maybe later." In fact, she had no idea, but she thought Anna would feel better if dawn were just a few hours away. Elizabeth was turning from the window to return to her bed when she saw—or thought she saw—a man in the door of the station house. She closed her eyes and looked again, but the shadow was gone.

"What is it?" Anna sat up, her face white in the darkness. "Did you see something?"

"No, nothing. There's nothing." Elizabeth got back in bed and wrapped herself in the blanket. "Don't worry, Anna. We'll be leaving in a few hours and never see that fellow again." But she too wished that time had come.

Finally she slept, waking to a cold, blue dawn. She and Anna dressed quickly, not bothering to light a candle. As she pulled on her shoes, Elizabeth imagined herself soaking in a deep tub of steaming water, scented with rose oil, and washing her hair with lemon soap. This would be the first thing she would do when she got to Fort Hays. Armstrong would arrange it, he was good about such things. Elizabeth was thinking of this when she opened the ambulance door. Gillespie was waiting with a smile on his face and a revolver in his hand. She heard Anna gasp behind her.

"Good morning, ladies," he said, with an elaborate bow. "I was just fixing to knock and ask you to join us. We're about to enjoy some coffee." He gestured with his gun toward the station house, where Benjamin Wilkins, his wife, and Romeo sat on the ground with their backs against the stone wall, their hands and feet bound with rope. Romeo had a knot on his forehead and a bruised eye that was beginning to swell. Off to the side, the white twins sat in the chairs Elizabeth and Anna had used the evening before, drinking whiskey from a bottle they passed between them. June Wilkins stood in the doorway, his face a portrait of confusion and misery.

"Where is Mr. Grover?" Elizabeth said.

"You mean Jack Gregory? Funny, I was just about to ask you the same thing," Gillespie said. "I thought maybe he was in there with you two. You never know with a man like him. But General Custer—Armstrong— he wouldn't like that much, would he?"

Elizabeth climbed down from the ambulance and walked to the house to stand beside Romeo. Anna followed. "I haven't seen Mr. Grover since last night," Elizabeth said.

"Well, he's around somewhere," Gillespie said. "That horse of his is still in the stable. Guess we'll just have to wait. I've got a score to settle with that son of a bitch."

Elizabeth's mind raced. Where was he? She scanned the flat and treeless horizon. The sky was just beginning to lighten. Surely Gregory—she was already beginning to think of him by that name—was watching them now, waiting to make a move. He wouldn't leave them at the mercy of scoundrels like these. All the while, Gillespie's eyes were on her, as if reading her thoughts. He gave her another of his yellow smiles.

"When does the next stage come through here, Wilkins?" he said, still eyeing Elizabeth.

"Nine o'clock," Wilkins said, "and it will be on time. Hank France ain't never late."

"Oh, he ain't? Well then, I guess we'd better get cracking." Gillespie walked to the center of the yard. "Gregory! I know you're out there. Show yourself or one of these nice people is going to get shot." He took a watch out of his coat pocket. "I'll give you three minutes."

"My God!" Anna said.

Elizabeth felt weak in the knees. She believed this man, Gillespie, could kill each one of them without a twinge of guilt. They waited. Time seemed to stand still. Occasionally June released a loud moan, otherwise there was no sound but the chirping of the peepers down by the creek.

"Do you know where he is?" Elizabeth whispered to Romeo.

"He was gone when one of those freaks woke me up with a gun in my face."

Elizabeth felt she would be sick.

"Two minutes, Gregory!" Gillespie raised the watch over his head and walked to the Wilkins woman, pressing the business end of his revolver to her head. June in the doorway whimpered like a kicked pup. "The old lady gets it first, Gregory," Gillespie said. "Then I'll shoot the simple." The boy turned and ran into the house.

"Take me," Benjamin Wilkins said. "Don't hurt my wife. Don't hurt the boy. June never did no harm to anybody. Take me instead." Wilkins tried to stand, but, because of his bound feet, could not.

"Shut up, old man," Gillespie said, not looking at him. "Don't try to be a hero. Nobody cares."

"How do you know Grover won't just shoot you from wherever he is?" Elizabeth said.

"He could," Gillespie said. "He very well could. But odds are I'll be able to get one shot off anyhow. The old woman still dies. He knows that."

"You ain't really going to shoot her, are you, Cave?" One of the twins got unsteadily to his feet, knocking over his chair. "You said your business was with the harelip, Gregory. You never said nothing about shooting a woman. Me and Lem, we don't support shooting females. Why don't we just keep these people tied up and be on our way? Meet up with that preacher fellow and do that thing like we planned?"

"Shut your mouth, Kemper. I don't give a damn what you support. The two of you together don't have the brains, or the eyesight, God gave a pinecone." He raised his watch again. "One minute, Gregory! Show yourself in one minute or I blow the old lady's brains out!" The nose of his revolver remained at the woman's temple.

"Here I am, Gillespie."

Elizabeth heard but could not see him. His voice seemed to be coming from above. She stepped away from the house and looked up to see Gregory standing on the roof, silhouetted against the rising sun.

Gillespie did not move. "Throw down your gun,

Gregory," he said. "Then get down here. Lem and Luther, you boys make sure he does like I say."

The twins walked to the center of the yard with their guns drawn. "You heard him, Gregory," Luther said. "Throw it down."

Elizabeth saw him hesitate. "He'll do it," she called to him. "He'll kill Mrs. Wilkins."

"Listen to the lady, Gregory!" Gillespie said.

Gregory tossed his pistol to the ground, then went to the rear of the house, where the twins met him, and jumped down. He walked alone to the center of the yard and stopped, facing Gillespie. Only then did he move his gun from the Wilkins woman's head. He walked toward Gregory with his gun pointed at the scout's stomach.

"Bet you thought you'd never see me again, huh, Jack?" Gillespie said. Though he was not smiling, Elizabeth could see he was enjoying himself. "Bet you thought you'd get away with making me look bad in front of the boys."

"You didn't need my help with that," Gregory said. "You do a good job of that on your own."

"You son of a bitch!" Gillespie shouted. "Nobody cared about those nigger women. Nobody! Quantrill didn't have no trouble with me before you came along. You had me run outta that camp like a dog. You shamed me in front of boys I rode with for five years, boys I've known all my life. All because of you, a goddamn nigger lover!"

He raised his arm, shifting his aim from Gregory's stomach to his head, and thumbed back the hammer.

Elizabeth closed her eyes and pressed her hands to her ears, but it was not sufficient to stifle the thunderous boom that seemed to shake the very ground. She opened her eyes.

Gillespie lay on the ground, his head exploded like a ripe melon. Gregory leapt forward to retrieve his gun and Gillespie's. He fixed the weapons on the twins, who stood frozen, then slowly raised their hands in the air, turning their green-goggled eyes toward the station house. Junior Wilkins stood in the door with a Henry rifle in his hands. With a sob, he threw it to the ground, ran to his mother, and began clumsily to untie her hands.

"Momma." His voice thick with tears. "Momma."

"I'm all right, Junebug," she said, stroking his head with her hand, the loosened rope dangling from her wrist. "Momma's all right. You are a good boy, Junebug. You are Momma's good boy. Where did you get that gun, son?"

He raised his wet face and pointed to Gregory. "He gave it to me last night, in the stables, before dinner. He said to hide it in the house and keep it a secret between us because that one"—he pointed to Gillespie's bloody corpse—"might try to hurt us. Did I do wrong?"

"No, Junebug, no," she said. "You did fine."

Gregory picked up the rifle and walked over to the boy, crying in his mother's arms. "Stand up, Junior," he said.

June looked at his mother, who nodded. When he was on his feet, Gregory extended his hand and June took it, tentatively. "You did a brave thing today, June," Gregory said. "You saved your mother, you saved your father, you saved all of us. It's an honor to shake your hand."

The boy's face reddened, for the first time in his life, with pride.

Chapter Ten

In preparation for his wife's visit, Custer had moved his tent to a cool, shaded bend on the water, apart from the rest of the camp, and ordered that screens of evergreens be set up around them to ensure privacy. The Custer compound also included separate tents for Anna and Tom Custer and a large white hospital tent so the ladies would have a cool place to lounge during the hot Kansas afternoons.

When their ambulance approached the camp, Custer ran forward to meet it, finishing with a perfectly executed handspring that landed him at the open door, where Elizabeth stood laughing. He was a splendid athlete, this no one could deny. He put his hands on her small waist and lifted her to the ground, as if she weighed no more than a box of groceries. When he kissed her, it was with such heat she was embarrassed.

"Libbie," he whispered, his mouth by her ear. "How I've longed for you."

"Armstrong, please," she said. "People are

watching." She was especially aware of Jack Gregory, who had followed the ambulance on horseback.

"What do I care?" Custer said. "Let them watch." He kissed her again.

"I've missed you too, Armstrong," she said, "but please, stop. You're making me uncomfortable." Finally, he let her push him to arm's length. "Let me look at you," she said. "It feels like years since we've been together."

"Don't call me Armstrong," he said, in a petulant voice. "You know I don't like it. Call me Autie, like you used to." Then he turned to Anna and lifted her from the ambulance also, pretending to struggle.

"Oomph." He grunted as he set her on the ground. "Miss Darrah hasn't missed many meals I see. Tom will have to pick up some to be ready for you."

Anna slapped him playfully on the shoulder. "He likes me just the way I am. Tom likes a woman with meat on her bones—he's told me so many times."

"Well, brother Tom's got some meaty bones with you, my dear," Custer said, laughing, "and lovely ones too. Where is that lazy bastard anyway? Let's go find him." He took each woman by the arm, stopping to speak to his striker, standing by. "Bring the ladies' bags, Doering. Mrs. Custer's things go in my tent, obviously. Miss Darrah is in the tent next to Captain Custer's."

Private Felix Doering, a cheerful young soldier with red hair and a face covered in freckles, responded with a brisk salute. "Yes sir, General Custer."

Captain Albert Barnitz, a handsome Ohioan with a headful of wild, blond curls, accompanied them as they walked to the compound. Barnitz wrote poetry in his free time, and though she considered his verse to be only mediocre, Elizabeth enjoyed his company. His wife, Jennie, sometimes joined him in the field, one of the few wives besides Elizabeth who chose to do so.

"Will Jennie be joining us?" she asked. "I hope so."

"Perhaps later," he said. His eyes were on six men shuffling across the parade lawn, their hands and feet in chains. Each man's head was partially shaven, in some cases so closely the skin bled. An officer marched at the front of the short column and a drummer brought up the rear, marking each step with a slow, funeral beat. Men lined their path, jeering at the miserable paraders.

"What's that about, Armstr—Autie?" Elizabeth said. "Why are those men being punished?"

Custer waved his hand dismissively. "Ignore them, Libbie. They aren't worthy of your attention. They're deserters, the worst kind of scum. I'm making an example of them."

Elizabeth recalled General Sherman's comments about morale in the Seventh Cavalry. "I see," she said. "How long were they gone? How did you manage to catch them?"

"I said ignore them." Custer spoke shortly.

Elizabeth watched the men, heads lowered and eyes downcast, as they shuffled back to the guard tent. "Please tell me," she said. "I'd like to know."

Custer heaved an exaggerated sigh. "I didn't catch them, they returned of their own accord. But that doesn't matter. They left without permission and that's desertion. We've had a plague of it this spring and I'm determined to put an end to it. But enough! No more talk of this. It's no concern to my precious girl." He put his arm around her shoulders and drew her to him.

She pulled away. "But if they returned on their own, is that desertion? Couldn't you call it something else . . . maybe absent without leave? Where did they go?"

Armstrong was getting annoyed. Anna drew her finger across her throat, but Elizabeth was compelled to know the answers.

"They went to Fort Hays, if you must know," Custer said.

"To drink or gamble? To visit a hog ranch? It must've been something awful to merit such public humiliation."

Barnitz, who until now had accompanied them silently, spoke up. "They went to the trader's store to purchase canned goods. Peaches, I believe. They were gone all of forty-five minutes and missed no roll call or any duty." Barnitz spoke carefully, but it was clear he disagreed with Custer's action.

"Armstrong!" Elizabeth withdrew her arm. "Surely this is too harsh for something harmless as canned peaches. Why, your men will hate you. They'll call you a tyrant." *They already do,* she thought.

Custer shot Barnitz an angry look. "It's not what they went for, Libbie, it's that they went at all. I just told you we've had a plague of desertions this spring. I can't have men leaving camp without authorization, it's simple as that. I've been very clear on this.

It's a challenge to my authority. A regiment runs on respect for authority, you know that. A commanding officer must be firm and consistent. He can't be concerned about his popularity."

"Obviously," Elizabeth said. She wished she could make him listen to her in these matters, that he could see how his actions affected both of them. Her fortunes were tied to his, but she had plans and designs of her own. She was more than his "precious girl"—in fact, her blood boiled when he addressed her in that patronizing manner. She was not a girl, she was a grown woman with a well-developed sense of what was right and appropriate and what was not. Others recognized her as a good judge of character and moral authority. He would be a more successful officer if only he would heed her advice. She did not intend to be a lieutenant colonel's wife forever!

"Enough of this," Custer said. His reunion with Libbie was not starting off the way he planned. The last thing he wanted to discuss with his newly arrived wife was the regiment's snowbird problem. Custer waved his manicured hand in the air as if shooing away a gnat. "So, tell me of your trip from Fort Riley." He winked at Anna. "Did you girls have any adventures?"

The two women exchanged a glance. "No adventures," Elizabeth said shortly. "It was really quite tedious."

* * *

Elizabeth had decided not to mention the experience at the stage station to her husband. The scout, Gregory, had something murky in his past, that was clear, but this was by no means unusual for men in his line of work and Elizabeth would keep his secret, for a time at least, even though he had not asked this of her. When she asked Anna to do the same, on their last day of travel, her friend had needed convincing.

"I don't know, Liz," she said. "What do you know of him, really? Maybe he did some terrible thing— maybe he killed an officer! Armstrong should know, so he can at least look into it. Think about it—there's a reason he's hiding his identity."

Elizabeth turned her head to study the passing country. There was nothing to catch the eye, only hard blue sky and rolling green hills. No houses, no trees, no water. The May afternoon was hot and both women were perspiring, even though they'd loosened their collars and shirtwaists. What a cruel, unforgiving country this was.

"I don't think a man who was troubled by the mistreatment of slave women would do anything terrible," Elizabeth said. "But if he did, he may have had a good reason."

Anna shook her head. "I don't understand you," she said. "You're married to one of the most famous, most admired men in the country—thousands of women would give anything to take your place—and you seem indifferent to it all, sometimes even to Armstrong himself. I don't think you appreciate what

you have in him, and I certainly don't know why
you'd risk any of it for a man like that scout, whoever he is."

Elizabeth's eyes fell on Gregory, riding his chestnut gelding beside the ambulance. Anna was right.
What she was doing was not rational. She had no
reason to believe in him, but she wanted to. Sometimes she caught him looking at her in a way that
made her heart beat faster. Even though she sensed
he was thinking of someone else, seeing another
woman, when he looked at her, she quite liked it.
It was a sensation she had not felt in some time.
And she had been impressed with the way he
treated the Wilkins family. They were not important people, just an aging couple and an afflicted
child. Armstrong would have been dismissive of
them, the way he was with store clerks or the servers
at restaurants. Gregory even showed leniency to
the Kemper twins. A cruel man would not have
done so.

"I don't want to deal with the law on this and I bet
you don't either," he had said to them. "Wilkins, do
you have a shovel in that barn?"

"I do."

"You boys go get it and put Gillespie under,"
Gregory said. "Then clear out of here. In the future
stay shut of men like Cave Gillespie. No good comes
of associations like that."

"Yes, sir," Luther Kemper said. "We will do it." He
and his brother hurried to the barn.

"Milo, help me drag him around back. We'll plant him in that cornfield. Is that all right with you, Wilkins?"

Benjamin Wilkins nodded. "Son of a bitch should make good fertilizer."

Chapter Eleven

When Gregory entered the smoke-filled tent, Custer motioned to an empty camp chair next to his. Gregory took it, joining the circle of Custer's officers, each smoking a pipe or cigar.

"Do you smoke, Grover?" Custer said. "No? Good man, neither do I. It fouls the lungs. I wish my associates felt the same. Anyhow, I'm glad you're here. It's high time we had a scout who knows Indians and how to find them."

Custer stood. "Gentlemen, this is Joe Grover, our new head scout. He comes to us from Fort Wallace, on loan from our friend, Captain Myles Keogh, who speaks very highly of him. Captain Michael Sheridan has worked with him a great deal also, and he tells me Grover knows the Smoky Hill valley better than any man alive. Yes, I firmly believe that if anyone can help us, this is our man."

Gregory looked at the ring of tired, bored faces. First to offer his hand was the surgeon, Major Adolph Higgins, a small fellow with wispy gray hair and thick eyeglasses. His shake was limp and his hand cool and soft, like a woman's. "Good to have you with us, Grover," he said. "Let me know if there's anything I can do for you." He moved in closer and, despite his heavy lenses, Gregory could see the physician was eyeing his scar. "I wonder, if you don't mind my asking, when was the cleft repaired? That is, how old were you?"

The question was not welcome, but Gregory answered. "I was six."

"I see." Gregory resisted the impulse to step back. "Was the palate involved, or the lip only? I am fascinated by congenital fissures and malformations. Your repair appears to have been expertly done."

Custer cleared his throat. "Is this necessary, Dr. Higgins? Couldn't this wait for later?"

"Yes, yes, of course. I forget myself. Apologies." He smiled and returned to his chair.

The next officer introduced, Major Wyckliffe Cooper, appeared intoxicated and seemed to have difficulty focusing his eyes. Other than Higgins, only one of Custer's staff regarded Gregory with any sign of interest. He wore the insignia of a captain, with a head of fluffy white hair, a dimpled smile, and the eyes of a well poisoner.

"So, Mr. Grover," he said, his dimples deepening, "that's an impressive introduction, but I wonder, what will you do for us our other scouts could not? After all, they came highly recommended too, especially Mr. Hickok, the so-called Wild Bill. As far as I can tell, he's nothing but a glorified courier and I could say the same for Messrs. Guerrier, Atkins, and Kincaid. No Natty Bumppos there either, I'm afraid."

A few chuckled. Custer did not. All eyes were on Gregory, awaiting his response.

"Those are good men. I would not put myself above them." Turning to Custer he said, "Do you have any Delawares with you?"

"Yes, a number of Delaware scouts, recruited from the agency south of Fort Leavenworth."

"Is a man called Fall Leaf with them? Older fellow, with gray hair and short, even for an Indian? Stands about here?" Gregory moved his hand, palm down, to a place well below his shoulder.

"I believe I've seen one who fits that description."

"Well, like I said, those names you mentioned are all good men, and experienced," Gregory said. "If you're having trouble, I'd say it's because you haven't been using your Delawares correctly. Fall Leaf is one of the best trackers I've ever met. I've never known him to fail." He was pleased to hear his friend was with the troop, though he knew the old Indian would be surprised to hear him go by the name of Joe Grover. He had no worry the Delaware chief would give him away; the red men Gregory had known in his life were generally—though not always—more trustworthy than the whites.

"And why should we put so much confidence in this Fall Leaf character?" the dimpled officer said.

"I just told you."

"So, you're saying it takes an Indian to catch an Indian?"

"That's one way of putting it," Gregory said. "The

Delaware have no love for the Sioux or Cheyenne, Fall Leaf in particular. He'll do the job for you."

"Well, if that's true why do we need you?"

"You probably don't," Gregory said. "I'd be happy to go back to Wallace."

"That's enough, Captain Benteen," Custer said. "Grover's here because I asked for him." A bugle sounded stable call and Custer looked relieved. "Benteen, aren't you officer of the day?"

"Yes, as usual," Benteen said. He rose with a sigh, gave Custer an exaggerated salute, and left the tent. The officers followed him out, but for Custer and one other.

"I apologize, Grover," Custer said. "Captain Frederick Benteen commands F Troop and he's a human skunk. He lives to make trouble, especially for me. I assure you, most of my officers are glad you're here. We've had a rough go, but now, with you along, things are going to turn around. I believe that."

"I'll do what I can," Gregory said. He waited for Custer to bring up the events at the stage station and the question of his identity, but it appeared Custer knew nothing of what happened there. Gregory was grateful for this, but confused at the same time. Why would Elizabeth Custer take a chance on him? The Darrah woman was easier to figure out; she would do whatever Mrs. Custer told her, and apparently Elizabeth had asked her to keep his secret as well. Anna would comply as long as it was in her best interest, but at the first sign of trouble she would talk.

Anna Darrah was one of those, but Elizabeth, she was a puzzle.

"Go on and get settled in," Custer said. "Keep your horse with mine, apart from the others. We've got a problem in the remuda, some disease is starting. I've supposed it to be glanders—they're running from the mouth and nostrils—but the veterinary surgeon thinks it lung fever, says the horses and mules need bran mashes. Bran mashes! He may as well have asked for shoes of solid gold." Custer paused on his way out the door. "Pitch your tent near ours, Grover. I want you to mess with Libbie and me also—not every night, of course, but often. I've got a lot to learn from you about the Indians, I want to know their habits, their signs and languages, all of it. I plan to make the most of our association. Is there anything you need?"

"For my tent, I'd prefer a Sibley, if your quarter-master has one to spare," Gregory said. Experience had taught him these cone-shaped structures held up better than a wall tent, even a well-anchored one, during a storm.

"I'll see to it," Custer said. Gregory expected the other office to follow Custer out the door, but he remained.

"Captain Albert Barnitz," he said, with a firm hand-shake. "G Troop. I'm glad we've got a few minutes to ourselves, Grover. I'm going to be candid with you, and I do not believe I'm talking out of school. So far, this campaign has been a disaster of the first water. You should know that. Everything, every single thing, has gone wrong, starting with the weather. We've been most unlucky there, snow, cold, wind—one old-timer told me it's the worst spring he's seen since forty-four. The bridges and roads were washed out and our supply trains couldn't get through, the whole prairie turned to a sea of mud. The men are hungry, they're eating bread that's five years old, and the animals . . . well, I heard Custer tell you they're ailing. No surprise! They've had no forage, hardly any grain and very little hay, and on top of that we've used them up on marches of eighteen, nineteen miles a day, sometimes without a single halt. Of course the horses are unwell—how could they be otherwise? Now General Hancock—Old Thunderbolt! ha!—he's returned to Leavenworth, having accomplished nothing but stirred up the hornets' nest. He's left the Seventh Cavalry with thousands of angry Indians to deal with and very shabby supplies with which to do it." Barnitz ran a hand through his unruly blond hair. "And our scouts . . . so, you know Hickok?"

"Mostly by reputation."

Barnitz laughed. "Yes, he's certainly got one of those. General Custer is quite taken with him; I am not. I arrested that mollycoddle in sixty-five, in Springfield, Missouri, when I was commanding there. He shot a man dead in the street—oh, he called it a duel, but I have no doubt it was a gambling matter. The charge didn't stick, but there's been bad blood between us ever since. He's not much of a scout anyway. He drinks too much, he's more interested in hair pomades and fancy clothing than finding Indians. I find him effeminate, to tell you the truth."

Gregory had heard others say this of Hickok, though never to his face.

"Anyhow, we've fooled away the entire spring," Barnitz said. "The Indians do as they please while we twiddle our fingers here in camp, knee-deep in mud, waiting for supplies. I suppose you heard about that village we burned on the Pawnee Fork? That was a big mistake too, there was no proof those Indians were responsible for the murders at Lookout Station, but we've certainly made enemies of them now! Then there's the desertions—sixty-five last month alone. As for Custer—well, I'll let you discover for yourself what sort of officer he is." Barnitz shook his head and put on his hat. "As I said, Grover, I'm telling you this so you'll know where you stand and what you're dealing with. I sincerely hope you can help us turn this ship around. A campaign like this could blight a man's career."

"Thank you for being honest with me, Captain Barnitz. Like I said, I'll do my best." Gregory followed the officer out of the tent and into the red twilight, wishing this assignment was over and he was back at Fort Wallace, waiting for Maggie to put his dinner on the table.

Chapter Twelve

Gunshots woke him just after midnight. Gregory threw off his blankets and ran from his tent just as Custer emerged from his. As he opened the flap, Gregory got a glimpse of Elizabeth sitting in their bed, her hair unarranged, her lovely face white in the darkness. She held a sheet, covering her breasts. She had beautiful shoulders.

"What is it?" Custer called to Benteen, who was running toward him. "More deserters?" Even as he spoke, they heard more gunfire, an exchange of twenty or thirty shots coming from the picket line.

"Yes, sir," Benteen said. "Four men broke through the guard and took off, armed and mounted. My boys fired on them and they returned fire. Fortunately none of ours was hit. I don't know about them."

Barnitz and Tom joined them on the run.

"Turn out the companies," Custer said to his brother. "Call the rolls. I'll find out who these cowards are and go after them! I will hunt them down like the dogs they are and make them suffer."

Within a few minutes the officers had their men lined up in rows by company. A roll call showed the four absent troopers, including a first sergeant, were from E Company. Custer wrote their names on a piece of paper and handed it to Gregory.

"Your first assignment, Grover," he said. "Go after them in the morning. Find them and bring them back. I don't care how long it takes and I don't care if they're dead or alive when they get here. I will make an example of them." Private Doering held a pierced tin lantern that swung in his hand, throwing crazy shadows on Custer's face.

"Like you made an example of those men yesterday?" Barnitz said. "I don't notice that had much effect."

Custer wheeled on him. "Damn you, Barnitz! Must you question every move I make? I'm warning you, I've had my fill of your whining and complaining."

Barnitz's face was red as Custer's. "General, I only worry that the men—"

"Yes! You worry, Barnitz, that's all you do—worry. My God, man, you remind me of my maiden aunt. Just do as you're told and leave the worrying to me." Custer turned from Barnitz to Gregory. "What will you need?"

"I'd like to take Fall Leaf along, and Mendoza too. We'll need a wagon, two mules to pull it and food for . . ." He considered. "Two days."

"Whatever you want, just bring them back. I know you won't let me down, Grover."

* * *

They left at dawn. Gregory and Fall Leaf rode horseback while Romeo drove an open wagon with his horse tied to a ringbolt in the back. The deserters' trail was easy to follow, as the fleeing men made no attempt at concealment.

"They keep together," Fall Leaf said, his eyes on the ground. "This is good for us. One is hurt." He pointed to a black splash of dried blood on the surface of a rock.

Gregory had expected the snowbirds to head south, toward Council Grove, which had become a sort of capital for desperados, road agents, and vagabonds. But these men were going west. Their track paralleled the Smoky Hill Trail.

"Could be they go to Colorado?" Fall Leaf said. "Maybe so."

Gregory nodded, thinking that's what he would do in their place. There were plenty of places for a man to disappear in a town like Denver.

They rode in silence with Romeo and the wagon rattling along behind. After a time Fall Leaf said, "Much time has passed since I last saw my friend. Since before the white man's long war. You were a boy with no hair on your face."

"Yes, the last time was that job at Fort Halleck," Gregory said. "The army hired us to find the woman killer, John Stubbs, and when we did they gave us five hundred dollars."

"Stubbs." The old Indian grinned, revealing tobacco-stained teeth. "When they hang him"—he put his hands on his ears and moved them forward in a throwing motion—"his head flies away."

Gregory nodded grimly. "That one was hard to forget," he said. "The hangman used too much counterbalance."

"My friend was called Jack Gregory in those days," Fall Leaf said, "and now he is called Grover. Why is this?"

Gregory considered, squinting into the rising sun. If he couldn't trust Fall Leaf he couldn't trust anyone. "I took some money that was due me," he said, "though the army might not see it that way. Then I had trouble up north, at a soldier fort in the Dakota Territory, not far from Fort Halleck. I do not blame myself for what happened, it was something I had to do and would do again, but the whites might lock me up for it. I call myself by another name, but I am the same man, no different."

Fall Leaf gave Gregory another nut-brown grin. "Does this one know?" He moved his head in the direction of Romeo following in the wagon, whistling the church hymns he called songs of glory.

"He knows as much as you do. He calls me Joe and doesn't ask questions."

"I will do the same," Fall Leaf said.

They rode for another two hours. By now the sun was fully up and the Kansas prairie yawned wide before them, endless in all directions. The only feature to catch the eye was a dark string of cottonwoods about a mile distant. Trees meant water, and the deserters had turned their horses toward them. The trail of their shod hooves was easy to follow. Fall Leaf, riding a hundred yards or so to the west, waved Gregory to his side.

"There," he said, pointing down to a second line of beaten grass. "Seven riders."

The tracks left by the unshod ponies were clear also. At this point, the soldiers did not know the Indians were behind them. Their big American horses were moving at a leisurely pace and in an ordered manner. This would soon change. Gregory scanned the sky for circling carrion birds. He did not see any, but this would change too.

They followed the soldiers' trail to the creek. Here they had dismounted, in the shade of the cottonwoods, and led their horses to water. Gregory and Fall Leaf did the same. As Jeff drank, Gregory looked around. Opened but still mostly full cans of sardines, tomatoes, and lima beans lay on the ground, many overturned. Close to the water was a pile of kindling, a newly dug fire pit, and an empty coffeepot. All around he saw signs of panic. The sandy soil was scored by the feet of running men and horses.

"This is where it started," Fall Leaf said, looking up the creek. "The end will not be far."

They heard Romeo arriving with the wagon, stopping the mules outside the trees. "Joe, what is it?" he called. "What do you see in there?"

Gregory and Fall Leaf walked out of the cottonwoods, leading their horses. Gregory walked around to the bed of the wagon where there were two Spencer carbines and boxes of cartridges. He took one of the guns, loaded it, and gave the other to Fall Leaf. Gregory and Romeo had Colt revolvers tucked into their belts and a Henry carbine lay at Romeo's feet.

"What is it?" he said again, shifting uneasily on the bench.

"We aren't the only ones after these birds," Gregory said. "Indians are on them too and I'm thinking they caught up with them not far ahead. Played out like they were, their horses couldn't hold out long. Keep your gun handy, Milo, in case the bucks are still around."

Romeo laid the carbine across his knees. "Hell, Joe, I thought we'd find those deserters and take 'em back to Custer. I didn't figure on fighting no Indians." He looked over his shoulder.

"We probably won't have to," Gregory said. "Just be on the lookout." He and Fall Leaf mounted their horses.

"The mules need water," Romeo said. "My horse too. You two go ahead, I'll be along directly."

"Don't be long," Gregory said. "We'll be needing that wagon."

He and Fall Leaf followed the trail westward, back onto the prairie. The track was different now, shod American horses and shoeless ponies, all jumbled together and moving at full speed. They rode for about a mile before spotting an object lying on their path. It was a dead horse, with the U.S. brand, shot in the head. Two arrows were buried in its flanks. The animal's equipment—saddle, bridle, halter— and the rider's saddlebags were still in place. Gregory removed the bags and examined their contents. The near side pouch held rations, including several tins of canned meat; the far pouch contained an extra pair of socks, drawers, two shirts, forty rounds of ammunition, a comb, and a razor. The drawers and shirts were marked with black ink: J. Stroup.

Gregory checked Custer's list and found *James Stroup, Private, E Company.*

Fall Leaf dismounted and examined the fletching on the arrows. The shafts were marked with bands of color, red and yellow.

"Sioux," Fall Leaf said, drawing a finger across his throat. "Pawnee Killer, the son of a bitch."

"You sure?" Gregory said. He suspected Pawnee Killer and his Oglala warriors were in the area, particularly when he heard of the grisly murders of the three workers at Lookout Station.

Fall Leaf nodded. "The arrows are Sioux, and see how the shafts are marked with the red and the yellow? This is Pawnee Killer."

Now Gregory was even more convinced they would find blood and sorrow at the end of the line. Before riding on, he turned and looked back, expecting to see Milo and the wagon. When he didn't, he thought about going to look for him. Milo didn't have much experience with Indians and he seemed nervous. Gregory thought he probably wasn't happy back there, all on his lonesome.

"Look." Fall Leaf pointed. "We find them there." Birds were circling in the sky ahead. They kicked their horses into a trot and before long came upon another dead horse. This time the rider lay nearby, a distance of maybe ten yards, with a line of flattened, bloodstained grass separating man and beast.

Gregory pictured the wounded trooper, his legs or back broken in the fall, dragging himself away from his horse in a desperate attempt to escape the un-escapable. Gregory dismounted and stood over the body. The man lay on his face, the back of his head crushed with a stone hammer or war club. He had not been scalped, probably because his hair was too thin to make an impressive trophy. Gregory walked back to the horse and examined the contents of the saddlebags. The rations were gone, but he found socks—Indians had no use for socks—and two shirts. *M. MacIntosh.* Another name on the list.

"Here!" Fall Leaf waved him to a depression in the ground about one hundred feet ahead. Gregory joined him, knowing what he would find. It was a scene of carnage such as he had not seen since that freezing night on Lodge Trail Ridge the winter before. All three of the men had been scalped. One had been sliced open from sternum to pubis, his entrails removed and unwound, like an obscene pink ribbon, through the grass. A second man held his eyeballs in the palms of his hands while his severed nose rested on his abdomen. The third had been draped, facedown, across the body of one of the dead cavalry horses. His pants were down around his ankles, and his bare buttocks had been used as target practice. It bristled with maybe twenty arrows; Gregory did not count them. He knew what the display meant: It was a sign of disrespect.

"He was not brave," Fall Leaf said.

"No." Gregory stood over the bodies. He figured they had maybe three hours of daylight left. Should they bury them or take the grim remains back to Custer's camp? But another, more pressing question weighed on him. Fall Leaf gave it voice.

"Where is your friend?" he said.

"Yes," Gregory said. "We should go back."

They urged their horses into a canter. Gregory had a bad feeling. Milo had plenty of sand, but he was afraid of Indians. He wouldn't say it, but he was. Gregory thought he shouldn't have left him alone.

They rode for an hour. Fall Leaf saw it first. He reined in his horse and pointed, then Gregory saw it too, a mile ahead on the prairie. A knot of fear tightened in his stomach as they got closer. It was the wagon, as he feared, with the two mules dead on the ground and still in harness. Milo sat upright on the bench. He was still, only his shirt and his long hair moved in the wind.

Gregory dismounted and approached the wagon. The young man's head hung forward so his chin almost touched his chest. The front of the shirt he proudly kept so clean was black with blood, clear down to his belt. "Milo," he said, not because he expected an answer, but because he needed to say his name. Though he was only mediocre with a gun—in practice he'd hit his mark only two times out of ten—Milo was a true friend and a man you could count on. He did not deserve to go out this way.

Gregory touched Milo's leg. He could not understand why he sat so stiffly. What was holding him up? Gregory walked around to the back of the wagon and climbed onto the bed. There, behind the bench, was a muddy boot print, with a cross carved in the heel. That was where the killer stood when he drove a long picket pin downward into Milo's spine, nailing his body to the wooden bench. Gregory prayed his friend was already dead when that was done.

Getting him free was hard work. When they laid Milo's body on the grass, Gregory saw his throat had been cut from ear to ear, clean through to the cervical spine. There was rage in it. The wound kindled an unwelcome memory in Gregory's mind, an image from that December night on Lodge Trail Ridge when he and Daniel Dixon found the remains of Captain Fetterman and his men. He had to study Fetterman's body for some time before he could make sense of what he saw, but finally, with a shock, he realized the officer's throat had been slashed and his tongue pulled through the slit. Then, as now, Gregory was awed by the passionate hatred that spawned such violence. How much hate would it take before such an act—or this thing that was done to Milo—would occur to a man?

After covering the body with a tarpaulin, Gregory walked around the site, trying to make sense of what had happened. He found a number of spent cartridges behind one of the mules. Clearly, Milo had taken shelter there and tried to fight off his attackers. At the same time, Fall Leaf studied the ground to the east, sometimes dropping to his knees in the buffalo grass.

"He wasn't killed by Indians," Gregory said when

they came together. "There's a boot print by the wagon and another one on the bed floor."

Fall Leaf nodded. "Yes, they rode American horses."

"How many?"

"Three."

Gregory removed his hat and wiped his face with a handkerchief. "We'll bury Milo and stay here tonight. Tomorrow we'll go back and get those others, take their bodies back to Custer. I will find the men who did this to Milo Mendoza, and when I do, they'll curse their mothers for giving them life."

Chapter Thirteen

Elizabeth lay on her back on the army cot. She was feeling uncharacteristically indolent, in no hurry to get out of bed. The sun was fully up and the shadows of the leaves on the cedar trees that surrounded their tent danced across the canvas walls. Armstrong was at his shaving stand, rinsing the soap off his face in a porcelain basin. When he straightened, his eyes met hers in the mirror.

"What?" he said, drying with a coarse muslin towel. "Why are you looking at me like that?"

"How am I looking at you?" she said.

"Like I've done something to displease you." He walked to the cot and sat beside her. With a smile, he took her hand and put it to his lips. "Have I annoyed my lovely girl?"

She returned his smile, even though he continued to ignore her request to stop calling her a girl. They had made love the night before and again that morning. It was better than it had been for a long time.

Maybe, she thought, there was hope for them after all. "No," she said, "quite the opposite in fact."

"Good." He leaned in and kissed her lightly on the lips. "I want my beautiful Libbie to be happy." He stood and crossed the tent to his clothes, hanging neatly on a taut line strung from one side of their tent to the other. Armstrong was well-known for his fastidiousness about his clothing, about his appearance in general. His brother and those few officers he was close to enjoyed chiding him about it.

"Anna asked me to talk to you about Tom's drinking," she said as he stepped into his blue serge trousers. "She says it's becoming more of a problem."

"Does she? Well, I haven't noticed anything." Elizabeth expected this. Armstrong had a blind spot when it came to his younger brother. Tom had won two Congressional Medals of Honor during the war and Elizabeth sometimes thought Armstrong was, if not intimidated by his younger brother, at least a bit in awe of him. He tolerated behaviors in Tom he would not have in anyone else.

"But even if I had, what does Anna expect me to do?" he said. "Tom's his own man. I don't tell him what to do."

"That's what I told her you'd say."

Custer tucked in his shirt and threaded his belt. "If Miss Anna Darrah is smart as she thinks she is, she'll be careful or brother Tom will put her on the train back to Michigan. That reminds me, have you had any luck convincing Kate to come stay? Tom asks about it. He'd like that. You would too, wouldn't you?

I've heard you say many times you prefer Kate's company to Anna's."

Elizabeth bit her tongue. Kate was her dear friend and a kind, sensitive person. She was cultivated and well-read, and Elizabeth valued their conversations. She could say anything to Kate and know her confidence would not be betrayed. Kate, she believed, felt the same. Much as Elizabeth wanted her to come, she did not want to put her friend in an uncomfortable position. Lately, Elizabeth was getting the feeling Armstrong used her as a procurer for her randy brother-in-law. "I've written, but she hasn't responded yet," she said. "Anyway, I don't think Kate is interested in Tom in that way. She's not like Anna, you know, she's not fishing for straps."

"Ha!" Custer laughed as he shrugged his shoulders into his jacket. "That's our Anna's game all right. If it's Tom's captain's straps she's angling for, I'm afraid she's going to be disappointed."

Elizabeth smiled, watching him button his coat. He did have a nice form, she noticed. Athletic and trim, Armstrong was unlike so many of the other officers who had let themselves go after the war. General Hancock, for example, had gone to fat and no longer resembled the handsome "Thunderbolt of the Army of the Potomac" who had distinguished himself at Gettysburg. The same could be said of General Andrew Smith, commander of the Seventh Cavalry and Armstrong's immediate superior, and Major Alfred Gibbs, commanding at Fort Harker, who was not only fat, but drunk most of the time.

A few of the officers were still attractive. Captain Thomas Weir, Smith's adjutant, though not particularly handsome, was charming and great fun to be with, though he drank too much. Sherman, of course, was still trim and fit. Maybe this would be a good time to mention parts of their conversation. . . .

"Autie," she said, "did I tell you I saw General Sherman on the train to Fort Harker? We spoke, briefly."

"Did you?" This drew his interest, as she knew it would. "I hope you didn't bore him with woman talk."

She cleared her throat. "No, I don't believe I did." Wouldn't her patronizing rooster of a husband be astonished to know what the great William Tecumseh Sherman, savior of the Union, had said to her, about the heat in his eyes when he spoke of his sleeplessness that night at Fort Riley? She smiled, inwardly. "He's concerned about morale in the Seventh Cavalry. He said he's been hearing things. In fact, he's been receiving letters from one of your officers."

She saw the blood rise up Armstrong's neck. Soon his face would be bright red but for a white ring around his mouth. She had seen this many times. It was the sign of rage. "The hell! Who is the goddam traitor? Benteen? I bet it's Benteen—or maybe Barnitz?"

"I don't know who it is," she said. "He didn't say and I didn't ask. He may not even know. The writer may have been anonymous."

"The hell!" Custer slapped his riding gloves against his open hand. "Isn't it enough that I'm stuck here in the middle of nowhere with no food for my sick animals and nothing but moldy, maggot-infested crackers for my men? Now I've got a traitor on my staff, poisoning Sherman's mind against me! Well, this is a fine thing—a fine, fine thing!"

He began to pace, then stopped and turned to her. "Why are you just now telling me this? Why didn't you say something earlier?" He walked to the cot and stood over her, looking down. Elizabeth sat, covering herself with the sheets.

"I'm telling you now," she said. "What difference does it make?" She hesitated, wondering if she should go on. He was already angry, but she decided she might as well continue. He would have to hear it sometime.

"He also mentioned your fondness for the men of the press. Pygmies, he called them; he thinks you court them and he doesn't like it. I got the feeling he suspects you of political ambitions."

"He said that? Jesus, Mary, and Joseph!" Custer's blue eyes blazed. "I don't control where the newspapers send their writers—does he really think I do? Does he honestly think I have that kind of influence?"

"Well, I notice that *Harper's* man is here," Elizabeth said. "Theodore Davis, or whatever his name is. Why is that? Did you invite him?"

"I did not invite him," Custer said, "but I didn't discourage him either. *Harper's* asked if a correspondent could accompany the Seventh Cavalry on campaign, or part of it, and I saw nothing wrong in it. I still don't. *Harper's* is an influential publication. The nation should know what its army is doing on its behalf. We're helping to build the railroads. These are essential to the country's future. The people need to know that I—rather, the United States Army—that we're doing our best to ensure the railroads get built in a timely manner, for the people's benefit. There's no personal glory in it. That's of no interest to me."

Oh please, Elizabeth thought, *I know you too well.* "All right, Armstrong," she said. "I simply thought you should know what the general said."

He returned to his shaving stand, unscrewed the lid from a blue glass jar, and scooped out a dollop of cinnamon-scented pomade, rubbing it through his long, strawberry blond hair. This was a new habit, one he had acquired on a recent trip to Washington, and Elizabeth despised it. Scented hair dressing was foppish and effeminate; one of the women he kept company with there must have introduced it. Once she would have questioned him about this, once she had seethed with jealousy when Armstrong wrote from New York or Washington about the attentions paid him by beautiful women, about his flirtations with women of the night or, as he called them, "*nymphes du pave.*" Once he wrote to her of attending a fabulous masked ball, dressed as a devil in a black velvet cloak and cape, with red silk tights and no drawers underneath, accompanied by two lovely women. Why would he tell her of such things, she used to wonder, knowing as he did how these dalliances of his humiliated her? But those days were gone. Armstrong was attractive to women, Elizabeth knew this, and she knew she was envied by unmarried girls and even by a number of wives. But Elizabeth would cheerfully surrender her famous, glamorous husband for a fully adult man who believed in his work for its own sake, who loved her for the intelligent, sophisticated woman she was, and who wanted a child, as much as she did, to make their union complete. If he could not give her these things, he could at least make her a general's wife. This, at the very least, he owed her.

"I'll see you this evening," Custer said. "We'll have dinner with Tom and Anna and maybe one or two of the other officers." He gave her a hurried kiss and left the tent without looking back. Elizabeth lay back on the pillow and covered her eyes with her forearm. She was conflicted. After her father died, she tried to accept that she could not leave her husband. She had tried to love him again, tried to see him as the dashing cavalier he had been during the war. She tried to see him as another woman would, and sometimes, when their lovemaking was at its best, she believed she was succeeding. Then he behaved as a self-absorbed child, without regard for the comfort of his men or the officers who served under him unless they were properly sycophantic. What kind of man was he? Was he a brave warrior, worthy of love and admiration, or a petulant, immature narcissist who thought of nothing but himself and his own pleasure? Would he ever give her the child she so desired? She reached down, picked up her shoe, and threw it across the tent, breaking her husband's shaving mirror.

* * *

The next day Elizabeth asked Jack Gregory to take her riding. He and Fall Leaf had returned with the bodies of the four deserters the evening before. "That is, if you're free."

"Yes, ma'am. There's not much going on here this afternoon."

"Good. I'll leave it to you to find me a horse. Mine was killed in April."

He nodded. "I heard. It hurts to lose a horse you're attached to, I understand, but I know a mare I think you'll like. She's sweet and smooth." He thought—but did not say—just like you, Elizabeth Custer. "I'll put your lady saddle on her and meet you at your tent. Will Miss Darrah be coming with us?"

Elizabeth put her head to one side, considering. "No, I think we'll go just the two of us." She thought—but did not say—and I'll expect those answers you promised me.

By mid-morning the air was hot and heavy and, for once, there was no wind. Most days it blew with a vengeance, causing women to do endless battle with their skirts. Elizabeth and Anna spent the previous afternoon sewing lead weights into the hems of their dresses. It spoiled the drape of the fabric, but was necessary.

For today's ride, Elizabeth asked Eliza, Armstrong's black cook, to prepare a picnic lunch, which Gregory packed in his saddlebags. They rode away from camp at about eleven o'clock with Gregory leading the way on Jeff. Elizabeth followed on a gentle gray mare named Sophie. She would have preferred to ride astride and even had a split skirt made for this purpose, though she had not yet dared wear it. Some of her husband's officers, she felt sure, would disapprove. As they were leaving camp, the journalist, Davis, trotted up on his big gray mule and asked if he could join them.

"Of course," Elizabeth said, though she wanted to refuse. She found the *Harper's* man pompous and boring, and anyway she'd hoped to have the afternoon alone with the scout.

Despite the heat, the day was fine. The sky was blue as her lapis lazuli cameo and the clouds looked like peaked mounds of meringue. The purple and yellow wildflowers she had admired from the window of the train were still in bloom. Other than the *clop clop* of their mounts' hooves and the occasional trill of birdsong, they rode in peaceful silence.

After about thirty minutes Davis said, "Are there Indians nearby, Grover?"

Gregory laughed. "You'd better hope not, Davis, unless you're wanting a haircut."

Davis sniffed. "The Indians I've seen so far don't seem much to be afraid of. Beggars and thieves the lot, far as I can tell."

Gregory shook his head. "The layabouts you saw back at Hays and Harker are like a wild Sioux or Cheyenne buck the same way a kitchen match is like a wildfire. The one tells you nothing of the other, and only a fool would think otherwise."

Elizabeth laughed. "It sounds like our scout just called you a fool, Mr. Davis."

Davis scowled but didn't say anything and neither did Gregory.

Despite his affliction, Elizabeth found Gregory nice to look at, with a strong but lean form, wide shoulders, and an easy way in the saddle. Lately she had taken up sketching and she thought she might ask him to sit for her. She would title the sketch "Native Son," or "Born to the Saddle."

After another hour of riding Gregory pointed to an outcropping of rock jutting up from the flat of the prairie. 'That looks like a good spot," he said, "and the horses could use a blow." Gregory dismounted and came to help her. He put his large, scarred hands on her waist—they almost encircled it, she was pleased to observe—and lifted her effortlessly from the saddle. She had never stood so close to him, and she noticed he smelled pleasantly of leather and wood smoke, without a trace of cinnamon.

As she unpacked the food, Gregory walked about, pounding the ground with the butt of his Henry rifle. "Driving out rattlers," he said, anticipating her question. "But if I see one, I won't shoot it. Like I said, I don't think there's Indians nearby, but no need to announce ourselves anyhow."

She spread a blanket in the shade of the rocks and they lunched on canned lobster, cove oysters, sweet corn, gingerbread, and plum cake. To her surprise, Eliza had even included a bottle of Madame Clicquot. Despite the poor rations the men received, officers still had access to a few "fine stores," though these too were rapidly dwindling and Elizabeth was surprised the devoted cook would part with these when her beloved "ginnel" would not be participating.

As they ate, Davis asked questions for an article he planned to write about Custer's chief scout. Gregory answered, seemingly without reluctance, though Elizabeth doubted much, if anything, he said was true. For instance, he told Davis he was from Texas, though he had previously confessed to her this was not so. He said he had never been east of the Mississippi River, never had a day of formal schooling, never knew his father. She doubted the veracity of these things also. Only when he spoke of his time as an Indian trader on the Upper Missouri, of winters passed in the dark, smoky lodges of the Sioux, Arapaho, and Cheyenne, did Elizabeth suspect he was being genuine. She heard respect in his voice when he described the Indians' spiritual beliefs, their gentle ways of raising children, the beauty and chastity of the Cheyenne women.

When the champagne was finished Gregory looked at the sun and said it was time to head back to camp. "We don't want to be out here after dark." He helped her to her feet and his hand, sun-browned and strong, engulfed hers entirely. Maybe it was the wine, but she felt a throb of excitement.

Elizabeth packed the remains of the food while Gregory and Davis resaddled Jeff, Sophie, and the mule. Finishing before them, she spotted a cluster of pale yellow flowers growing under a shelf of rock. They would look pretty on the evening's table, she thought, and nicely complement the cream-colored Irish poplin dress with leg-o'-mutton sleeves she planned to wear. She dropped to her knees and reached in for the flowers with her ungloved left hand, thinking she would ask Gregory to join them for dinner.

The snake's flat, anvil-shaped head flew up and out at her with muscular speed, striking the fleshy tip of her small finger. Her scream brought the men running. Gregory kneeled beside her, took her hand, and examined the bleeding punctures while Davis raised his pistol and prepared to shoot the serpent.

"No!" Gregory said. "No guns, Davis. Beat it with your gunstock." Gregory turned back to Elizabeth as Davis bludgeoned the rattler, though this took some doing as it was fully four feet in length and thick as a man's wrist.

"Lie still, Mrs. Custer," Gregory said. Her heart was beating so loud she could barely hear his voice. "Keep your head down. Now, I want you to stay calm. It won't be easy, but you can do it. Take a deep breath." She did so, and then another. "All right," Gregory said. "Now we've got to get that ring off."

Her entire hand was already beginning to swell and the gold wedding band did not come off easily. At last he succeeded and dropped it in his coat pocket. Then he pulled a handkerchief from his pants pocket and wound it tightly around her forearm, knotting it just below the elbow.

"What are you doing?" she said as he unsheathed the knife he wore on his belt. "What are you going to do with that knife?"

"I've got to get that poison out," he said. "It'll hurt some, but I've got to do it. Hold still." She watched him make a small incision on each puncture, slightly enlarging the wound. After the cuts were made, he put her finger in his mouth and began to suck, his cheeks hollowing with each pull. She closed her eyes after watching him spit a mouthful of her contaminated blood on the ground. Her finger was red and growing by the instant.

Elizabeth felt a hot, crushing pain that surged with each beat of her heart. Her head swam, she felt nauseous, she felt herself drifting away, back to her childhood and the Christmas Day her father accidentally closed a carriage door on her hand. She had not known such excruciating pain since. Elizabeth struggled for consciousness, like a drowning swimmer fighting for the surface. When once she opened her eyes she saw Davis's bone-white face suspended over Gregory's shoulder, like a giant man in the moon. Sound was magnified tenfold. Insects buzzing in the grass were loud as a sawmill and when Gregory spoke—"The poison is working fast"—his voice boomed, as if he were yelling though a horn.

Elizabeth tried to raise her head, for she needed to see her hand. All her life she had been careful of them, always wearing gloves when out of doors. As a result, her hands were white as porcelain and unmarked by freckles. Her fingers, like her mother's, were long and slender. When she saw the red, bloated thing Gregory held in his hand, she hardly recognized it as part of her body. It was almost comical-looking, like a man's oversized glove inflated with air.

She noticed her arm below the tourniquet was

also red and swollen, and waves of panic washed over her, worsening her nausea. Was she going to die? Would it all come to smash, here, on the lonely Kansas prairie, her dreams and goals unmet? Overcome by a wild, irrational need to run, she pulled her hand free from Gregory's, but when she tried to stand, her legs collapsed and she fell, landing on her poisoned hand and arm. The pain was so intense she vomited.

"All right, now, all right," Gregory said. He felt for his handkerchief, realized it was already in use as her tourniquet, and wiped her mouth with the hem of her dress. Elizabeth was too distraught to care. "Don't jump around so, Mrs. Custer," he said. "It's the worst thing you can do. Calm down, Elizabeth, you must calm down." He had never spoken her name before and, for some reason, it seemed to soothe her. Gently, he pushed her back onto the grass. She closed her eyes and he brushed her hair back from her perspiring face. "You're going to be fine," he said, "long as you keep still. I'm almost done." He took her hand and began again to draw out the poison. The pain was unbearable, and she fainted.

When she opened her eyes it was fully dark. She and Gregory were alone. He sat beside her, smoking a cigarette. She had never seen him smoke before. The air had grown cool, but she was warm. Lifting her head, she saw he had covered her with his jacket.

"How long have I been asleep?" she said. "Where is Mr. Davis?"

"You've been out a couple hours. I sent Davis back to camp for a wagon and he took Sophie with him. You won't feel like riding for a while."

Every part of her body ached as if she had been dropped from a great height, and her hand was swollen to at least three times its normal size. The skin on her little finger was stretched so tight, she thought it would burst.

"You'll feel bad a day or two," he said, "but it could've been worse. That was a big snake."

"I'm just glad you were there and knew what to do. I've never been bitten before."

"I've seen it plenty times. I was bit myself once. A Sioux woman saved me, but the snake that got me wasn't near big as yours. You had me scared, tell you the truth."

"You don't do much of that, do you? Tell the truth?"

He extinguished the glowing end of his cigarette on the sole of his boot. "I admit, I stretch the blanket when it suits my purpose. I think most people do—the people I know, leastways."

The night sky was bright with stars and the prairie quiet as she had ever known it. There were no men's voices, no camp noises, no mules braying. "Back at the station house you said I'd get answers," she said. "Now would be a good time."

Gregory rolled another cigarette. "I'll tell you why I'm calling myself Joe Grover instead of Jack Gregory, which was the name my mother gave me. I'll tell you the whole thing and then it will be up to you to do what's right."

"I can keep my mouth shut if I choose to. Haven't I proven that?"

He smiled and lit the cigarette. "Yes, you have. You've also proved that you are a very brave woman, Mrs. Custer. I don't know what you'll think of me after you hear my story, but whatever you decide I respect your courage. I want you to know that."

Elizabeth was glad of the darkness.

Gregory exhaled a cloud of smoke and looked out over the prairie. "I don't know why people complain about Kansas," he said. "It's beautiful—the country, leastways. I'll never have much love for Kansans, as you will see.

"Anyhow, before the war, me and my family had a farm in Cass County, Missouri, near a town called Harrisonville. It was a pretty good-size town back when I was a boy, had almost seven hundred people living there before the war. Now there's hardly nobody. Harrisonville, the war pretty much killed it.

"On September ninth, eighteen sixty-three, Kansas Jayhawkers came to our farm looking for sesesh they thought was hiding on our land. There was a Yankee officer with that Kansas trash, he was the one in charge. When my pa told them he wasn't hiding rebels on his land—and he wasn't—they locked him in the barn and set fire to it. Burned him alive, burned the house, burned everything. My ma and sisters begged that Yankee officer, told him we were a Union family, that their only son—me—was away fighting for the Union at the time, but he did not care. It was him gave the order to fire the barn. When I heard of it, I promised Ma I'd find that Yankee devil and kill him. Well, I found him at Fort Phil Kearny last December, and I killed him." He did not tell her about the stolen payroll, he'd said enough.

It took a moment before Elizabeth could process what she had heard. "My God. You're talking about Mark Reynolds. *You* killed Lieutenant Reynolds?"

"I promise you, his passing was a whole lot less painful than my pa's."

"I met him once or twice," Elizabeth said. "Lieutenant Reynolds, I mean. He was a great favorite of General Sherman's, or so I heard. His wife, Rose, I liked her very much. Everyone did. They were a lovely couple, and beautiful to look at, the both of them."

Gregory rubbed out his cigarette. "Rose Reynolds is a fine woman who did not know the truth about the man when she married him. It's strange, but you remind me of her."

I knew there was someone, Elizabeth thought, flattered by the comparison to the beautiful Rose Reynolds. "I can understand your need for revenge," she said, "but did you have to shoot a dying man in his sickbed? Surely there was a better way."

Gregory shrugged. "I do not castigate myself." He went back to a clear and cool September day when he returned to his home to find a charred ruin, his farm a wasteland. His ride through the Burnt District, as that part of western Missouri came to be known, was the most dismal of his life, more soul-crushing than his flight from Fort Phil Kearny. Four counties of rich and generous farmland, home to generations of hardworking Missouri families, including his own, were reduced to a graveyard of smoke-blackened chimneys. Survivors called these Jennison's Tombstones, after the most ruthless of the Kansas Jayhawkers, the horse thief and renegade Charles R. Jennison. Gregory believed it was Jennison and his men who rode with Reynolds that black day.

The rattle of a wagon's iron wheels recalled him to the present. Elizabeth remained motionless beside him, still looking at the sky. The question hung in the air, unspoken. Would she tell her husband who his new scout really was?

"Was a warrant issued?" she said. "Are the authorities looking for you?"

"The army thinks Jack Gregory is dead, killed trying to get away from Phil Kearny. If men are looking for me, they're not from the government."

Elizabeth considered. Gregory was guilty of the same crime he accused Reynolds of, killing a man in cold blood and an officer, a brother in arms, at that. On the other hand, it was pure evil to burn a man alive, even in wartime. No legitimate officer would countenance such a crime. But maybe Reynolds was not truly guilty of this, maybe it was another of Gregory's lies? He admitted his fondness for, what did he call it, "stretching the blanket." But no, she believed him. If he were going to invent a life history out of whole cloth, surely he would have come up with something more favorable to himself. By now the wagon and riders were almost upon them.

"I will keep your secret, Mr. Gregory. Please don't give me reason to be sorry."

Gregory nodded his thanks, then got to his feet and hailed the approaching horsemen.

Chapter Fourteen

Custer jumped from his horse and ran to his wife,
dropping to his knees beside her. "My darling, my
darling, are you all right? Are you in pain?"

"I'll be fine, thanks to Mr. Grover," she said. "Just
take me back to camp, please. I want to go back."

Custer got to his feet and confronted Gregory.
"You fool! What's the matter with you? She might've
died!" He reached back with his right arm and swung.
Gregory caught his balled fist before it made contact
with his jaw.

"Don't do that," he said.

"Armstrong!" Elizabeth cried. "Don't be an idiot—
he saved me. This wasn't his fault. Just take me back
to camp. Please!"

"We'll discuss this later," Custer said to Gregory.
He carried his wife to the wagon where a bed had
been prepared, complete with mattress, pillows,
and blankets. It was a long, silent ride back to camp
and late, half past ten, when they arrived. Gregory
wanted only to go to sleep, but Custer, who slept less

than any man Gregory had ever known, called him to his headquarters tent after Elizabeth was settled.

"What the hell were you thinking?" he said, throwing his riding gloves on the desk. "How could you take Libbie out there after what happened to your friend Romeo and those deserters? I thought you were smart, Grover. I thought you knew what you were doing. Now I'm not sure."

"I am sorry about Mrs. Custer's injury," Gregory said. "You're right, the ride was bad judgment on my part. I'm willing to resign if that's what you want." Part of him hoped Custer would accept his offer.

The general paced before Gregory, standing in the center of the tent, hat in hand. "Whose bright idea was it in the first place?" Custer said, not waiting for an answer. "Thank God there weren't any Indians around—I can't even think about what might have happened if there were." His face was bright red but for a ring of white around his mouth.

"There was no danger of that. The hostiles have moved west."

"So you say! How can you be so sure where they are and what they'll do? The Cheyenne have been killing settlers and raiding stage lines and railroad crews all along the Platte. Sherman says he may have to close the Denver road."

"Like I said, General, if you doubt me, I'll go back to Fort Wallace tomorrow. Captain Keogh has work for me and I've got a hay ranch that could use my attention."

Custer stopped pacing and stood before him. They

were about the same height and practically nose to nose. Gregory got a strong whiff of cinnamon.

"If I had the luxury of time I might send you packing, Grover, but I don't. I've got orders, it's time to move. The tents I've been waiting for finally got here and the grass has been up long enough that the horses are ready. My orders are"—he pulled a paper from his coat pocket and read—"'to hunt out and chastise the Cheyennes and that portion of the Sioux who are their allies between the Smoky Hill and the Platte. It is reported that all friendly Sioux have gone north of the Platte and may be in the vicinity of forts McPherson or Sedgwick. You will, as soon as possible, inform yourself as to the whereabouts of these friendly bands and avoid a collision with them.'" He folded the paper and returned it to his pocket. "I'm leaving tomorrow with six companies and rations for fifteen days and I'm depending on you to help me find the damn Indians and separate the friendlies from the hostiles. I don't know how the devil I'm supposed to tell them apart, they all look alike. I need you, Grover. Don't let me down again. Don't make me sorry I asked for you."

"No, sir." Gregory recalled Elizabeth's nearly identical words just a few hours earlier. "I won't."

As it turned out, Custer and Gregory did not accompany the six companies of the Seventh Cavalry when they left camp on the morning of June 1. Instead it was Major Cooper, apparently sober, who rode at the head of the column of three hundred and fifty men and twenty fully loaded supply wagons. Captain Barnitz's G Troop would remain behind to protect the camp and the women. At the last minute, Gregory convinced Custer it was important to move the ladies' tents from the secluded compound to a site nearer Fort Hays. He suggested a knoll four or five feet above the valley floor and distant from the water.

"It's too far from the creek," Custer said with a frown. "They'll have trouble getting water."

"That's not a problem," Gregory said. "The men will haul water for them. The problem is that creek. It'll come up fast if we get a hard rain, and the farther they are from it, the better. I grant you, that little rise don't look like much, but Mrs. Custer and Anna will be glad of it if a flood comes."

Custer laughed. "Flood? Why, Big Creek's hardly more than an irrigation ditch."

"Even so."

Custer seemed unconvinced, but agreed. They worked for hours, moving the two hospital tents, each roomy enough to accommodate ten men, anchoring them securely and staking down carpeting of empty coffee sacks. It was midnight when they were finally ready to leave. Gregory waited with the horses as Custer said good-bye to his wife. Listening to the low, murmuring voices and long silences, Gregory imagined what it would feel like to hold Elizabeth in his arms, to kiss her the way Custer was doing now, the same way he used to imagine holding Rose Reynolds. Jack Gregory had had many women in his life, Indian and white, and some had been

beautiful. Waynoka, the Cheyenne girl he had known
in Nebraska Territory soon after he first left home,
was probably the loveliest—of any race—with soft
brown eyes, long curling lashes, and hair black and
shining as a raven's wing. She was good to him,
cooked the foods he liked the way he liked them,
and had an unfailingly sweet disposition. Waynoka,
whose name meant *sweet water* in her native tongue,
was a woman Gregory thought he could spend his
life with. She was undemanding, with a way of letting
him know what she thought and what she wanted,
without actually saying anything. Her brothers,
though, did not cotton to the notion of a white trader
for a brother-in-law and took her away. Gregory
grieved but did not fight for her because he did not
want to come between Waynoka and her people.
Eventually she would resent him for it—Gregory had
seen that play out often enough. Now he had another
Indian woman, Maggie, a Sioux, who waited for him
at the ranch. She was a good woman, she cared for
him, and in return he took care of her. He felt obliged
to do this, but he did not love her as he wanted to love
a woman, and he would not want Elizabeth Custer, or
his mother or sisters, or any woman he respected, to
know of their association. He was ashamed of her.
This was unfair to Maggie, but there it was. If she
didn't like it, she was free to leave.

As he waited, Gregory wondered if there was a
chance he would find a woman like Rose or Elizabeth, a woman who was not only lovely but kind. In
Gregory's mind, kindness was as important as beauty,
and essential to true femininity. All his life, he had

dreamed of finding a partner like that, but in his heart he did not truly believe it would happen. Why would such a woman find anything to love in him, a lowly scout and a harelip to boot? He looked down at his hands, holding the horses' reins. They were scarred and dirty, the nails bitten to the quick. These were not the hands a genteel, well-bred woman would want on her white, scented skin.

Finally Custer emerged from his tent, took the reins from Gregory, and mounted his horse. To Gregory's surprise, the general's eyes were full of tears. "It's hell to leave her," he said. "You wouldn't how that feels, to part from a woman who loves you the way Libbie loves me. It's tough, every time, and it never gets easier. You know, Grover, I envy you in a way. I really do. Free as the wind, with no attachments to weigh you down."

Gregory looked at Custer, who smiled with self-satisfaction as he adjusted his neckerchief, then pulled on his riding gloves. The man was a horse's ass, perhaps the most complete example of that part of a horse's anatomy Gregory had ever known. About a mile out of camp, he reached into his pocket for a toothpick and found that he still had Elizabeth's wedding ring. He held it in his palm, a bit of gold shining in the starlight. He should return it to her, or give it to Custer, he knew that. Instead, he let it slip through his fingers and fall to the prairie floor.

Chapter Fifteen

The moon was bright, lighting the plain in shades of silver, black, and gray. They traveled all through the night, following the north fork of Big Creek for more than twenty miles, seeing no living things other than small herds of antelope and a few buffalo they startled into flight. The cavalry's trail was easy to follow, even at night, and they arrived at Cooper's camp just as the bugler was sounding reveille. Tom Custer met them as they rode in.

"Major Cooper's drunk as a lord," he said, "and has been since we left Big Creek. Apparently he brought a keg of whiskey along. I found it in his tent last night after he passed out."

Custer cursed as he dismounted. "That's all I need. Pour it out. If he can't ride this morning, throw him in a wagon, the hell with him. Anything else?"

"Three men took off when we stopped at midday. I sent a detail out after them, but they took our best horses. We couldn't catch them."

Custer slapped his gloves against his palm. "If the

Sioux don't kill those cowards I will. Well, brother, any other happy news?"

"I don't know if it's happy, but we picked up three railroad workers today, said they got separated from their crew during an Indian attack. I told them they could travel with us a while, I didn't think you'd mind. They're a queer lot—two are twins, albinos and blind as bats, far as I can tell. I can't see how the railroad got any work out of them."

Gregory hoped he wasn't about to regret his decision to let the Kemper brothers go.

"No, no, that's fine." Custer waved his hand dismissively. "They'll probably be more useful than those goddamn snowbirds anyway. Come on, Grover, let's have some of brother Tom's coffee. We'll ride with the column today."

Gregory was saddle sore, bone tired and needing a rest, but Custer wasn't going to give him one. Gregory was fit and strong, but it took all he had and then some to keep up. No wonder the men called Custer Iron Butt.

At Tom's fire they sat cross-legged on the ground, drinking coffee, while Tom went to remove the hogshead of whiskey from the major's tent. Cooper woke while Tom was at it. His angry voice, hoarse and slurred, carried throughout the camp.

"Hey! What gives you th' right to come sneakin' into my tent and steal my belongings?" Cooper shouted. "Tha's mine! Give it here!" There was the sound of a scuffle followed by the crack of breaking wood. Gregory imagined Tom pushing the drunken man back onto his cot, splintering the frame.

"I'm acting on the general's orders," Tom said. "He told me to confiscate this whiskey and pour it out and that's what I intend to do. Just look at yourself, man! You're a disgrace."

Around the camp men went about their morning tasks, eyes down, embarrassed for Cooper, who was popular and a decent officer when not in his cups. Lately, though, it had become obvious to all that John Barleycorn had gotten the better of the major. His wife was expecting their first child, and many suspected this was the reason for his dissolve. Indeed, it was to escape that very responsibility that a good number of Custer's men had cast their lot with the Seventh Cavalry.

Gregory finished his coffee wanting nothing more than to spread his bedroll under a tree and sleep the morning away. His eyelids felt as if they were lined with sand. "General," he said, "are you sure we can't grab just a few hours' sleep and catch them up later? I could use some shut-eye."

When he got no response he looked at Custer, sitting ramrod straight, coffee in hand, fast asleep.

At six o'clock, Custer moved out in columns of fours. They rode in a northwesterly direction, across rolling plains, through muddy lowlands still wet with winter's traces, up and down dry arroyos, finally reaching the Saline River by mid-afternoon. The water and grass were good here and they found abundant fuel in the cottonwoods that lined the riverbanks. Custer ordered a halt and the men began to make camp.

Gregory's head and body ached from lack of sleep, but instead of climbing into his bedroll, he and Fall Leaf were charged with exploring the country downstream. About two miles out they came across the remains of fires and great, bloody patches of ground littered with piles of animal bones. They dismounted and walked through the campsite, looking for signatures. The air was heavy with the smell of blood and the buzzing of blowflies.

"What do you think?" Gregory said. "Sioux hunting camp?"

Fall Leaf shrugged. "Maybe so. Could be from the big village the bluecoats burned. The people have many to feed."

"How old is it?"

"Three days, no more."

Gregory nodded, looking over the primitive abattoir. Whoever they were, they'd been successful. Most of the bones were elk, and they had killed scores of them. Because of the encroaching white men, the buffalo population was dwindling and the Indians had old people, children, and women to care for. Custer's job was to "hunt out and chastise" these very Indians, whose village the soldiers had burned, who were fleeing for their lives and fighting to protect their families and traditions. Gregory's task was to help Custer find them. More and more, he found himself regretting he had accepted the assignment. Weren't the soldiers doing to the Sioux and Cheyenne the very thing Mark Reynolds and his Kansans had done to his family in the fall of 1863?

Gregory shook his head, reminding himself there was no point in thinking that way. All he had to do was keep his head down, get this job for Custer done, and collect his pay. Then he could go back to Fort Wallace and his ranch. His meadows would be ready for cutting soon. If he was lucky, he could be harvesting his first crop of the season in a few weeks.

In the late afternoon, as Gregory and Fall Leaf were returning to camp, they saw the Custer brothers and Davis riding away in the opposite direction. Gregory sighed. Now what? He sent Fall Leaf back to camp and followed the three horsemen. Before long, he saw the object of their attention: an Indian burial on a twenty-foot scaffold. By the time he reached them, the Custers had pulled it down and were stripping the body of the skins and blankets that wrapped it.

"Just in time, Grover," Custer said. "I've always wanted to see what's inside one of these bundles."

Gregory turned in the saddle, scanning the horizon. He hoped they weren't being watched. "You shouldn't do that, General," he said.

"Why not?" Custer did not look up.

"How would you like it if some Sioux buck dug up one of your relatives to see what was in the hole?"

By now the body was exposed. Custer, kneeling by the decomposed corpse, which looked to be that of a young boy, squinted up at Gregory. "These people aren't Christians, Grover, and this isn't a Christian burial. It's nothing like the same."

"It is to them."

Custer shrugged, winked at Tom, and went back to examining the grave goods. These included a pair of beautifully beaded moccasins, two pieces of store-bought peppermint candy, a bow and quiver, sized for a child, a scalping knife, a war club, a red clay pipe, three pieces of dried meat, and part of a scalp. This last item Custer held aloft. The hair was long and wavy, with a reddish cast.

"My God, Tom, look at this—it's the hair of a white woman!" From a kneeling position, he leapt to his feet. Not for the first time, Gregory wondered if Custer had springs in his legs instead of muscles. "Yes, it's the scalp of a murdered white woman!"

Davis and Tom Custer regarded the ragged thing with interest though Davis, Gregory noted, wrinkled his nose and was careful not to get close to it.

"Why, it sure as hell is," Tom said. "That red hair is from the head of some poor man's wife, some poor child's mother. Goddamn, I can't wait till we catch up with those red devils—they will feel my steel!"

Davis pulled out his notebook and began to write. Gregory could see pages were filled with sketches and descriptions.

"No, General, you got that wrong," Gregory said. "That hair came off another Indian. The Sioux don't scalp women, Cheyenne neither. They just don't."

He was still on his horse and the others had to look up at him.

"The hell," Custer said. "Just look at that color, that red color. Indians don't have hair like that. No, it's from a white woman. It's clear as day." He turned to Tom and Davis for affirmation.

Gregory shook his head. "Indian scalps can go that hue. I've seen it plenty times. Davis, if you write Custer found a white woman's scalp, you'll get folks whipped up for no reason. You'll make things hotter than they are over a thing that's not true." Davis's writings and artwork for *Harper's Weekly* influenced thousands of people, including lawmakers in Washington, D.C.

"I don't know, Grover," the journalist said, not lifting his eyes from the page. "It looks like a white woman's hair to me."

"Your objections will be noted, Grover," Custer said. "Davis, write it down, what he said." He squatted again by the grave goods scattered on the ground and picked up the moccasins. They were made of the softest white deerskin with beautifully beaded flowers. "I'm taking these. Small as they are, they might fit my Libbie. You gentlemen want to take something, go ahead." Tom chose the quiver of steel-tipped arrows, also covered with exquisite beadwork. Davis selected the red clay pipe.

"What about you, Grover?" Custer said. "Don't you want a souvenir? Something to show the grandchildren?"

"No. This is wrong what you've done here, and we may well pay a price for it."

Tom walked toward him, the quiver swinging in his hand. "Say, Grover, you aren't one of those Interior Department, Indian-lover types, are you?" He spoke with a smirk, cutting his eyes to his older brother. "Worried about Lo, the noble savage? That would surprise me, man in your line of work."

"It's not that," Gregory said. "But I don't see any good in unnecessary troublemaking and that's what's happening here. We should put that child's grave back as we found it. We ought not to leave him food for the wolves and carrion birds."

"Well, if you think it's so important, you go right ahead and do that, Grover," Custer said, remounting his horse. "Me, I'm hungry. I'm going back to camp for my supper."

Gregory said, "I could use a hand getting that scaffold back together."

"Would that be something either of you is interested in?" Custer said, grinning at his brother and Davis.

"Not me," Tom said. He put a foot in the stirrup and swung into the saddle. "I'm going back with you."

"Nor I," Davis said with an apologetic smile. "Sorry, Mr. Grover."

"Well, Joe, looks like it is a one-man job after all." With a laugh, Custer turned to Tom. "Last one back does fifty push-ups!"

They kicked their horses into a gallop and took off, racing across the prairie. Davis scrambled to follow on his big mule, leaving Gregory alone with the child's rotting body. He rewrapped the corpse with its remaining goods and covered it with the platform and saplings that were the scaffold. These would do little to keep the predators at bay, but it was the best he could do.

He climbed into the saddle, but neither he nor Jeff was in any hurry to get back. They stood motionless, listening to the quiet and feeling the breeze.

The sky was beginning to darken. This was the best time on the prairie, the peaceful interval between day and night, when the sky glowed a fiery red and orange, the air cooled, and the wind began to stir. It was a time for reflection, time for a man to take stock of where he was in his life and where he wanted to be. If he was lucky, these were one and the same. This was not true in Gregory's case. He did not like or respect Custer, and he did not like working for him. It was dangerous. Custer's arrogance, coupled with his brazen ignorance, was likely to get people killed. Not only that, Gregory was sick of being reminded every day that Elizabeth was Custer's wife and shared his bed. Like Rose Reynolds, she was a beautiful woman wasted on a smug, self-satisfied rooster.

Gregory was swept by the powerful urge to turn Jeff's head west and ride home to Wallace. The hell with the job and Custer too. This campaign was not going to end well, Gregory was sure of that. As Barnitz said, Hancock had already washed his hands of this war that bore his name and was back at Fort Leavenworth, licking his wounds, leaving Custer adrift on the land with an army at his disposal. When a man like Custer went down, he pulled others with him, and Jack Gregory did not want to be one of the many sucked into the vortex.

The arrival of the Kempers and the mysterious third man was an additional complication. He didn't need this trouble. He could leave. Custer would complain to Keogh, and Gregory's stock as a scout and guide would go down for a time, but in the end he'd have plenty of work. There weren't many men in Kansas who could do his job as well as he did.

But he did not ride west. Instead he kicked Jeff into a trot and headed back toward camp. If he deserted Custer, he would never see Elizabeth again. And for now, that was reason enough.

Chapter Sixteen

The day's heat broke at sundown and with the
darkness came a merciful breeze, sweetly scented
with the promise of rain. Elizabeth and Anna sat in
camp chairs before their tent, sipping sherry, though
Elizabeth would have preferred a jot of whiskey. She
had a bottle in her medicine box, but Anna would
be scandalized if she took some and Elizabeth was
not in a mood for approbation. Maybe she would
have a taste later, when she was alone.

Elizabeth felt more content than she had in weeks.
Her worry about Armstrong's stalled career had
retreated, temporarily at least. Nothing had changed,
but for now she was happy to close her eyes and surrender to the elements: the darkness, the light caress
of the wind that lifted the loose strands of hair about
her face. She enjoyed the stillness. Even the usually
talkative Anna had been quiet of late.

After a time the first fat drops of rain began to fall,
making little craters in the sandy soil. Elizabeth stayed
as she was until a long, ragged bolt of lightning

struck close by, followed immediately by a crash of thunder that boomed like the report of a cannon. The ground shook with its power. She and Anna jumped from their chairs and ran for the tent where they wrapped blue army blankets around their shoulders against the sudden cold and waited for the storm to pass.

But it only intensified. The skies opened up and the wind blew a hurricane, rattling the tent poles and shaking the canvas like a puppy with a handkerchief. After a few minutes of this, the tent fly tore loose and slapped against the canvas walls with the crack of a pistol shot. The lightning came in chains, each burst throwing a hard blue light that cast the tent's interior in stark relief. The torrential rain, driven by the wind at its zenith, penetrated the canvas walls so they dripped water.

"Liz!" An ashen Anna grabbed Elizabeth's arm after one especially violent blast of wind almost lifted the tent from its moorings. "We're not safe here! What shall we do? Where shall we go?" She had to yell to be heard.

"Go? We can't go anywhere," Elizabeth said. "I must see what's happening." She went to the door and began to open the flap. This took some doing, for Armstrong, worried about his wife being inadvertently exposed to prying male eyes, had ordered the saddler to reinforce the entry with straps and buckles. At last she succeeded, but the rain blew horizontally and she could not see anything. She could hear, however; it was a sound that at first she could not identify, but then made her heart rise in her throat.

No, she thought, it couldn't be. She must be mistaken, Big Creek was just a stream! But there was no denying it—she heard the roar of rushing water, not a gentle stream, but a raging river. And there was something else . . .

"Do you hear it?" Anna stood close, at Elizabeth's shoulder. "There—you hear? It's a man screaming!"

It was faint, barely audible above the keening of the wind and roaring of the water. As her eyes adjusted to the darkness, she saw that Big Creek had burst its banks, running wide and wild on either side of the little hillock where their tent stood. They were an island in the middle of a white-water river, and still the rain was falling and still the water rose. It was less than a yard from their tent. And, yes, there were voices—not just one now, but several—men screaming for their lives.

"Help me! Please, somebody help me!" In a blue flash of lightning Elizabeth saw a white face in the running black flood, a man clinging to a tree still anchored to the bank. The terror on his face was dreadful to behold, a thing she had never seen before. And there were others, also calling out to God and their fellow men.

"Oh, Liz," Anna said, clutching her arm. "It's the end of the world!"

"It's no such thing. It's just a storm and I think it's weakening." Elizabeth spoke with an authority she did not feel. She was, however, confident of one thing. If Gregory had not convinced Armstrong to move their tent, she and Anna would be out in the water now, fighting to survive.

They stood in the doorway, soaked through to the bone. Elizabeth's teeth chattered, not only in fear, for the night was quite cold.

"There!" Anna pointed into the darkness. "What—who—is that?"

Elizabeth could barely make out the dark shapes of two men, struggling through thigh-high water toward their tent. They were having much difficulty and she feared they wouldn't make it. An idea came to her.

"Anna," she said, "where is that clothesline we were going to hang tomorrow? Is it still in the tent?"

"Yes, just here." Anna ran to her cot and pulled from beneath it a coiled length of rope. She gave it to Elizabeth who began unwinding it.

"Yes, this should be long enough," she said, peering at the two men, who were no longer moving forward, but fighting to hold their own. She now recognized them as captains Albert Barnitz and Tom Weir. "Anna, we're going to throw this rope out to them and pull them in. Help me—we'll need something to weight the throwing end."

They cast about in desperation. Anna reached for her small clothes iron, one specially made for travel. "Here, try this!"

Elizabeth shook her head. "It's too heavy. I can't throw it that far."

"I can," Anna said, taking the rope from Elizabeth's hand. "I'm bigger than you, and stronger. I can do it."

Elizabeth watched with admiration as Anna

wound the rope around the iron's handle, knotting it securely. Her friend had talents she had not suspected. Anna stepped out into the storm, paid out some line, swung the iron around her head three times and let it fly. It splashed into the water beyond Weir's reach. Anna reeled it in and threw again, just as a jagged streak of lightning split the sky, landing so close both women jumped. This time Weir was able to grab the rope.

"Help me pull!" Anna said.

Elizabeth got behind her and put her arms around Anna's waist. They planted their feet in the wet, slippery soil and stood firm as the two men advanced toward them, hand over hand. It was hard going, and twice the women fell in the mud, but after about twenty minutes Barnitz and Weir were standing beside them, breathing hard and dripping water on the tent floor.

"We came to see if you ladies needed help," Weir said to Elizabeth. He looked so bedraggled, such an unlikely rescuer, she could not help but laugh. At first he was offended, but then, because her laughter was infectious, he joined in. As their tension eased, their laughter built until, despite the continuing storm, Weir and Elizabeth collapsed on the muddy canvas floor, holding each other and laughing helplessly.

Barnitz and Anna looked on, unsmiling.

Chapter Seventeen

They marched for days, through heavy rains, through marshy plains and streams swollen with rushing, dirty water, without seeing a single Indian. Always impatient, Custer's temper was now on a hair trigger. He was distracted, and had barely a civil word for anyone other than Tom. He was obsessed with getting to Fort McPherson as soon as possible so he could send a telegram to Elizabeth.

"I've got to see her, Grover," he said that evening as they sat by the fire. "I want her to meet me at Wallace." They were camped on Muddy Creek, a foul-smelling stream they had crossed and recrossed three times that day. On one occasion they had to corduroy the creek bed to get the wagons across. Custer stared moodily into the flames. "Once you get used to being with a woman like that, not only in bed but all the time, you can't stand to be away from her," he said. "When you're apart, it's like you're not living, like your life is on hold. You worry that something is going to happen to spoil it, that maybe you've already spoiled it yourself with something stupid you've done."

Gregory stirred condensed milk and sugar into his coffee. It occurred to him to throw the scalding liquid in Custer's pink, freckled face. Instead he said, "You're a lucky man, general. No doubt about that. Plenty of men would like to trade places with you."

Custer choked on his coffee. "What do you mean by that, Grover?" he said. "Have you heard talk? Why did you say that?"

Gregory continued stirring. "I mean Mrs. Custer is a fine woman and you're fortunate to have her. Just that."

Custer turned back to the fire and resumed his brooding. His eyes landed on Major Cooper, sitting on the opposite side, picking at his food. Cooper's long face was gray and his eyes were sunken, like two holes burned in a blanket. Although the night air was cool, he was sweating.

"What's the matter with you, major?" Custer said. "You look like hell. My God, man, you're turning into a skeleton. Eat those beans. You'll need your strength for that baby you've got on the way."

Cooper said nothing, though Gregory thought he saw him shudder.

"Yes, when is baby Cooper due to arrive?" Tom said.

"Three months or so. We're not exactly sure." Cooper kept his eyes on the beans he was pushing around on his plate.

"You don't seem too happy about it," Tom said.

"I'd be happier if you hadn't poured out my

whiskey." Finally Cooper raised his head, fixing blazing eyes on Tom. It was the first emotion he had shown in days. "You had no right to do that, Custer. No right at all! I paid good money for it and you had no right to throw it out."

The camp fell silent. Tom's eyes cut to his brother, who nodded before Tom spoke again. "I acted on the general's orders, Major, and it was for your own good. You're drinking too much and it's interfering with your ability to do your job. Everyone sees that. When you sober up and get back to yourself, you'll be grateful. And Sarah, she'll be grateful too. Just tough it out, man. You'll feel better. You'll see."

"I am not grateful, captain, nor will I be. You Custers have no right to decide what's best for a man in his personal life. I am not a child, I am fully capable of making my own decisions." Cooper's lower lip trembled and his eyes filled. The other men looked away. It was bad form to gawk at a man when he was overcome, and clearly Major Wycliffe Cooper had come to the end of himself.

"Listen, Wycliffe," Custer said, "why don't you go to your tent and try to get some rest? You're tired, I can see that. Hell, we're all tired. Get a good night's sleep and you'll feel better in the morning."

Gregory was confident Cooper would not feel better in the morning. If anything, he'd feel worse as the bottle ache tightened its grip. Gregory had seen it before; the shakes and sweating had already started, and pretty soon Cooper would be seeing things that weren't there—bugs were common— then he'd start crying and tearing his clothes off because the bugs were crawling all over him. Maybe he'd seize up altogether—Gregory had seen that too. The symptoms were always worse at night. Sometimes a man died.

Cooper stood and smoothed his trousers, clearly struggling to compose himself. "Yes, I am tired. I believe I will go to my tent. Good night, General Custer. Good night, everyone." He saluted and walked off into the darkness. His fellow officers sat for a time in contemplative silence.

"Too bad," Custer said, finally. "Cooper did well for himself during the war, especially in Georgia and again at the capture of Montgomery. That's when the drinking started getting bad, or so I hear. I feel bad for his wife. Sarah is a lovely lady, a real Southern belle." He shook his head. "I only hope the rest of you can see what happens when a man lets John Barleycorn get the better of him." Here he looked pointedly at his brother.

"Oh, I see," Tom said, reddening. "Anna's been at it again, trying to get you to—"

He was silenced by a shot, fired at close range. "Indians!" A soldier yelled and several of the men at the fire jumped to their feet. Custer and Gregory remained seated. Their eyes met. Both knew at once what had happened.

"It's not Indians," Custer said, standing. "That shot came from Major Cooper's tent. Grover, you and Tom come with me."

They found Cooper on his knees, facedown on the ground, with his revolver in his right hand.

"Jesus," Tom said. "Hell of a thing to do to his wife."

Custer said, "Grover, go get my officers and bring them here." Gregory thought the general meant to move Cooper's body to a more dignified position, but when he returned the corpse was still ass-up.

"Gentlemen," Custer said, "take a look. This is not the death of a soldier. I believe this disgusting example says everything required about the evil of drink. I need not say more." He ordered that Cooper's body be wrapped in a blanket and transported by ambulance to Fort McPherson, some twenty-seven miles to the north, for burial.

"You, Tom, I hope you took a good, long look," Custer said as two enlisted men carried Cooper's corpse from the tent, leaving the Custers and Gregory alone. "That's where you're headed, little brother, if you don't straighten up. And this isn't about Anna. I promised Mother I'd keep an eye out for you and I feel obliged to say this, before you end up like the major."

Tom laughed. "Brother, I am offended. Wycliffe Cooper was a run-of-the-mill whiskey soak. I'm sorry to say it but it's true. You can't possibly put me in that hard company. Armstrong, I know you've been listening to Anna, to her whining and complaining, and I am tired of it. In fact, I'm tired of her. Let's send Anna back to Michigan, shall we? Wouldn't we all like that? What do you say, Grover? Don't you think Miss Darrah's worn out her welcome?"

Tom looked pointedly at Gregory. "It's nothing to do with me," Gregory said. Tom turned back to his brother.

"Let's bring Kate out instead," Tom said. "Is Libbie working on that?"

Custer cuffed Tom on the ear, playfully. "You can't treat a woman like that—like she's a coat you wear for a while and then discard for another. I'm tired of this one, bring me that one. You can't treat a woman like Anna like a squaw."

"Oh, is that what I'm doing?" Tom said, with a wink at Gregory. "Well, you should know. You've had plenty of experience in the squaw department." Custer cuffed him again and they fell to slapping and shoving each other like a couple of barefoot boys without a care in the world. Gregory walked alone to his tent, wondering, not for the first time, what bound Elizabeth to George Armstrong Custer. Was a famous name and a general's rank, brevet at that, so important to her? He found it hard to believe Elizabeth was that kind of woman, but he'd been wrong about a woman before.

It was still dark the next morning when he and Fall Leaf prepared their horses for the day's scout. The rope line was strung by the creek and a thick haze hung over the water. As Gregory tightened the cinch, three men, black silhouettes, emerged from the mist. He recognized the unmistakable Kemper twins, Lem and Luther, and a third man, tall and heavyset.

"So, you're Grover, the scout I keep hearing about?" the tall man said.

"I guess I am." Gregory looked at the Kempers, who regarded him with identical blank faces. Even in the morning mist they wore their dark glasses. If they recognized him, they weren't letting on. "I suppose you're the railroad hands Tom's boys came across the other day," he said.

"Yes sir, that would be us." He stepped forward and offered his hand. "Indians rode down on our crew while we was grading a bed, we was working out ahead of the others. The boys went one way, the three of us went the other, and we got separated. Cheney's the name. Louis Cheney."

He stepped in close and offered his hand. The skin on the lower half of his face was raised and thickened and deep purple in color. *The mark of the devil.* Those were the words Jack's mother had used to describe one of the "government men" who came to the house, looking for him and the stolen payroll. This man was one of them and Gillespie was the other. Of that Gregory had no doubt.

"Say, friend," Cheney said, "will you and your group of pioneers be scouting clear to McPherson today?"

He smiled, trying to look friendly, but the effect was so comical, Gregory almost laughed. Instead he turned to Jeff, who was up to his old trick of holding a belly full of air while being saddled. Gregory had to give him the knee to make him release it.

"I don't have a group of pioneers," he said. "It's just me and Fall Leaf. And yes, we plan to scout to the road to McPherson."

"Well, would you mind if me and these two boys ride along? It'll take days to get there with Custer and that lot."

"What's your hurry?" Gregory said. "I can't think of anything at McPherson I'd be in a hurry to get to."

Cheney shrugged his heavy shoulders. "All the same."

"Me and Fall Leaf ride alone," Gregory said. "No exceptions."

"I'm asking you to reconsider, friend. There'll be forty dollars in it for you, you let us ride along."

Gregory moved his eyes from Cheney to the Kempers. Did Cheney know who he was? He didn't think so, but Tweedledee and Tweedledum could identify him after that business back at the stage station. But their vision was bad, their eyes pale and pink-rimmed behind the dark glasses, and they had been drinking. Gregory wasn't sure what they remembered or even took in. But if they weren't after him, there must be something at McPherson. Whatever it was, it would be trouble. Gregory wanted no part of these three. He was about to tell Cheney he could keep his forty dollars when he happened to see the man's prints in the damp soil. There was a cross carved in the right boot heel. Fall Leaf's eyes met Gregory's. The Indian saw it too.

"I guess I could use forty dollars." Gregory looked at his partner with raised eyebrows. "What do you say? Should we take them along?"

Fall Leaf shrugged and turned his hands palms up.

"All right, Cheney," Gregory said. "Saddle up and meet us yonder, on that ridge." He pointed toward a low hillock just beginning to take shape in the blue predawn light. "I'll give you ten minutes."

"Thank you, friend," Cheney said. "We'll be along presently."

Gregory watched the three men hurry away to saddle their horses and collect their gear. "Food for the wolves come evening," he said.

Chapter Eighteen

The morning came bright and sunny, a dramatic contrast to the black hours of terror that preceded it, a night resounding with the screams of drowning men and animals. Six men perished. Though most of the bodies were washed some distance from the camp, along with trees and earth and rubbish caught up in the maelstrom, one corpse was embedded in the mud not far from Elizabeth's tent. The man was naked to the waist and partially buried, with only his head and half of his upper body exposed. His eyes bulged and his mouth was open wide, filled with mud. The bile rose in her throat and she turned away, wishing she had not seen the body. The drowned man was Felix Doering, the young private who served as Armstrong's striker when he was in camp.

"A horrible way to die." Captain Weir stood beside her. He and Barnitz had remained with Elizabeth and Anna throughout the night, all fearing the tent would go down with the others. As it turned out, they needn't have worried, for Gregory, well-acquainted with plains hurricanes, had seen to it the poles were planted deep. He further secured the tent by fastening stout picket ropes to both ends of the ridge pole and anchoring these to the ground with iron pins. Unlike most that terrible night, Elizabeth's canvas home remained in place.

"Poor Felix," she said. "I must write to his family." Only then did it occur to her that Armstrong might be blamed for the deaths, for it was he who selected the campsite. Tom Weir read her mind.

"No one could have anticipated this, Elizabeth," he said. "It was an act of God."

She nodded absently. "I suppose." Did Weir know that just before leaving camp, Armstrong had moved her tent to higher ground—a precaution extended to her and Anna, but not the others? If he had any negative feelings, if he felt ill-used by his commanding officer, Weir would never say so. He was one of Armstrong's most loyal staff members.

They picked their way through the detritus of the storm, finding bits of clothing and torn canvas, broken tent poles, rope and picket pins, a soggy bag of potatoes. As they walked toward Fort Hays, Elizabeth prayed she and Anna could find fresh clothing and a place to bathe, but the closer they got, the less likely this appeared. Elizabeth surveyed the wreckage and shook her head. How could this happen? How could a stream that was barely a trickle become a raging wall of water in just a few minutes? She shuddered. What other horrors lay in wait for her in this wild country?

The damage at Fort Hays was even worse than she feared. The flimsy log structures listed badly or were gone altogether. While the post's few stone buildings fared better, even these were mud-filled and unusable. Dead mules and horses lay on the parade beside upended wagons and the stench of death was already poisoning the air. Colonel Smith wandered through the ruins, stooping occasionally to retrieve a book or other soggy bit. He responded listlessly to Weir's salute.

"Five of my orderlies died last night," he said dully. "Five strong young men, drowned. This time yesterday they were alive and healthy, and now . . . so senseless. Such a senseless way to die." He shook his head.

Weir nodded. "Yes, sir. Very sad."

Elizabeth looked about, turning a complete circle. It was becoming clear she and Anna would have to make due with whatever clothing they could find at camp. A bath, well, that would have to wait. Her stomach grumbled loudly and she realized she was hungry. "Is there anything to eat?" she said. Smith appeared not to hear her.

"What will you do, Colonel?" Weir said. "Will you rebuild?"

"Yes, captain, but not here. I'll not let this happen again!" He looked up and only then did he register Elizabeth's presence. "Mrs. Custer! Thank God you're all right. I could not have lived with myself if anything had happened to you or Miss Darrah. She is unharmed, I trust?"

"Yes, Colonel, Anna's fine. We had a fright, but our tent withstood the winds."

"And thank the heavens for it. Well, as I said, I certainly won't risk anything like this again. You and Miss Darrah will be on the first train back to Fort Riley. This country is no place for a woman. If there was ever any doubt—and I've never had any!—what happened last night puts it to bed. I've said it before and I'll say it again, women and children do not belong in the field. They weren't allowed in my day. It's insane. I only hope General Sherman takes note of what almost happened here."

Elizabeth's heart dropped to her shoes. Fort Riley! The most boring place on the face of the earth, where one long, tedious day led to the next and the next. No, she would not go back there, she would not rot in that east Kansas hole while Armstrong had so much at stake. His future—their future—was on the line.

"No, Colonel Smith," she said, using her sweetest voice, "I am not going back to Fort Riley. Armstrong expects me to meet him at Fort Wallace. It's been arranged. I have letters to prove it."

"Fort Wallace?" Smith shook his white head. "Mrs. Custer, that's absurd. Fort Wallace is smack in the middle of Indian country. Why, it's the most dangerous post on the Smoky Hill Trail. I won't send you there. It's out of the question. You will go back to Riley immediately, by way of Fort Harker."

Elizabeth inwardly counted to ten. She was tired and overwrought and needed to keep a lid on her temper. Anger and shrillness, she learned long ago, were not effective in negotiations with a man. She forced a smile. "Colonel Smith, you don't understand. You see, the general expects me. As I said, he's made arrangements. The plans are in place."

Smith turned to Weir. "And what do you think, Captain? Is it a good idea to send this lady to Fort Wallace, where the Sioux and Cheyenne are thickest and most aggressive? Wouldn't that be something like sending a snowball to the beach?"

Weir raised his hands palms up. "It's not my call, sir. It is true that General Custer expects her. He's arranged for some of his men to escort Mrs. Custer from here to Wallace, where he plans to meet her in about two weeks' time."

"There, Colonel," Elizabeth said. "You see?"

"Yes," Smith said, with obvious irritation. "And I don't care. What happened last night changes all of that. For one thing, you couldn't stay here for two weeks, even if I were to allow it. There's no place for you to stay, nothing to eat, you can see for yourself—everything's buried in mud. I should think most women would be keen to get away as soon as possible."

"Well, Colonel Smith, I am not most women. I will wait here for my husband's men and I will go to Fort Wallace." And with that she turned, lifted her skirts, and began picking her way through the mud back to the camp on Big Creek.

Chapter Nineteen

The Indians had become increasingly active as the summer progressed. Tribes that were previously divided on whether to close the white man's Smoky Hill Road and stop the railroad now were united. The peace chiefs who negotiated with the Cheyenne agent Edward Wynkoop the preceding fall were pushed aside and the warrior societies of the Sioux and Cheyenne became ascendant, led by the Cheyenne's Dog Soldiers and southern Sutaio. Hancock's April decision to burn the Sioux and Cheyenne village on the Pawnee Fork, an action that resulted in the immolation of 250 lodges and all the Indians' belongings, only fanned the flames of hatred and distrust.

The tribes escalated their raids on the stage stations, stealing livestock and killing the station keepers. The Overland Stage route to Denver became so dangerous few passengers were willing to attempt it, and even the drivers refused to work without a military escort. Likewise, railroad crews of the Union Pacific's

Eastern Division, working along the Smoky Hill Trail, frequently were attacked and workers killed. Construction basically came to a halt during the months of May and June, 1867.

Many of the raids were led by a Kiyuksa Oglala warrior called Pawnee Killer, a fearless fighter who had earned his name in bloody action against his tribe's traditional enemy. He was tall for an Indian, and sturdily built, with eyes black as obsidian and a deeply pockmarked face. Unlike the other chiefs, who adorned themselves with silver pendants, armlets, and scalp locks dressed with strings of silver disks, Pawnee Killer wore no decoration other than a white man's broad-brimmed hat with a single feather affixed to the band. He often smiled, though a careful observer would find no warmth in his glittering black eyes.

Jack Gregory first encountered Pawnee Killer when Gregory was a twenty-year-old trader, working the stage and pony express routes along the south bank of the Platte. For the past four years he'd been junior partner in a concern owned and operated by a pipe-smoking Frenchman named Constant Prevot and a cheerful Canadian, Thomas Sun. Unlike the larger outfits, Prevot and Sun did not wait for the Indians to come to their storefront on the Platte Road, but instead ventured out to the villages to trade with their customers in their smoky lodges. Most of their business was with the Cheyenne and Sioux, and Gregory found himself captivated by their vagabond and carefree way of life. He spent happy months living shoulder to shoulder with his customers, learning their languages and ways. Some lessons were harder learned than others.

In the fall of 1862, Prevot, Sun, and Gregory traveled to a rendezvous on the Cache la Poudre River, in the free territory of Colorado. It was held on a wide, grassy meadow in a favored spot where cold, crystal water comes rushing down from the mountains to begin its easterly flow across the plains. Pawnee Killer was a headman with the Kiyuksa, or southern, band of the Oglala Sioux, whose people made their camp with White Horse's Cheyenne Dog Soldiers and the southern Sutaio. Gregory saw that Pawnee Killer was a man of importance by his dignified manner and the way others deferred to him.

"You'll want to stay away from that one," Thomas Sun said to Gregory. "He's a right devil to do business with."

But Gregory was flattered when the Oglala warrior singled him out for special attention. When Pawnee Killer invited Jack to sit with his people in the evenings, he accepted with pleasure. It did not hurt that a young woman seated at his fire was far and away the prettiest in camp, and one Gregory had his eye on since the rendezvous began. He spent every evening there, eating bowls of meat soup and smoking Pawnee Killer's tobacco. The Oglala warrior was pleased when Gregory spoke to him in his own tongue and he commended the young man on his mastery of the Sioux language. Gregory thought Thomas Sun had been unfair in his judgment of the Indian's character.

"Do you know why I like you, Jack Gregory?"

Pawnee Killer said. "It's your face. You have the face of a rabbit. I like rabbits."

Gregory was not pleased with this comparison and his disappointment must have shown for the big Sioux laughed and clapped a warm hand on Gregory's shoulder.

"I mean no disrespect. The rabbit is a brave and wily fellow and I will tell you why this is so." He launched into a story about a rabbit who lived in a lodge with his grandmother. The rabbit was a successful hunter who provided meat for many lodges. One morning when he was hunting he saw that someone with a very long, pointed foot had been there before him and taken all the game. This happened again the next morning and the next. His grandmother and the others were hungry and the rabbit became enraged, vowing to catch this poacher. So one night he set a trap using a stout bowstring as a snare. When he returned in the morning he saw that he had indeed captured the poacher, who was none other than the Sun himself! The rabbit ran home to tell his grandmother, who was very frightened and told him to return to the forest and free the Sun at once. When the rabbit got back, the Sun was violently angry and the rabbit quaked in terror. Still, he gathered his courage and ran in to cut the bowstring. The freed Sun soared into the heavens, but not before teaching the rabbit a lesson. He reached out with a long finger, white hot with a nail sharp as a knife-edge, and sliced the trembling rabbit's lip clean to his nose. Despite his injury, the rabbit brought home much game for his grandmother and the hungry village and was hailed as a hero. "So, you see?" Pawnee Killer said. "The rabbit's mark is a sign of his bravery and courage."

Gregory nodded, unconvinced. He stole a glance at the young woman, whose name was Mapiya, hoping she shared Pawnee Killer's admiration for rabbits, but her lovely face remained impassive, revealing nothing.

Later, as Gregory stood to leave, Pawnee Killer said he would like to buy a horse from his outfit. The animal he identified was a particularly handsome black stallion that would command top dollar. "He will make a gift for my sister," the Oglala said, nodding toward Mapiya. "That one's mother. This fine horse will make my sister and my niece very happy."

At this Mapiya looked into Gregory's eyes and smiled radiantly. "Yes," she said. "Very happy."

Gregory's heart went to pounding like a foundry hammer. She was beautiful, almost as beautiful as his lost love Waynoka, with soft brown eyes and straight white teeth.

"What will you take for him in trade?" Pawnee Killer said. "How many skins?"

Gregory tore his eyes away from the woman and cleared his throat, not trusting his voice, before answering. "I'll have to check with my partners," he said. "The price for that horse will be dear."

"Oh? Then you will not object if I ride him first, to make sure his gait is smooth and he is not too much horse for my sister to handle. Tomorrow is the last day of the rendezvous and I must be sure he is worthy of a high price."

Gregory hesitated. The more experienced Prevot usually handled negotiations of this nature.

Pawnee Killer gestured dismissively. "Of course. You are merely a baby. You must get the approval of your bosses first."

"They aren't my bosses," Gregory said, feeling his face redden. "I am equal to them in the partnership."

"Well then?" Pawnee Killer raised his eyebrows.

Mapiya moved next to Gregory, standing so close he could feel the heat from her skin. "Yes, all right," he said. "Just a short ride, though."

The three of them walked together to the corral where Gregory separated the black from the others. Mapiya stroked the stallion's muscular neck as Gregory slipped on a hackamore. Pawnee Killer examined the animal's teeth.

"A fine, young horse," he said. "Yes, my sister will be happy. Maybe this will sweeten her shrewish nature. Maybe now she will stop her arguing ways."

Mapiya laughed and said in English, "Maybe so."

Pawnee Killer grabbed hold of the stallion's mane and jumped onto his back. The horse bucked and kicked with his rear legs, but the Sioux warrior was a strong and confident horseman and the stallion did not fight long. When the horse had calmed, Pawnee Killer extended a strong arm and said, "Come, niece." Mapiya gripped his arm and he lifted her up behind him on the stallion's back. He winked at Gregory, who felt an uneasy stirring in his stomach as Mapiya wrapped her arms around the warrior's midsection. There was something not uncle-like in the way he stroked her thigh. The Sioux turned the horse's head, kicked him in the ribs and they were off, Pawnee Killer and Mapiya and the fine black stallion, vanished into the night.

Gregory felt vaguely ill as the pounding of the horse's hoofs grew fainter and fainter and then disappeared altogether. He sat up all night and in the morning he went to tell Constant Prevot and Thomas Sun how he had lost their prize horse. So great was his shame, it took all his courage to meet their gaze.

Before leaving the rendezvous, Gregory visited the Oglala camp and told Pawnee Killer's relatives that he would find the warrior and punish him for his treachery. "We will tell him, Rabbit," a young man said, with a broad grin. "Yes, we will tell him."

Chapter Twenty

The trail to Fort McPherson took them through miles of broken country the Indians called Badlands. It was marked by a series of ridges, deep ravines, and canyons, some as deep as fifty feet. Fall Leaf led with way, with Cheney and the Kempers following. Gregory brought up the rear because he didn't want to be expecting a bullet in the back all day. The going was hard and no one did much talking other than Cheney, who repeatedly asked if they were getting close to the fort.

"I told you this morning we had twenty-seven miles to cover," Gregory said. It was late afternoon and they had stopped in a shady canyon for a meal of water and jerky. "Why are you in such a powerful hurry? What's there to interest you boys anyhow?"

Cheney sat on a boulder, chewing a piece of meat and squinting at the sinking sun. "The railroad. I just want to get back to work, that's all. I want to get back with the boys."

"You that hot to go back to grading beds and laying track?"

"A man needs a paycheck."

After a time, Gregory said, "You want it known you're a religious man, ain't that so, brother Cheney? It's something you're proud of."

"Yes, indeed. I fear the Lord and encourage others to do likewise."

"Is that why you carved that cross in your boot heel, to show your fear of the Lord and encourage others?"

"We all labor under the curse of Cain, Mr. Grover," Cheney said around a mouthful of jerky. "We all do, me included, but some of us strive harder than others to resist the temptations of the mortal flesh. Some of us use our God-given strength to stand against the devil's fiendish persuasions. The sign of the cross is a reminder to me, and to all who walk with me, to follow his teachings and turn our backs on temptation." He reached for his canteen and took a long swallow, washing down the meat.

"Cheney, you are full of shit," Gregory said. "Right up to your eyeballs. You know it, I know it, and if there is a God in heaven, he knows it too."

Quiet followed, broken only by the munching of the horses in their linen nose bags.

"Why, brother Grover, that is not a very Christian thing to say," Cheney said with a smile. "And what leads you to this uncharitable assessment of my character?"

"Couple things," Gregory said, getting to his feet and drawing his .38 caliber Smith & Wesson. "One, I happen to know there'll be an eastbound shipment of Montana gold on a train that's coming through McPherson tomorrow. I looked into it. There had to be some reason you and the Tweedle twins were poking around this neck of the woods."

Cheney bit off another piece of jerky. "What's the other?"

"The other was a young man named Milo. Does that name ring a bell, brother?"

Cheney said nothing, but Gregory saw something move behind his eyes.

"Milo? The name means nothing to me."

"Well, maybe I can help you remember. Most folks called him Romeo on account of his good looks. He was young, just turned eighteen, and always real particular about his appearance. Me and the boys, we had fun with him on account of it, but he didn't care, he said a man who respects himself is careful about how he presents to others." Gregory smiled. "The women flat-out loved him, I've never seen the like. Milo, he was like a brother to me, and now he's dead."

"Well, I am sorry about your friend, but like I said, it's nothing to do with me." Cheney drank from his canteen and wiped his purple mouth with the back of his hand. "You know, Grover, maybe you'd be a happier man if you improved the level of your associations. Mexicans aren't reliable because they're soft. That's why they don't last out here, they haven't got the sand for it."

"How'd you know Milo was part Mexican?" Gregory pointed his gun at Cheney's head and thumbed back the hammer. "I'll tell you how. You're the one who killed him."

Cheney heaved an exaggerated sigh. "You and your Mexicans. Wasn't it a greaser you were working with up at Reno last summer, when you stole that payroll money? I don't know why you hook up with trash like that, I honestly don't. You should stick with your own kind. You'd have been better off—and your greaser friends too, for that matter." Cheney seemed mighty relaxed for a man with a gun at his head, so Gregory was not surprised when he heard the voice behind him.

"Drop the gun, Grover or Gregory or whatever the hell your name is."

Gregory dropped his revolver and turned to see one of the Kempers behind him, holding a .44.

"What took you so long?" Cheney said, brushing off his trousers. "Where's the pygmy?"

"Dead." Kemper said. "The little redskin's dead. Lem's taking care of the body so won't nobody see him when Custer comes through."

"I didn't hear a shot."

"I cut him." Kemper grinned and put his hand on the leather sheath hanging from his belt. "So, what you want done with this one? I'd be happy to give him the same he gave Cave, back at the stage station. I'd be all right with that."

Cheney shook his head. "So much violence. Who would've thought making one's way in God's great world would involve such pain and bloodshed? You ever ask yourself that question, brother Gregory? No, I suppose not. I believe, in your case anyhow, we can put all this sorrow and misfortune down to not loving the Lord as he would be loved." Cheney raised his arms and eyes heavenward. "'And we know that in all things God works for the good of those who love Him, who have been called according to His purpose.' That's from Romans."

"You know, I've always thought it's real funny," Gregory said, "the way gasbags like you go on about the Lord this and the Lord that, while if he was here he wouldn't have anything to do with the likes of you."

"See, friend, that's your problem," Cheney said, walking forward. "A heart full of hate will never gain heaven." As he bent over to pick up the Smith & Wesson, Gregory brought his knee up hard against Cheney's fleshy face, feeling his nose explode on impact. As Gregory dove for his gun, he felt the albino's bullet graze his right shoulder. Gregory rolled onto his back as he hit the ground and raised his revolver, all in one fluid motion. Kemper's second shot was high, not even close. Before he could get off a third, Luther Kemper was dead, a bullet hole in the middle of his forehead, like a Hindu jewel. Cheney was on his hands and knees, dripping bright red blood from his nose and mouth.

"Get on your feet," Gregory said.

"You son of a bitch." Cheney spat out a tooth.

"Now." Gregory pressed the business end of the revolver against Cheney's temple, and the big man stood, unsteadily. Gregory looked toward the mouth of the canyon, now in shadow. He saw no sign of the dead man's twin.

"Go sit over there." Gregory pointed with the gun's barrel to a spot at the base of the canyon wall. Once Cheney was seated, Gregory took a length of rope from his saddle and bound him, hand and foot. This done, he tied a kerchief around Cheney's head, covering his bloody mouth.

"Now, brother," Gregory said, "you just sit there and think about that God you love so much. You enjoy that and I'll be back in no time." Cheney muttered as Gregory crept toward the canyon entrance, gun in hand. Luther Kemper had come from that direction and Gregory figured Lem would too. By now it was getting on to six o'clock and the evening shadows were playing tricks on his tired eyes. He moved forward, cautiously, holding to the canyon walls, then following a dry streambed for about half a mile until he neared the ruins of a burned-out stage station. The Overland Stage used this route, back when the site of Fort McPherson was a tiny settlement known as Cottonwood Springs. Gregory knew the country well. When the ruins came into view, he stopped, not trusting what his eyes were telling him. It didn't make sense, maybe it was another trick of the light.

But as he drew closer, he realized he was seeing the nude body of Lem Kemper. Arrows had been shot through his open palms, in effect nailing him to the charred log wall, the only part of the station house still standing. Lem had been scalped and a small bit of the tissue, with long, white hair still attached, lay beside him on the ground. His nose had been slit from nostrils to eyebrow, the lenses of his glasses shattered and thrust into his eyes, his legs cut from hip to knee. Muscle protruded from his lacerated thighs like sausage from a burst casing. Through his

chest was a third arrow, like the others marked with
bands of red and yellow.

Gregory spun on his heel, straining to see, sensing
a watcher in the gathering darkness. Pawnee Killer
was there. He could feel the Indian's black eyes burning into his flesh. He wondered if he still rode the
black stallion.

"Pawnee Killer!" He called in the language of the
Oglala Sioux. "Show yourself! You hide in the shadows
like a woman. Come fight me, you coward!" He did
not expect Pawnee Killer to respond, neither did he
think him a coward. He knew the Oglala was toying
with him, the way jay hawks he used to observe as a
boy in the Missouri woods would play with a field
mouse before devouring it.

He turned and started back to the canyon. Along
the way he stumbled over the remains of Fall Leaf,
partly buried in a shallow grave. He supposed Kemper
had been in the process of burying him when
Pawnee Killer surprised him. Gregory kneeled to
examine the body and saw Fall Leaf's throat had
been cut. He turned the body over and found that
the initial injury, the one that brought him down,
was a deep stab wound to the back.

"I am sorry, friend," Gregory said. "You deserved
a more dignified death." He cut Fall Leaf's beaded
fire bag from his belt and trotted back to the canyon.
When he arrived, Cheney and the horses were gone.
In their place was a dead rabbit, pinned to the hard
ground by an arrow, marked with bands of red and
yellow.

Chapter Twenty-one

Custer paced before his tent, watched closely by his dogs. Gregory was overdue. He and Fall Leaf should have been back in camp hours ago, with a report on the next day's route.

"Something's wrong," Custer said. "I'm sure of it. Grover's reliable, he knows I expect him back tonight. No, something's happened and I'll bet those missing railroad workers have something to do with it."

"Could be," Tom said. He sat in a camp chair, cleaning his fingernails with a pocket knife. "They were a strange lot, that's for sure. Good riddance, I say. As for Grover, we can get to McPherson without him. The old stage road will get us there. We can be there by tomorrow night, probably."

Custer was not placated. "Yes, that's not what bothers me. I'm worried about Libbie. I asked her to meet me at Fort Wallace and I was going to send Grover back to Big Creek to get her—and now this. What's happened to him, dammit? It's a nuisance."

In the camp, men were singing around their fires, "Old Hundred" and other sentimental songs of home. The scene was peaceful, with their tents, lit from within, glowing in neat rows like Japanese lanterns.

Tom cleared his throat. "Do you think that's a good idea, brother? Bringing Libbie to Wallace? Things are much rougher there than back at Hays." He couldn't see Custer's face, but he could picture the scowl and the reddening skin.

"I know what I'm doing, Tom. You think I don't? I wouldn't do anything to put her at risk. This Indian threat is overstated—you know that well as I do. We've spent weeks chasing down wild rumors started by hysterical settlers who're getting everybody all exercised over nothing. The Indians don't want war—isn't that obvious? That's why they're running from us, hiding from us. There's only one thing we're accomplishing out here and that's ruining our horses! My God, Tom, it's pitiful what the U.S. Army has become. It makes me sad."

Tom waited. He'd learned a long time ago it was no good, trying to talk to his brother when he was in a state. "Well," he said at last, "what do you want to do? Do we wait for Grover or go on to McPherson without him?"

"We move tomorrow," Custer said. "No point sitting around here."

Despite an early start, the column made only twenty miles during a long day of difficult travel and stopped seven miles short of Fort McPherson. Custer called a halt near the Forks of the Platte where they found plenty of good grass for the horses. They were close enough to the fort to hear the boom of the evening gun and the whistle of the train as it neared the station.

That evening, as the men were pitching their tents and making their cook fires, eight Indians rode into camp, causing a commotion. They quickly identified Custer and went directly to his Sibley. They spoke no English but, with signs, identified themselves as Oglala Sioux and said they wanted to parley. Custer called on one of the Delawares to translate. The Indians and officers sat cross-legged in a circle in front of Custer's tent. His orderly served the Indians coffee, liberally laced with sugar and canned milk.

"I am Pawnee Killer," the tallest of the Indians said when his cup was drained. "I have come to talk to Yellow Hair for an important reason. I have come to say the Sioux people want peace with the Long Knives."

Custer smiled broadly when the translation was complete. "There, you see?" he said to Tom, sitting beside him. "It's just like I told you, these Indians don't want war. No, this whole campaign is nothing but a waste of time and money and energy. I've been saying it all along. Maybe now General Sherman will listen to me." To the translator he said, "Tell Pawnee Killer the bluecoat soldiers want this also." Custer put his hand on his breast. "I, Yellow Hair, also want peace."

Tom leaned over and put his mouth close to his

brother's ear. "Armstrong, don't you recognize that name—Pawnee Killer? He's the one who killed those men at Lookout Station. We should make him our prisoner, we should bring him in to Fort McPherson to answer charges."

Custer turned on Tom with a face like thunder. "Are you crazy? I will not take him prisoner! No one knows who killed those station workers. There's been lots of talk, lots of suspicion, but I certainly don't know who did it and neither do you. Why the hell would I make a prisoner of this man who's come to us—voluntarily—to sue for peace? No, I'll convince him to bring his people to the fort, where the army will give them food and supplies and make sure they keep away from Cheyenne troublemakers. Then this Indian business will settle down and we can all get on with our lives and I can finally spend time with my wife."

Custer ordered the Delaware to deliver his offer. Pawnee Killer listened closely, nodding and smiling. The flickering firelight accentuated the deep, pitted scars on his face.

"Yes, Yellow Hair, I understand you," he said. "You want me to bring my people to live by the soldier fort. It would be good to settle. But then I remember how you bluecoats burned our village before. Why should I trust you, Yellow Hair? Maybe you will hurt us again."

Custer waved his hand as if shooing an insect. "That was a mistake. I agree, your village should not have been burned, and anyway I had nothing to do with it. Your people will be safe at Fort McPherson, I promise you."

Pawnee Killer narrowed his black eyes. "All right, Yellow Hair, I will bring them, but to you only. I do not trust the other Long Knives. For this reason, I need to know where you are going, when you will leave this place, and when you will return. Otherwise I cannot do what you ask."

Custer shook his head. "You don't need to know that. Bring your people to the solider fort near here, the one on the river. They will be safe, even if I'm not there at the time. I will make all the necessary arrangements."

The Sioux men received this translation with frowns and sounds of displeasure. "No, this is not what I want," Pawnee Killer said. "I said I will bring them to you only, but you will not say where you are going or when. I do not know when you will be at the fort to receive my people. No, this will not do." He stood, signaling the parley was over, and the rest of his men stood with him.

"Wait!" Custer said, jumping to his feet. "I will give you gifts to demonstrate Yellow Hair's good intentions. And there will be more, much more, including fresh beef, for your people when they come." To Tom he said, "What have we got?"

Tom shrugged. "Coffee, sugar, crackers. The usual."

"Well, give it to them and plenty of it. As much as they can carry."

The Indians left the camp loaded down with supplies, Pawnee Killer having assured Custer he would move his people to the soldier fort as instructed. "What fools these bluecoats are," Pawnee Killer said to his friend, Red Lance. "Yellow Hair is the biggest fool of all." And the two men laughed as they rode away on their heavily laden ponies.

Chapter Twenty-two

Colonel Smith was more obdurate than Elizabeth anticipated and she did leave for Fort Riley after all. Despite all her charming, pleading, and, eventually, weeping, he would not relent. Even General Sherman weighed in on this matter, advising her in a chilly letter to "remain quietly" at Riley for her husband would be on campaign, scouting in the Division of the Platte, all summer and it was unlikely she would be able to reunite with him before fall. The letter's tone was so different from the warmth Sherman expressed on the train, she wondered if it was written by the same man. *Maybe he regretted his heartfelt confession,* she thought. Oh, well, so much for the devotion of—how did he describe himself?—a "shabby old soldier."

On the afternoon of Sunday, June 16, Smith told Elizabeth and Anna to be ready to move out at nine o'clock that evening. He would escort them personally, along with Captain Weir and ten soldiers. "Every day brings new reports of depredations," a visibly distraught Smith said, "and each is more violent than the one before. Why, just this morning I learned that a large number of Indians, probably a Cheyenne war party under Lean Bear, passed Fort Larned a day ago and are heading this way. I was also told of an attack on Walker Creek, where women were violated and two men killed. No, I need to get you ladies to safety as soon as possible."

They spent the afternoon packing their trunks. Their soaked clothing had been dried in the sun, hung over bushes or from tree limbs, and was stiff as board as a result. Elizabeth tried to fold a particular favorite—a Nile-green silk that showed her gray eyes to great advantage—but gave up in disgust and simply stuffed it into the trunk. A skilled laundress might be able to save it, but she thought it was probably ruined. All her clothes were ruined. Only the dress she wore that night, a blue-and-green plaid, was undamaged. If she had known she would have only one dress to carry her through the summer, it was not the one she would have chosen.

"Why are you so upset, Liz?" Anna asked after Elizabeth released an especially heavy sigh. "I don't understand why you're so keen to be with Armstrong just now. To tell you the truth, I've had the feeling you were quite put out with him."

Elizabeth stopped packing and walked to the tent door. Because of the heat the flap was tied open, but along with the breeze came biting black flies. One landed on her neck and she killed it with a slap. "Yes, it's true," she said, "I have been annoyed with him lately. He seems such a child. Tom is part of the problem.

They shouldn't campaign together. All that skylarking—they simply encourage each other in their immaturity. Even their mother acknowledged this was a problem."

Anna nodded. Though she had not said anything, something was troubling her. Elizabeth could tell. Anna simply wasn't the flirtatious woman with the rapacious smile she had been when she first arrived. Elizabeth supposed this was because she and Tom were on the outs, and earlier that day she asked Anna about it, but she merely shrugged her shoulders. Maybe it was time Anna went back to Michigan.

"But you're right," Elizabeth continued, "I do feel it's important Armstrong and I be together just now. His career is at a delicate juncture, and I don't trust him to make good choices—his judgment is faulty, he's impulsive, he doesn't think things through. My greatest fear is that he'll make some terrible mistake that results in disaster. And he has enemies, so many enemies, who would simply delight in his undoing. Captain Benteen, for one, and lately maybe even Albert Barnitz. How I wish I could show Armstrong to get along with people, or at least how not to offend them. He needs to cultivate men, other than Phil Sheridan, who can advance his career."

Anna kept her eyes on her packing. Before closing the trunk, she dropped in several leaves of fresh rosemary to lend the clothing a fresh scent. "Really, Liz, Armstrong is a grown man. Don't forget what he did during the war. He's still the same man, is he not? My goodness, have some confidence in him."

"I wish I could, Anna, I do. But the fact is I simply cannot shake the feeling that something horrible, something truly ruinous, is going to happen, either to him or because of him, if I'm not there to stop it."

"Are you sure that's all it is?" Anna asked with a studied casualness.

"What do you mean?"

Anna was careful to keep her eyes down, away from Elizabeth's, as she locked her trunk. "I was thinking there might be another reason you want to be in the field with Armstrong. Joe Grover is there too. I merely wondered if that might have something to do with it. He's not a bad-looking man, even with the harelip."

"Anna, please!" Elizabeth said. "Don't be ridiculous!" Even as she spoke, Elizabeth felt disloyal and shabby.

Despite Smith's admonition to be ready at nine, it was midnight when the short column finally rolled away from Fort Hays. A light rain began to fall as they started, and the soft patter on the canvas, coupled with the swaying of the ambulance, soon lulled Elizabeth to sleep. She dreamed of the scout Gregory, saw him among the Indians in a dark, smoke-filled lodge. A lovely Indian girl stood at his side. Suddenly Elizabeth was in the lodge also, frightened and alone, trying without success to draw his attention. "Why won't you help me?" she said to him when at last she succeeded. "I'm all alone here. Why won't you help me?" He looked at her with disdain, then drew the Indian girl to him and turned to kiss her on the lips. "You aren't what you pretend to be," he said to

Elizabeth. "You're an imposter. You'll have to take care of yourself." And he turned back to the Indian woman, kissing her again while his hand stroked her shoulder and breast.

They arrived at Fort Harker at sundown. The glowing colors did nothing to enhance the three-company post, which appeared as forlorn and gloomy to Elizabeth now as it did in the spring, when she arrived on the train and first met Jack Gregory. The commanding officer, Major Alfred Gibbs, offered the women his quarters for the night. This was perhaps the garrison's most attractive structure, a one-story sandstone home of good size, maybe eight or nine rooms, and Elizabeth very much wanted to stay there, in a real bed, with a private bathroom where she could have a long, hot soak. But she knew she and Anna would inconvenience Mrs. Gibbs and the couple's two small boys, so she declined. Instead she asked the men to roll the ambulance to a narrow alley between two warehouses and stretch a tarpaulin between the buildings to provide a shelter for their cook fire. She and Anna had a meal of canned meat, beans, and coffee and went to bed early. As she was changing into her white cotton nightdress, Elizabeth noticed the ring finger of her left hand was bare. *Jack must still have it,* she thought. Funny, she hadn't missed it till now. She climbed into bed and fell asleep immediately.

At midnight she woke to a strong, keening wind that whistled down the narrow alley between the two buildings and rocked their little wagon like a toy in the hands of an angry child. Anna was already awake.

"God, it can't be," she said, "not another storm!"

Elizabeth was frightened too, but pretended not to be. "At least we don't have to worry about a flood," she said. Fort Harker was a mile from the Smoky Hill River and on a hill as well. No, she thought, their greatest danger came from the ambulance's location. The alley concentrated the wind's force, threatening to rip the wagon to pieces. Already the canvas's fastenings were strained to the limit.

The rain started, a horizontal deluge that quickly found its way around the canvas. Soon the women's blankets were sodden. Elizabeth looked out under the billowing canvas just as the tarpaulin stretched across the alleyway filled like a sail, pulled free of its moorings and flapped away like a giant bird. The two women huddled together in a corner, wrapped in their wet blankets, and prepared to wait out the night. Thunder boomed, lightning crashed, the wind blew like a typhoon. Elizabeth no longer tried to conceal her fear. She and Anna held each other, shivering in cold and terror. Elizabeth almost wondered if they had done something to anger the prairie storm gods, who now conspired to teach them a lesson.

In a blue-white flash of lightning, Elizabeth saw a poncho-clad sentry at the head of the alley, passing on his rounds, and almost called out to him, but stopped herself at the last second. It was a cardinal sin to talk to or distract a guard on duty, every army wife knew that, but she immediately regretted her decision when a violent blast lifted the ambulance from its moorings. It bounced once, twice and then, to her horror, broke free of the picket pins and ropes that anchored it in place and started rolling. This time there was no hesitation; Elizabeth and Anna screamed at the sentry for all they were worth and brought him running. He and others grabbed hold of the trailing ropes and pulled the wagon back to its place in the narrow alleyway. But Elizabeth and Anna had had enough. Inconvenience or no, they asked to be taken to the commanding officer's quarters where they were received warmly and passed the remainder of the night in warm, dry clothing and warm, dry beds. The Gibbs boys had to sleep on the floor, but Elizabeth was past caring.

Chapter Twenty-three

Gregory rode into Custer's camp from the south, just as a short column headed by General William Tecumseh Sherman's custom-made Dougherty ambulance arrived from the north. Gregory took advantage of the excitement to slip in quietly, hoping for a few hours' sleep, but Tom Custer waved him over.

"Where the hell have you been?" he said before Gregory had even dismounted. "We expected you days ago. Where's Fall Leaf? What happened?"

Gregory climbed down from the saddle and stroked Jeff's sweating neck. He was tired; the horse's head hung almost to the ground. He had earned a rest and a nose bag of oats and Gregory would see to it he got them. "We had trouble with those three drifters you picked up," Gregory said. "They weren't railroad workers, by the way. Fall Leaf is dead. One of those albino freaks killed him."

"Killed Fall Leaf? Why?"

"They wanted to rob us."

Tom laughed. "Rob you? Of what?"

"They thought I had something I didn't. One of the twins killed Fall Leaf and I killed them. I don't know what happened to Cheney. I think Indians might have him. I hope so anyhow."

Tom shook his head. "This doesn't explain where you've been. What have you been doing all this time?"

"I had to bury Fall Leaf and then there was some personal business I had to take care of." In fact he had ridden sixty miles to deliver the Indian's fire bag to his widow on the Saline River. "I knew you wouldn't have trouble getting to McPherson. A baby could follow that road."

Tom narrowed his eyes. The scout had disobeyed orders, but he was not at all sure what to do about it.

"What's he doing here?" Gregory nodded toward Sherman, just emerging from his ambulance. Custer met him with a brisk salute and a smile. Sherman returned the salute but not the smile. His naturally grim face looked grimmer than usual.

"I'm not exactly sure," Tom said. "We didn't know he was coming until this morning. It might have something to do with some Indians we met with recently. A group of Oglala Sioux."

"Was one of them tall, wearing a white man's hat? With a scarred face?"

"Yes, that sounds like Pawnee Killer. You know him?"

"I know him. What did he want?"

"He came to make peace. He's going to bring his people in to Fort McPherson. He was reluctant to do it, but Armstrong got him to agree."

"And I suppose you gave him gifts in return?"

"Yes. It seemed right, a gesture of goodwill."

"I see," Gregory said. He knew now why Sherman was paying Custer an unexpected visit, and why he wore a sour face. "Pawnee Killer won't bring his people in, no matter what he said. He skunked you. He'll never surrender to the Long Knives, not for all the beef and sugar in the world."

Tom's face reddened and a white ring appeared around his mouth. Must be a family trait, Gregory thought. "You don't know that, Grover," Tom said. "I was there, you weren't. Armstrong warned him if he didn't do it, his people would suffer."

Gregory shrugged. "All right. Wait and see for yourself." As he walked Jeff to the picket line, he saw Custer and Sherman on their way to Custer's tent. Sherman was doing all the talking and Gregory could imagine what he was saying. *"What's the matter with you, Custer? I thought you knew how to handle Indians. Don't you know that damn Sioux, that Pawnee Killer, and his warriors were responsible for that butchery at Lookout Station? Goddamn it, Custer—he walked right into your hands. You should have arrested him or at least taken some hostages until he complied with your demands. What, were you born yesterday? I expected more from you!"* Gregory smiled to himself. Yes, he was confident Custer was getting a hiding. Maybe it would make Goldilocks's feathers fall some.

That night Gregory was wakened from a deep and satisfying sleep by an orderly shaking his shoulder, saying Custer wanted him in his tent right away. Gregory swore under his breath as he threw off his blanket. "What time is it?"

"Midnight."

"What's it about?" Gregory said as he began pulling on his boots.

The orderly shrugged. "I don't know, but he don't look happy."

The camp was still as they walked to Custer's tent. Even the dogs were quiet. As usual when he was stressed or anxious, Custer was pacing.

"Come in, Grover," he said. "Orlie, you're dismissed."

The interior of Custer's tent was immaculate. There was none of the clutter some men surround themselves with. His cot was neatly made, his clothes for the following day folded on a camp chair, his razor and toothbrush on a shaving stand beside a clean, folded towel and a blue glass jar. Whatever was in that jar, Gregory thought, probably accounted for Custer's Christmas candy aroma.

"Sit down, Grover," Custer said, pointing to a second camp chair. Gregory did as instructed, expecting a dressing down for his unauthorized absence. As it turned out, Custer had other things on his mind. He paced as he talked.

"My orders have been changed. Sherman wants me to scout to the south, to the forks of the Republican, then back up to Sedgwick for supplies and fresh orders. Then, if nothing changes, I'm to continue west along the Republican all the way to the Platte. Sherman is impatient, he wants the Indians put away yesterday."

Gregory suppressed a smile. He suspected Sherman

had said a lot more than that, and about one Indian in particular.

"I had expected to resupply at Fort Wallace," Custer continued, "not Sedgwick, and I asked Libbie—that is, Mrs. Custer—to meet me there, at Wallace. I posted that letter days ago; she's probably en route or maybe even already there. So, Grover, I need you to go to Fort Wallace and get her. If she's not there when you arrive, wait for her. If, say, three days go by and still she doesn't arrive, go to Fort Hays. And if she's not at Hays, then find her. Wherever she is, go there and bring her to me."

He stopped at Gregory's chair, looking down at him. The quiet was absolute, other than the chirping of crickets and the thud of a moth against the lantern glass.

Gregory cleared his throat. "General Custer, I'm not sure I understand. What if Mrs. Custer isn't at Wallace or Hays? What if she's back at Fort Riley, or even Leavenworth? I could be gone for weeks. Not only that, but then I'd have to bring her back. Have you thought about that? We'd be traveling clean across Kansas, without an escort or a minimal one at best. If she was my wife, I wouldn't—"

"Well, she's not, and I don't remember asking for your opinion, Grover. You're my scout, I'm giving you orders and I expect you to obey them. May I remind you that you are being well paid, Grover— three times what a trooper makes!—but if you can't do what I ask I'll find someone who will."

It was on the tip of Gregory's tongue to tell him to

go ahead. No one knew this part of Kansas better than he did, and Custer knew it. Gregory would enjoy watching him try to find a scout to replace him. But he'd do what Custer asked. He was more than happy for a chance to see Elizabeth again, and he also welcomed the opportunity to get back to Fort Wallace. He'd go by his ranch and see how his crop was progressing. No telling what his hired man was doing—or not doing, more likely—in his absence. Still, Custer's request was strange. There was more here than just a pining for his pretty wife.

"When do I leave?" Gregory said, getting to his feet.

"As soon as Sherman moves on. I think he plans to stay another day. I'd rather he not know of this . . . assignment I've given you." Custer walked to his shaving stand and began washing his hands. "He may not approve."

You're not lying, Gregory thought.

"Meanwhile, Grover, get some rest. Tom told me about that business with Fall Leaf and those three drifters, and you've got a lot of riding ahead. Oh— we've got an Indian in the hospital tent. He's hurt, a patrol brought him back this afternoon, just before Sherman arrived. Talk to him in the morning, find out who he is, what he knows, and so forth."

Gregory walked back to his tent and crawled into his bedroll. The night was chilly and his woolen blanket felt good. He turned onto his side, looking toward Custer's tent, still brightly lit. The last thing he saw, before sleep overtook him, was the general's pacing silhouette against the canvas wall.

* * *

The hospital tent was pitched next to the surgeon's Sibley. Gregory pushed aside the flap and entered. The dark interior stank of corruption, like a piece of meat left in the sun.

"Water." The word, spoken in English, came from the shadows. When Gregory's eyes adjusted, he saw a man lying on a low army cot. "Please, I need water." Gregory popped a match to flame with his thumbnail and held it to the wick of a spirit lamp hanging from the tent pole. The yellow circle of light fell on the lower half of the man's body, his right leg exposed. Above the knee was a red, meaty hole with slivers of white bone sticking out of it, like bits of broken pottery. Just looking at it made Gregory's insides pucker.

"A patrol brought him back yesterday afternoon." Major Higgins, the regimental surgeon, had entered the tent soundlessly. "As you can see, he's been shot in the leg." Higgins was small and slight with a carefully trimmed beard and sweet, almost womanish, features. His immaculate uniform bore the gold-embroidered laurel wreath designating an officer of the Medical Department. He wore round gold-rimmed eyeglasses that reflected the lamplight as if a furnace burned behind them.

Gregory stepped closer to the man on the cot and spoke to him in the language of the Cheyenne. "What is your name?"

The Indian tried to sit, briefly bringing his face

into the yellow circle of light. He was very young, probably no more than sixteen years, and clearly relieved to hear his native tongue. "Little Wolf," he said. "I am called Little Wolf." He fell back on the cot in pain and exhaustion. "Please, I need water."

There was a small barrel by the tent door. Gregory filled a tin cup and gave it to the boy, who drained it in two gulps and asked for more.

"Just half a cup, Mr. Grover," the surgeon said. "Wouldn't do to give him too much."

When Little Wolf was finished drinking, Gregory said, "Who are your people?"

"I am from the village of Turkey Leg," he said, naming a chief Gregory knew well, a customer during his time with Prevot and Sun. "I was hunting with my cousins and brothers when the Long Knives attacked us for no reason. We were north of the Republican River, where you whites allow us to hunt, and we did nothing wrong, but they did this thing anyway. I fell from my horse and one of my cousins was killed. I didn't see what happened to my brothers. I want to go home." His thin face was very pale.

Gregory translated for Higgins, who pulled a clean white handkerchief from his coat pocket and touched it to his perspiring forehead. "Are you all right?" Gregory said.

"Oh, yes, I'm fine," the older man said. "Only that it's rather ripe in here. Does the smell bother you?"

Gregory shrugged. It was bad but he'd known worse.

"Then I'll ask you to help me," Higgins said. "I

need to examine the boy's wound and I'd appreciate it if you would hold the light above his leg."

"Why don't I carry him outside?" Gregory said. "You could see it in the daylight."

"No," the surgeon said, offering no explanation. "We'll do it this way."

"All right," Gregory said. "You're the doctor." He took the lantern from the pole and held it aloft as Higgins knelt beside the cot and probed Little Wolf's injury with a metal instrument. The boy cried and thrashed and the surgeon instructed Gregory to tell him to keep still. Throughout all this, Gregory admired the physician's obedience to his craft, his willingness to discomfit himself for the good of another, regardless of the sufferer's low station. Days before, Gregory had watched Higgins pull a recruit's rotted tooth and lance a teamster's festering boils. It was repulsive, stinking work, yet the old man never showed any sign of disgust. Though he did not speak of it, Gregory had heard that during the war Higgins voluntarily had taken charge of a quarantined hospital for Confederate prisoners on an island in the Mississippi River near Alton, Illinois. It was a posting shunned by other Federal surgeons and a place avoided by all civilized men. The Saint of Pox Island they called him, or so Gregory was told.

"Yes, the joint is filled with pus." Higgins stood, wiping his hands on his handkerchief. "Serum infiltration the length of the leg, high as the apex of Scarpa's triangle." He inhaled deeply, flaring his delicate nostrils. "That smell, Mr. Grover, is the beginning of putrefaction."

Little Wolf looked up at Gregory with wide, frightened eyes. "What does the old man say?" Gregory did not answer.

"The leg must come off," Higgins said quietly, "and the sooner the better. Tell the lad, Mr. Grover. Make sure he understands the urgency."

Gregory relayed this to the boy.

"No!" he shouted hoarsely. "Without my leg I will be unable to ride, to hunt. I will not be a man! Take me back to my people—please—the healer will cure me. I've seen him cure worse, much worse." This too Gregory repeated for the surgeon.

Higgins shook his head as he picked up his bag. "There is no other way, I'm afraid. Amputation or death, those are his choices. And he needs to decide quickly. In cases like this, every minute counts."

He leaned down to give the wounded boy a pat on the shoulder. It was meant to be reassuring, but Little Wolf recoiled, an expression of horror on his face. The surgeon sighed and exited the tent, leaving Gregory alone with the Indian. He felt bad for the lad, damaged and alone among the Long Knives. How would Gregory feel if it was him on that cot instead of Little Wolf?

"Don't worry," he said as he returned the lamp to its hook on the pole. "That old man is one of the best surgeons in the U.S. Army. I know this is hard, Little Wolf, but it's better to be a one-legged than dead in the ground. When you are recovered, I will take you to your people in Turkey Leg's village. I promise this." He doubted Custer would like the idea, but Gregory would do it anyway—if the boy survived.

Little Wolf pushed himself up on one elbow. "The old man hates Indians. He is a demon. I see this in his eyes behind the glass. Please don't let him cut off my leg. Please."

At that moment the wind kicked up. A powerful gust set the lamp to bouncing on its pole, throwing shadows and creating a dizzying sense of motion. Gregory had the strange sensation that he and Little Wolf were the only passengers on a tiny vessel, tossed about by towering waves. He felt nauseous.

"You must believe me." The boy was pleading now. "The old man is a demon. I am a seer, I am known in my village for my way of knowing. Help me, please."

The dancing light played across Little Wolf's frightened face. Gregory was torn. He wanted to help the boy, but what could he do? The leg was starting to rot, that was obvious. If the surgeon said it had to come off, that was what had to happen. Still . . . Gregory felt an urgent need to get out of the stinking tent.

"Get some rest," he said. "I'll be back with food and water." Little Wolf wept as Gregory stepped outside, filling his lungs with clean air. The camp smelled of burning cottonwood and boiling coffee. Before returning to his tent he glanced toward the surgeon's conical Sibley, which stood apart from the others. The flap was open and Gregory saw Higgins inside, hunched over a desk. What was he doing? Reading from some obscure medical text? Writing maybe? If so, to whom? Gregory had never heard the surgeon speak of family, never known him to receive a personal letter.

Back in his own tent, he pulled off his boots and
stretched out on his cot, looking forward to a day of
rest. He slept most of the day and was not pleased
when the captain of the guard woke him at sundown
to say Higgins was asking for him in the hospital tent.

"What does he want?" Gregory said, rolling onto
his side.

"It's about that Indian," the soldier replied, "he's
raising a racket. Can't nobody understand what
he's saying."

With a curse, Gregory got up and dressed, tucking
in his shirttails as he crossed the camp. A sentry
called the time—"seven o' clock and all's well"—
starting the round-robin that moved from post to
post.

The stench in the hospital tent had worsened.
Little Wolf's face was gray in the low light and his
head was wet with sweat. He appeared to be sleeping.
Higgins sat on a chair beside him.

"I gave him a sedative," he said. "He was yelling,
out of his mind. I will operate immediately and I
would like you to assist me."

"Me?" Gregory said. "Why me? I don't know about
these things."

"You speak the boy's language and he appears to
trust you. I want you to be there."

Gregory looked down at Little Wolf. He did not
want to see what was about to happen, but maybe, for
the boy's sake, he should be there.

"Carry him to the quartermaster's wagon and
lower the gate," Higgins said. "That will suit as an
operating table. Cover it with a rubber blanket, then

round up five or six lamps and a basin of water. Move quickly. Time is of the essence. I may be too late already."

Gregory had a bad feeling as he went about these tasks. He remembered Little Wolf's eyes when he said, "That old man is a demon."

Little Wolf began to moan as Gregory and an enlisted man carried him to the quartermaster's wagon. Six coal oil lanterns burned brightly in the wagon bed, throwing a stark light. As he lifted the boy from the stretcher, Gregory remembered a story he'd heard years before, read aloud around a campfire, a ghoulish tale of grave robbing and unnatural passion.

Higgins arrived carrying a black leather field case that he placed on the wagon bed beside the moaning Little Wolf. Gregory was struck by how fresh the old man looked, how bright-eyed, despite the hour. A small smile tugged at his lips as he opened the case and withdrew a long, gleaming blade.

"This is a Liston's long knife, Mr. Grover," he said, holding the instrument aloft and turning it so the light played along the polished nickel. "Sharp enough to split a hair. Beautiful, isn't it?"

"I guess." Beautiful was not the word Gregory would have used to describe it.

The surgeon placed the knife carefully, almost lovingly, beside Little Wolf on the rubber blanket. "And this, a tenaculum." He lifted a long-handled device with a sharp claw, like a witch's curled fingers, at its business end. This too he held to the light. He repeated this procedure with a series of instruments, introducing each by name: catling, scalpel, retractor, artery forceps, bone saw. Gregory kept his eyes on the surgeon's face during this strange exercise, sensing he was seeing the old man for the first time. When the tools were aligned in a neat row, Higgins waved his arm and four men approached.

"What are they for?" Gregory said.

"Why, to hold the lad down. You see, I have no anesthetic. No chloroform, no ether."

Little Wolf opened his eyes and looked at Gregory. He was coming around.

"Use some more of that sedative. Whatever you gave him is wearing off."

The boy struggled to sit.

"That was the last of my supply," Higgins said. "It's gone too, I'm afraid. I wish I could provide anesthetic, but I can't."

Gregory looked at Little Wolf's leg. Dark streaks ran from the wound to the groin. The surgeon removed his eyeglasses, cleaning them on a handkerchief. At that moment Little Wolf's eyes came into focus, fixed on the old man's face. They widened in terror.

"Demon!" he screamed. "Your eyes! I see you! I see you!" He retched, the soured contents of his stomach splashing onto the ground.

"What's he going on about?" Higgins said.

Gregory looked at the surgeon and saw nothing unusual. "He says you're a demon. He also says you hate Indians."

Higgins replaced his eyeglasses before pulling a

full-length linen apron over his head. "He's out of his mind. Get behind him, hold his shoulders down. The rest of you, each take a limb."

Little Wolf continued to cry and plead as the four men came forward. Gregory did not move.

Higgins turned to him. "Well? Will you stand there while this boy dies?"

"I want nothing to do with this," Gregory said. "You'll have to do it without me." He retreated to the river where the horses were picketed and walked up and down the rope line, calming the agitated animals as Little Wolf's screams resounded through the camp.

Later, when all was quiet, the surgeon joined him. His rolled shirtsleeves and linen apron were stained with blood.

"Well?" Gregory said.

The surgeon shook his head. "It was a simple, double-flap amputation." He spoke softly, sorrowfully. "I've done hundreds like it, but the hemorrhaging was uncontrollable. He bled out, I'm afraid."

A soft wind moved like a whisper through the cottonwoods and moonlight shimmered on the shallow, fast-moving water.

"You know, Higgins, I've been thinking," Gregory said. "You had chloroform when you yanked Magruder's tooth the other day, and the same for Callahan's boil. How is it you had nothing for that boy tonight? Or maybe you did."

The surgeon kept his eyes on the water, saying

nothing. When his bloody sleeve brushed against his jacket, Gregory recoiled.

"What happened tonight?" he said. "Why'd you torture Little Wolf like that? Because he was Cheyenne? Maybe he was right. Maybe you do hate Indians."

A stone grew in Gregory's throat as he waited for a reply. When at last the surgeon turned to him all the womanish softness had vanished from his face. The pale flesh tightened and flattened against the skull until Gregory found himself looking at a leering death's head, terrible in the silvery light.

"A man does what he must," the surgeon said, his smile widening as Gregory stepped back. "You, me, Little Wolf, we all have our duty, a place in his plan. Some, like the Indians, like the Confederates on Pox Island, some must pass through fire to be cleansed. Little Wolf is at peace now."

He laughed, a girlish giggle that slowly rose in pitch and volume and turned Gregory's blood to ice water. He turned and scrambled up the riverbank toward the camp, fast as his shaking legs would carry him.

Chapter Twenty-four

Gregory was so shaken he was unable to sleep. He felt he had been in the presence of something indecent, unclean, and he wanted shut of it. But nothing, not even his mind-bending trick, could free him of the image of Little Wolf's frightened eyes as begged for help. *"The old man is a demon. Please help me. Please."*

The boy's leg looked bad. Maybe it did need to come off. Gregory was no judge of these things, but he had no doubt Higgins had anesthesia available. What did he say? *"Some must pass through fire to be cleansed."* Little Wolf had been tortured and died a horrible, screaming death right in the middle of their camp and no one seemed to care, or even notice, just as scores of Confederate prisoners on that island in the Mississippi must have died before him. Again, Gregory was tempted to pack up and ride away from Custer and his moving cavalcade of misery. Nothing good, he was sure, would come of any of it.

After a long and restless night, he was glad to see the sun rise and gladder still to see General Sherman preparing to move. That meant Gregory could leave too. As he walked to Custer's tent, he passed a two-man grave detail. Little Wolf's body lay beside them on the grass, his severed leg on his stomach. Gregory quickened his step.

He found Custer brushing his teeth, standing so close to the shaving mirror, he spattered its surface. He didn't stop brushing when Gregory arrived, but motioned for him to sit. Watching the general's morning ablutions, Gregory thought he had never known a man who groomed himself so carefully, thoroughly, and often. It was almost womanlike. If he weren't such a hard-ass, Gregory could almost believe Custer to be a mollycoddle, the kind of man who sits down to pee.

"No changes to your orders, Grover," he said when at last he finished, "but it's good you came by." He went to his desk and picked up two envelopes. "This is for Libbie," he said as he handed Gregory the first. It was sealed and addressed to "Mrs. General Custer." Gregory put it in the pocket of his field coat. "And this"—Custer gave him the second—"is for Captain Keogh or whoever you find commanding at Wallace when you get there. It instructs him to free up a squadron to escort you and Mrs. Custer to my camp. I'm moving out today as well. I really don't have men to spare, but I suppose I could find someone to accompany you if you want company."

"No." Now that Fall Leaf was gone, Gregory would just as soon travel alone.

"All right then," Custer said as they shook hands. "Bring her to me. Be safe."

At the rope line Jeff was ready and waiting. Gregory transferred Custer's letters from his jacket pocket to his saddlebags. Then, with a sense of relief, he climbed into the saddle and turned Jeff's head south for the long ride to Fort Wallace. He was looking forward to his solitary journey and relieved to be seeing the last of this camp on the forks of the Platte. Something evil had happened here, something Jack Gregory could have—should have—prevented, but had not.

He rode over high rolling ground, broken by creeks and ravines, and across wind-blown prairie covered with dry brown buffalo grass. Though he saw not another living creature, man or beast, it was obvious that Indians, and many of them, had covered the same ground not long before. Wide bands of earth had been scored by the hooves of unshod ponies and by the long lodge poles they pulled behind them. In several places these streams of scored earth came together and the path widened, looking for all the world like a farmer's plowed field. The Indians were gathering and, like him, moving south toward Wallace.

The sun was so hot his ears rang and the wind carried grit that burned his eyes, got in his mouth and coated his teeth. He covered the lower half of his face with a handkerchief, but the dirt found a way in anyhow. When he drank from his canteen, the first

sip made a sticky paste that he washed down with the
second. After about eight hours of riding, Gregory
decided to rest in a stand of scrubby cottonwoods by
a stream. He loosened Jeff's saddle and led him to
the water. As he drank, Gregory stretched out on a
flat, grassy stretch of beach and bathed his face and
head in the cold, running water. Refreshed and glad
to be out of the wind, he picketed Jeff with ankle
ropes, spread his roll on the ground, and slept.

Something woke him. He sat, his heart pounding.
It was almost dark. Jeff, cropping grass nearby, raised
his head, ears forward, nostrils flared. It came again:
men's voices, the voices of Indians. Gregory crawled
to Jeff and led him deeper into the scrub, keeping
the horse's head down with a hand on his nose. They
stood together in the darkest part of the thicket and
waited. Jeff was a confident, tranquil animal by
nature, and he and Gregory trusted each other, a
trust that had deepened these weeks on campaign.
Gregory moved his hand from Jeff's nose to his
neck, holding it there with a steady, reassuring pressure. The horse would keep quiet. The voices were
coming closer and they were Cheyenne. Three riders,
Gregory thought, though he could not be sure. He
thanked a God he did not believe in for the darkness. The Indians did not see his trail.

They were laughing. "Maybe you should ask your
wife before you do that," one said. "You know how
Plum gets when she is angry. You don't want to have
to hide from her again, like you did last time." This
brought more laughter.

"I do not have to ask her," a different voice said.

"Plum has learned her lesson. I taught her. Now she does exactly as I tell her." More laughter and hoots of derision.

Now Gregory could see them, three men on ponies, dark shadows moving across the prairie. *Hunters,* he thought. They led a fourth pony, probably laden with meat. One of the riders was smaller than the others, a youth. They were taking their time, enjoying the pleasant evening. Thinking they would pass him by, Gregory breathed a sigh of relief. But at the last moment the smallest rider broke away.

"I am dry as a chip and my pony too," he said. "I'm going to the water. Go on and I'll catch you up." He kicked his pony into a trot and made for the creek. With a sinking stomach, Gregory saw the boy heading for the grassy beach where he had taken the water earlier. If the Indian lay where he had done, he would have a clear view of Gregory and Jeff, hiding in the shadows.

The boy slid from the pony's back and walked him to the water, but the pony would not drink. His head was up and his ears were forward. The animal sensed the presence of Gregory and Jeff, but the boy seemed unconcerned. He dropped to his knees and stuck his face in the cold water, drinking and bathing his head. When he sat up, he looked directly into Gregory's eyes. The boy jumped to his feet, reaching for his pony's bridle.

"Stop." Gregory spoke in Cheyenne as he stepped forward, hands outstretched to show he held no weapon. "I mean you no harm, no harm. I want no trouble." He glanced toward the other two riders, now disappearing over the crest of a hill. The Indian, who appeared to be no older than twelve or thirteen, looked at them too. As far as Gregory could see, the boy was unarmed. "I am alone," Gregory said.

The Indian looked around to confirm the truth of this, and Gregory saw him relax a bit.

"What are you doing here?" the boy said.

"I am resting on my way to the soldier fort south of here, on the Smoky Hill River. I am delivering papers to the fort they call Wallace. Look, let me show you." The boy tensed as he reached into his saddlebag, but eased when Gregory pulled out the two white envelopes. "See? Papers. Only that."

The Indian's eyes cut again toward his two companions, now out of sight. If he called to them, Gregory was in trouble. This boy he could take, but the other two? He held out the letters.

"I don't want to fight you," Gregory said. "I don't want to fight your friends either. I want to go to the soldier fort and deliver the papers."

The boy studied Gregory's face, measuring the level of the white man's fear. This *wasichu* appeared not to be one of those who would lose his head and act foolishly. Still, the boy resolved to try his luck. He pointed to Gregory's gun. "Give it to me, or I will call my uncles."

The boy had sand, no doubt of that. It occurred to Gregory that maybe this child held the avenging spirit of Little Wolf, come to exact punishment for his failure to save him from Higgins. It was a chilling thought, but Gregory forced himself to smile and shook his head. "You know I won't do that." He steeled himself for the cry that would bring the uncles. If that happened he would have to kill the lad and he didn't want to participate in the death of another Indian boy.

The boy considered. "Give me your *wasichu* papers."

"That I can do." He closed the distance between them and handed him Custer's letters.

The boy tore open the envelopes, examined their contents, and returned them to Gregory. "Tell me what they say," he said, "and don't think you can trick me. My uncle has a white woman for a wife and I know what these symbols mean."

Gregory did not believe that, but he read the letters honestly. The one addressed to Keogh was as Custer described, instructing the Fort Wallace commander to assign a squadron to escort Gregory and Elizabeth to Custer's camp. The second letter to Mrs. General Custer was more interesting.

Near Fort McPherson
June 18, 1867

Darling girl, I hope to be holding you in my arms in just a few short days. Never, never in all my years have I so longed for a woman, to hold her, kiss her, taste her.

The Indian boy laughed and moved his pelvis back and forth in a thrusting motion. Gregory smiled and nodded. If the boy was gone too long the uncles would come looking.

Obviously I hope this finds you at Fort Wallace, but if it doesn't, Grover will find you and bring you to me.

Now, for this most important business: Have you been successful in your mission? Has my minxish little spy learned who is working to poison General Sherman's mind against me? I am eager to take action! Another question has occurred to me since last we spoke and I want you to apply yourself to this as well. Perhaps my traitor has been writing to others in addition to Sherman. Colonel Smith, for example? Find out what you can. Of course, your discoveries must be delivered to me in the flesh (yes indeed!), not put to paper and entrusted to the vagaries of the mails.

Then, when we are reunited, we will decide upon a proper punishment and set the wheels in motion to ensure he suffers. No one is better at plotting tortures than my pretty little wife.

Until then, I remain, your loving Autie

When Gregory finished, the corners of the boy's mouth turned downward. "This is worthless, it says nothing of soldier intentions, nothing that will help my people against the *wasichus.*"

Gregory shrugged. "I read what was written. You can have the papers if you like to show to your uncle's wife. Now, let us go our separate paths. I do not want to make you bleed."

The boy's eyes narrowed.

"You have courage, son," Gregory said, "I see that, but I have the gun. That's the only thing you need to think about. If you call your uncles, I will kill you. I do not want to, but I won't fight three if I can fight only two. Do you want to end your life here, as a young man who has not yet fully lived, when you can grow to be a great warrior with a beautiful woman and many fine children of your own? It is time to decide."

He was a brave lad, but not ready to die. "No, I will not call them," he said.

"Good." Gregory walked to Jeff and tightened the cinch he'd loosened when they arrived. Once in the saddle, he kicked Jeff forward through the water and leaned down to loop a rope through the Indian pony's headpiece. "I'm taking him with me, but not to keep. I'll turn him loose after a mile or two. I don't want you hotfooting it back to your uncles and following me. You'll get your pony back unharmed, I promise." The boy scowled, but said nothing.

Gregory gave Jeff a hard kick in the ribs and they bounded out of the cottonwood thicket, trailing the pony behind them.

Chapter Twenty-five

The rain had turned the roads to gumbo and carried away the bridges, so Elizabeth and Anna found themselves stranded at Fort Harker for a week. While waiting to leave, they were joined by a third woman. Alice Sterner was the pretty, young wife of a contract surgeon stationed at Harker and newly with child. She was eager to leave Kansas.

"Oh, Mrs. Custer, I hope you and Miss Darrah don't mind me tagging along," she said. Her husband, Captain Richard Sterner, and Major Gibbs brought her to a tent set up for Anna and Elizabeth after the storm. "I am so grateful and I'll try not to make a nuisance of myself, but I'm very anxious to get home, now that I'm in a delicate condition . . ." She blushed prettily as her husband put a proud, protective arm around her and drew her close. "Richard is keen to get me back to Ohio, so my mother can look after me."

"That's right," the surgeon said. "Much as I'd like

to have Alice with me, this is not the place for her right now. I wish I could put her on the train tomorrow."

"We're glad to have you, Alice," Anna said. "Very glad. Aren't we, Elizabeth? The more the merrier."

But as the days passed, Elizabeth found the pretty Mrs. Sterner annoying. Not that she was unkind or unpleasant to be with. Neither was she one of those women—all too common in army circles—who could not stop talking. She was not grand, not always reminding others of her husband's brilliance or her family's wealth back in the states. No, what Elizabeth found intolerable was the way Alice Sterner repeatedly apologized for her "condition," the way she constantly touched her stomach as if to communicate with the tiny son or daughter growing there. It was as if the Sterner woman were saying to childless Elizabeth, "Look, see what I have? Don't you wish you had one too?" She realized this perception may be unfair; after all, Anna did not view Alice's behavior in this way. Still, Elizabeth disliked Alice Sterner intensely.

The day before they were to board the train for Fort Riley, Alice complained of feeling unwell. She lay listlessly on the cot, allowing Anna to pack for her.

"I'm so sorry to be such a bother," she said, for what seemed to Elizabeth the one hundredth time. "Usually I've got plenty of energy, but all day I've felt completely spent."

Anna placed the back of her hand against Alice's cheek. "You don't have a fever," she said. "Maybe it's because of your pregnancy. I've heard others say it's normal to feel exhausted the first months."

Alice smiled weakly. "Yes, I'm sure that's it. Would you mind bringing me some water, Anna? I'm so thirsty. No matter how much I drink I'm still dry."

"Shall I fetch your husband?" Anna said. "After all, he's a physician. Perhaps he could do something for you."

"Oh, no, no, please don't." Alice tried to sit, but fell back on the pillow. "Richard is so busy just now. He's on service tonight and the ward is full, all twenty beds. I don't want to worry him. I'll be fine, I'm sure." She placed her hands on her abdomen. "That is, we'll be just fine."

Elizabeth rolled her eyes at Anna, who whispered, "I think she needs a doctor. She doesn't look good, and it's strange she drinks so much water yet still feels thirsty."

Elizabeth said with a shrug, "I guess she knows if she needs a doctor or not."

She woke at midnight to the sound of Alice vomiting into a basin by her cot. She continued retching as Anna helped her to her feet and out to the privy. When they returned, Alice was leaning on Anna's arm.

"I'm sorry to wake you, Mrs. Custer," she said. "It must've been something I ate."

"Please, don't apologize," Elizabeth said. "These things happen to all of us." She was alarmed by the pregnant woman's appearance. Her face in the flickering lamplight was white as bleached bone.

The sequence of vomiting and diarrhea returned

about twenty minutes later. This time, Alice was too weak to make it to the privy, even with Anna's help, and fell to the tent floor, soiling herself. She wept in shame and distress as the other women cleaned her and helped her into fresh clothing. Elizabeth insisted they go for her husband but again, Alice refused.

"No, I feel better now. I do, honestly. If you'll just bring me another cup of water I believe I can sleep. I'm so tired." She drained the cup and slept immediately.

"I don't care what she says, she needs a doctor right away," Anna said. She and Elizabeth stood over the cot, looking down at the sick woman. "Look how fast she's breathing and how sunken her eyes are. This is something more than pregnancy sickness, I'm sure of it. See how dry she is, look at her hands."

The tips of Alice's fingers were wrinkled and prune-like, as if she'd spent an hour in the bath, and it seemed to Elizabeth her skin was taking on a bluish cast. "You're right," she said. "I'll go. You stay with her."

The night was chilly and Elizabeth wrapped her plaid woolen shawl tightly around her shoulders as she hurried to the hospital. She felt guilty and ashamed. Perhaps if she had liked Alice more, if she hadn't been jealous of her pregnancy, she would have taken action sooner. Now it may be too late. She picked up her skirt and started to run, arriving at the hospital flushed and out of breath. A steward met her at the door.

"I need a physician," she said, "and right away. It's Alice, Captain Sterner's wife, she is very ill. Please, find someone at once." At that moment Richard Sterner himself entered the office. He wore a white linen jacket and was wiping his hands on a towel.

"Mrs. Custer," he said. "What brings you at this hour?" Her expression must have provided the answer, for the blood drained from his face before she spoke a word. "My God, is it Alice? Please tell me it's not Alice."

"I'm sorry," Elizabeth said.

He tore off his linen jacket and threw it and the towel to the floor. He turned to the steward. "Jenkins, find Dr. Robertson and tell him to take charge here. After that, come to my wife's tent. I'll need assistance."

Sterner ran through the camp, with Elizabeth following. They entered the tent to find Alice leaning over the basin, with Anna holding her head. Exhausted, she fell back onto the pillow. When she saw her husband's stricken face, she groaned.

"Richard," she said, "I'm sorry. I'm losing our child."

"How long has she been like this?" he said, dropping to his knees beside his wife's cot and taking her hand.

Anna answered. "She said she wasn't feeling well earlier today, but she didn't start vomiting until midnight or so. We should have come for you earlier." She shot a reproachful look at Elizabeth.

"Yes," Sterner said. "You should have." He put his

head to his wife's chest and listened, eyes closed. Then he took her arm and pinched a bit of skin between his thumb and first finger. The flesh had no elasticity but remained peaked. "My God, Alice," he whispered as he pushed a sweaty lock of hair off her forehead. After examining her hands, he lifted the sheet to look at her feet. Her toes, Elizabeth noticed, were as wrinkled as her fingers. Sterner asked Elizabeth to fetch a cup of water and held his wife's head as she drank it.

"Has there been diarrhea?" As he asked this question, the steward, Jenkins, arrived.

"Yes," Elizabeth said.

"Would it be possible to for me to examine the stool?"

"She soiled her nightdress," Anna said. "I guess you could look at that. I put her things outside the tent. Come, I'll show you."

Elizabeth sat on the tent floor by the sick woman's cot, holding her hand. Alice's hand was limp and her eyes were closed, she seemed unaware of Elizabeth's presence. There was no doubt, it was no trick of the light, Alice's skin was turning blue. What could that mean? She touched Alice's cheek, finding her skin cold and clammy. Elizabeth could not help but wonder how Armstrong would act if it were she who lay stricken. Would he be willing to examine her fouled underthings in an effort to diagnose her illness, and thereby save her? No, she thought not.

Alice's eyes fluttered open. "Where is Richard?" she said.

"Here's here, just outside for a moment," Elizabeth said. "He is a very capable man. He'll help you."

Alice moved her head on the pillow. "I'm beyond help, Mrs. Custer. I am dying and my little child with me."

Elizabeth gripped her hand more tightly. "Don't say that. You'll get better, you and your baby will be fine." Again, she felt crushing guilt. She had not been kind to Alice Sterner. The woman was dying, clearly, and she deserved to have a genuine friend beside her, not a poseur like Mrs. General Custer.

When Sterner and Anna returned, Elizabeth saw the fear on the physician's face. "Mrs. Custer," he said, "you and Miss Darrah must pack your things and find new quarters at once. I am quite sure that my wife"—his voice broke and he struggled to compose himself—"that my wife has cholera. I have two men in the hospital with similar symptoms. One of them is near death." Turning to the steward, he said, "Jenkins, bring me two jugs of the salt-and-sugar solution we've been giving those others." As the steward left, Sterner paused, looked down, and ran a hand through his hair. "Ladies, I was about to suggest you stay with Major Gibbs, but, on second thought, I think it better that you have a fresh tent. I'll have the men get one ready for you. Please, be careful that you wash your hands thoroughly and often. This is important. Wash your hands immediately after leaving here, Miss Darrah, you especially."

Anna and Elizabeth looked at each other, each

seeing her own horror reflected on the other's face. Cholera! The very word struck terror. Elizabeth had not considered this dread possibility; she suspected Alice was suffering with something more than pregnancy-related sickness, but cholera . . . perhaps she and Anna were already poisoned. Perhaps they too were doomed. Elizabeth's heart was beating so she could barely hear herself think. But when she spoke, her voice, she was relieved to hear, was calm and measured.

"Our trunks are already packed, doctor, as we were planning to leave for Fort Riley later this morning," Elizabeth said. "As for a tent, there's no need. It must be nearly three o'clock. Anna and I will go to the station and wait on the platform. The train is due at nine. We'll be fine there."

Richard Sterner looked from Elizabeth to his wife, whose breathing was becoming labored. "Yes," Sterner said absently, "whatever. Take care, be aware of any signs of illness. It's the loss of fluid that kills."

"Yes, of course." Elizabeth gathered her shawl and bag and began to follow Anna out the door. Before leaving, she turned. Sterner sat beside his wife, holding her hand, stroking her hair, speaking to her in a low voice. Elizabeth could not hear, but was sure they were sweet words of love and devotion. Richard Sterner was not especially handsome, neither was he rich or famous, but Alice was fortunate to have been loved by such a man, Elizabeth thought. "Good-bye," she said. "I'm sorry." Neither appeared to hear her.

* * *

Elizabeth and Anna sat on the platform for hours, in view of the tent. There were no comings or goings, other than Jenkins and the men who retrieved for their trunks and belongings.

"We should have gone for him sooner," Anna said. "I wanted to. Maybe if he'd started that solution sooner . . . I shouldn't have listened to you."

"I see," Elizabeth said. "I suspected that was what you were thinking. Heavens, I had no idea the poor woman had cholera. If you suspected something so serious, you shouldn't have let anything I said stop you." The women did not speak again until the train arrived.

As Elizabeth took her seat by the window, she saw Jenkins and another steward carry a sheet-covered body on a stretcher from the tent, followed by an ashen Captain Sterner. *Cholera has come to Fort Harker,* she thought, *but it won't stay here. It will gain, may already have progressed, with the troops, from one post to the next. How many will die before it runs its course? Will I be a victim?*

Chapter Twenty-six

Gregory arrived at Fort Wallace at sundown to find it in panicked disarray. Earlier that day a large Cheyenne war party had threatened the fort, which was badly undermanned, and all feared they would return. The first person Gregory encountered was a newspaper correspondent named Declan McManus, who described the day's action as "complete mayhem." It started at about eight o'clock that morning, he said, when warriors struck Pond Creek Station, two miles to the west. Because of the pure prairie air, observers at the fort could see the attack.

"There were hundreds of them," McManus said, "two hundred at least, maybe three hundred. It's hard to tell the way they circle around, in no clear formation. They stampeded the station's horses and mules and started driving them north, up to Beaver Creek. A detachment went after them—I rode along—but we hadn't gone far when even more warriors appeared on those hills." He pointed at a range of high bluffs. "I don't mind telling you, Grover,

when those Indians rode up on those hills, well, my
stomach heaved, I thought I would puke. We turned
right around and started hightailing it back here to
the fort, and they come after us. It was a close thing
too, with their little ponies being so much faster than
our horses. There was lots of shooting, rifle and carbine fire, going both ways, I was just as likely to be hit
by one of our own as the Indians. The fighting lasted
about two hours total I'd say, and those were the two
longest, most terrifying I have ever experienced in all
my thirty years, worse even than a line of Rebel cavalry." He said the Indians were led by a big fellow on
a fine-looking white horse, an American horse, not
an Indian pony. "One of the boys said it was Roman
Nose, others said it was the squaw man Charlie Bent.
Me, I don't know. Whoever he was, he had sand. I'll
give him that."

It was Bent, Gregory thought. Bent rode a white
horse in battle, Roman Nose a gray. But even beyond
that, there was no mistaking the two. Roman Nose
was a giant, by far the larger man, and an impressive
physical specimen. Both were bold warriors, crafty
and fearless, but the Cheyenne chief could not hold
a candle to the half-breed Bent when it came to
hating. Charlie Bent was a passionate, dedicated
hater. The son of a white trader and a Cheyenne
mother, Charlie once told Gregory he hated his
father so much he would kill him, scalp him, and
make a necklace of his fingers if ever their paths
crossed again. Charlie and his half brother, George,
adopted their mothers' Indian lifestyle and no

full-blooded Cheyenne fought the *wasichus* with more ferocity.

Four troopers had been killed that morning. One was a sergeant named Dummell, who charged the Indians with a force of ten, but at the last minute one of his men, another sergeant, Hamlin, turned and retreated, taking five others with him. Dummell and his three followers, unaware of Hamlin's retreat, rode into the Indians and fought bravely, though all were surrounded, knocked from their horses, and quickly killed with lances and stone hammers.

"Hamlin showed the yellow feather," McManus said. "Dummell and them might be alive now if not for Hamlin's cowardice. If it was up to me, I'd have him drummed from the garrison with nothing but a toothbrush and the clothes on his back."

As he listened to McManus's account, Gregory recalled the converging trails he'd seen on his ride to Wallace. *How many Indians were they up against?* he wondered. This post, the westernmost of the Smoky Hill forts, had always held a precarious place, with Arapaho, Kiowa, Apache, and Comanche to the south, Cheyenne, Sioux, and Pawnee to the north. So dangerous was its position, Gregory was surprised more Wallace soldiers hadn't been killed in the roughly two years of the fort's existence. And things were getting even hotter now, mostly because of Hancock's boneheaded campaign. Gregory regretted he'd ever signed on.

He prayed Elizabeth Custer wasn't here, but if she was, he would have to escort her through miles of hostile country to her husband's camp, wherever that was. Gregory wanted to see her again, but not under these circumstances. Fort Wallace, Kansas, especially now, was no place for a woman like Elizabeth Custer. It was no place for a woman, period.

Gregory walked to Keogh's office only to learn the captain and forty troopers, all of the post's cavalry, were away, escorting General Hancock to Denver. Keogh's adjutant, Lieutenant Joseph Hale, was commanding in his absence.

"All the cavalry?" Gregory thought he had misheard.

"Yes, it was a bad decision"—Hale shook his head—"and I said so at the time. They'll be gone all week. I'm left with some infantry and a few civilians, fewer than fifty men total. I'm expecting Barnitz with his G Company, along with a party of engineers surveying for the railroad. I hope they get here and soon. We need help."

Gregory asked if Elizabeth Custer and Anna Darrah were present.

"No, I'm glad to say the Queen of Sheba and her handmaiden are not here." Some officers did not believe wives had a place in the field, and Hale was one of them. "Did you hear about the flood at Fort Hays? She and the Darrah woman were lucky to survive. I'm told the fort was pretty well destroyed, and Custer's camp on Big Creek too. The women were sent back east, to Riley. She may be there already, for all I know—or care."

Gregory was both relieved and disappointed. The question was, what to do now? Should he follow her, as Custer instructed, even if it took him all the way to

Riley? Or should he stay here, where an extra gun clearly was needed? Fort Wallace was under siege, or soon would be, if the signs he saw along the way meant what he thought. On top of this, he felt a keen need to get to his Rose Creek Ranch, eight miles to the south. He wanted to check on his meadows and Maggie. He needed to know that she and his hired man, Sharp Willis, were on top of things.

Hale decided the matter for him. "Grover, I'm asking you to stick around for a while," he said, "maybe a week or so until Keogh and the cavalry get back. I don't know what orders General Custer gave you, but we're in a bad way here. I need you."

"I will," Gregory said. Custer wouldn't like it, but he didn't give a damn. "But I need to get out to Rose Creek for a few hours. I'll be back tonight and I'll stay as long as you need me."

Hale came around the corner of his desk and shook Gregory's hand. "Be careful, Grover. You won't be any use to me if you get yourself killed."

He crested a low hill and there it was, still standing, a small frame house, needing paint, shaded by a few cottonwood trees. Every time he rode away, he thought he might never see the place again. So far, he'd been lucky. The Indians let him alone, but who knew how long that would last?

Truth was, he'd been lucky in many regards; lucky to get the property, known as Fitch's Meadows when he bought it for a song from old man Fitch, who was ailing, mourning the death of his wife and anxious to be shut of the place. He'd been lucky to get a hay contract with Fort Wallace at twenty-five dollars the ton, lucky to harvest upward of two hundred tons a year. His meadows were the only ones in the area, which allowed him to command top dollar. And he'd been lucky when Maggie came to him. He had been surprised when she showed up, as it had been years since last he'd seen her. She was no longer a beauty, it hurt him to remember how lovely she once was, but she was clean and a good cook. In fact, Maggie was good to him in all the ways a woman should be. He did not love her as he wanted to love a woman, but Maggie was not bad company.

Gregory was less sure of his hired man. Sharp Willis was a hard worker and, despite his age and short stature, the strongest man Gregory had ever known. He once saw Willis free a wagon that was stuck in the mud by singlehandedly lifting it clear of the sucking muck. He was in the field now, cutting timothy. They had harvested a field early in the spring, just before the bloom, when the head was still covered with velvet. Gregory had been called away before the cut was complete. He'd left it to Willis to dry the hay and deliver it to the fort. Now Gregory was anxious to know what they got for it.

At Gregory's approach, Willis stopped swinging his scythe and raised it above his head in greeting, the blade flashing in the sun. Gregory lifted his hat in return. Ten years older than Gregory, Sharp Willis had been hired as head scout in 1865, the year Fort Wallace was established, to protect emigrants and a stage line traveling the Smoky Hill Trail from a point

150 miles west of Fort Hays to 200 miles east of Denver. The two men worked well together when Gregory first arrived, but his superior skills and knowledge of the Indians quickly became obvious, and Keogh gave Gregory—Joe Grover—top job. Willis still took occasional work with the army, but when Gregory offered him full-time employment on his ranch, he accepted. Gregory was respectful of the older man, but he knew resentment was a passion, strong as any other, born of injury. There was a divide between them that could not be bridged.

Maggie walked out on the porch. She wore a store-bought dress of red calico and was wiping her hands on an apron. She waved. Tall and slender, Maggie was once as beautiful a woman as Elizabeth Custer or Rose Reynolds, and would be still, Gregory thought, if not for the scar.

"Hello, Maggie." He dismounted, looping Jeff's reins loosely around the porch rail.

"I did not expect you." She spoke in her native Sioux. "Is your job with Yellow Hair finished? Are you back to stay?"

Gregory shook his head. "No, I've got to go back to Wallace in a few hours. I came to see about things here. Give Jeff a bag of grain, will you, and make me something to eat. What have you got?"

"I can give you chicken stew and biscuits. One hour."

"I'll be back then." He could not see how her eyes followed him as he walked to the field to join Willis. He waded through the tall grass, breathing in its fresh scent. He was pleased with the look of things, especially the field of timothy where Willis was cutting now. "Hello, Sharp," he said, shaking Willis's sweaty hand. "You've done well here. What did you get for the first crop?"

Willis wiped his brow with a dirty handkerchief. Gregory recognized it as one of his. "Same as the rest, twenty-five dollars the ton." Willis had a deep, baritone voice that was startling in a man of his stature. "I tried to talk the quartermaster higher, but no go. He said the horses didn't like it any better than the other, and it didn't put weight on faster neither. It's not worth the extra work—my opinion anyhow."

Gregory looked over the field. "Could be you're right, but I want to give it another season."

Willis shrugged. "You're the boss. So, you done with that job for Custer? You here to stay for a time?"

"I wish I was shut of him and his outfit, but I'm not. Custer doesn't know what the hell he's doing. Fact is, nobody in the whole Department of the Platte does. If the generals and the railroad bosses had their way, we'd kill every red man down to the very last one. Custer's only making it hotter. You and Maggie have any trouble here?"

Willis smiled and looked toward the house. "No. The Indians leave us alone. That Maggie, she's got more sand than most men I know. Hell, I pity the man, red or white, who tries any funny business when she's around." Willis shifted his gaze from the house to Gregory. "She's quite a woman, Joe. You don't know what you've got there."

"I don't need you to tell me that, Willis."

"I think you do."

Willis's sunburned face was getting even redder, and Gregory was not in a mood for confrontation. "All right, Sharp," he said. "I'm just saying things are hot now. Don't leave Maggie alone out here, not even for a little while. She needs looking after."

He gave Gregory's words back to him. "I don't need you to tell me that."

They worked in the field for an hour, with Willis cutting and Gregory stacking the cut stems. They would dry in the sun for three or four days before Willis would put the hay in the wagon and take it to the fort. If he had his way, Gregory would stay here, sweating in the hot sun, cutting, lifting, stacking. It was purifying, physical toil that required no thought, only muscle power. Then, after the day's labors were done, he'd go to his clean, comfortable house for a nourishing meal, maybe a glass of whiskey on the porch in the cool of the evening, and finally to bed with fresh white sheets that smelled of soap and sunlight. If he wanted her, Maggie would join him. That's how it would be if he had his way, but he didn't.

She stepped out on the porch and rang the bell that called them to dinner. Willis dropped his scythe in the field and he and Gregory walked together to the house without speaking. Jeff stood in the shade of the cottonwoods, munching in a linen nose bag. His coat was gleaming and Gregory saw that Maggie had brushed him.

She had prettied the dinner table with a clutch of yellow wildflowers, standing in a glass pitcher. Gregory thought of Elizabeth, who had also wanted wildflowers for the table. He saw her stricken white face, the fear in her eyes when he took her hand to examine the bite, finally the way she looked lying in the grass that evening as they waited rescue.

"What do you see?" Maggie said as she put a bowl of chicken stew before him. "What makes you smile?" He looked at her, at the angry, puckered scar on her left cheek drew her mouth upward, in a continual sneer, and pulled her left eyelid downward, in constant sorrow.

"Nothing," he said as he reached for the plate of steaming, perfectly browned biscuits. "I don't see anything." He cut one open, slid in a slab of fresh butter, and, when the butter melted, spooned apple butter on each half.

"This stew is mighty good, Maggie," Willis said, "and I've never had a lighter biscuit. You are a fine cook. Yes, you are."

They ate without talking. Gregory was hungrier than he realized, quickly finishing his bowl and raising it for a refill. He ate four biscuits.

"Maybe you and Willis should come back to Wallace with me tonight, Maggie," he said, wiping his mouth with a cloth napkin. "Just because the Indians have left us alone so far doesn't mean they'll keep on. There was a big fight at the fort yesterday. Sounds like Charlie Bent was riding with the Cheyenne."

"I am not afraid of Charlie Bent," Maggie said. "I will stay."

"I told you, Joe," Willis said. "I'll stay with her, like I said."

Gregory stood, dropping his napkin on his plate. "I appreciate your loyalty, the both of you, I do, but I don't expect you to die for the place. If you get to feeling nervous, come on to Wallace. I won't hold it against you."

Maggie and Willis watched him go to the bedroom for a clean set of clothes, pack them in his saddlebags, and walk out the front door, closing it behind him. By the time he had Jeff saddled and started back to the fort, it was almost dark. At the crest of the hill he stopped and turned back. Maggie stood on the porch, her dress a splash of red in the yellow circle of lamplight.

Chapter Twenty-seven

"Halt!" A sentry on a platform challenged him as he approached the fort. "Stop and identify yourself!" Before Gregory could answer, the soldier raised his carbine to his shoulder and fired. He was a better shot than most; Gregory felt the wind from his bullet.

He jumped from the saddle and lay belly down on the ground, praying the idiot wouldn't kill his horse. "Don't shoot! It's Grover, the scout. Don't shoot!"

The man lowered his gun and Gregory got to his feet, leading Jeff the rest of the way in. He planned to give the sentry a string of hard words, but he was just a boy, maybe sixteen or seventeen, and he was clearly shaken. "Sorry, man," he said with an Irish accent. "I guess I'm a little jumpy. I didn't hurt you then?"

"I'm all right, but next time, give a man time to answer your challenge. A Cheyenne buck wouldn't ride up on you like that anyhow."

The boy hung his head. "No, I reckon not."

"Not bad shooting, though," Gregory said.

The sentry smiled bashfully. "I'm glad I was no better."

After tending to Jeff in the stables, Gregory went to his quarters, a small frame cabin next to the enlisted men's barracks. It was a spartan dwelling, its only furnishings a cot, heating stove, shaving stand, and small water barrel. A mirror hung from a nail on the wall. He didn't like the place—it was hot in the summer, cold in the winter, and didn't even have a window—but he rarely used it. He prayed Rose Creek would continue to be spared during this latest round of Indian trouble. He sometimes wondered if Maggie's presence gave him protection. He knew little about the circumstances surrounding her departure from her people, only what she told him.

As he started to undress, there was a knock at his door. He opened it to find Barnitz and Sergeant Frederick Wyllyams, an Englishman who was new to the Seventh Cavalry, swaying in the doorway. The two had been drinking.

"Hello, Grover," Barnitz said. "I just heard young McCoy almost shot your head off. I'm sorry about that, he's one of mine. Good lad, fine marksman, but maybe I should've given him some rest before assigning watch duty. We got here a few hours ago and we had a hard pull. Anyhow, I thought I'd come by, make sure you're still in one piece."

"It was a close thing," Gregory said. "You're right about his marksmanship. If all your G Troop shoots like McCoy, we're in good shape."

"Jus' like a mick," Wyllyams said with a hiccup. "Here all of two hours and almost kills our top scout.

By Jove, your Uncle Sam shouldn't allow that lot in his army. Micks and dagos, the regiment is chockablock with 'em. Tha's a problem."

"If not for that lot, as you call them, Uncle Sam wouldn't have much of an army," Gregory said.

"True enough," said Barnitz. "Say, we're getting up a game of poker, take the edge off. Things are wound too tight around here. Care to join us?"

Gregory shook his head. "I think I'll turn in."

"Suit yourself. Wyllyams, you go ahead. I want a few words with Grover." When they were alone, Barnitz said, "So, Grover, what are your orders from Custer? What brought you here to Wallace and where do you go next?"

Gregory hesitated. There was no reason not to tell Barnitz of Custer's instructions, but he didn't want to. He was embarrassed about playing Custer's cupid, traveling the width and breadth of Kansas to deliver the general's ladylove. Despite his admiration for Elizabeth, he felt the work was beneath him.

"Very well," Barnitz said. "I won't press you, but can you tell me where he is with his companies? Could he be brought to assist us if necessary?"

"I left him near Fort McPherson. From there he's supposed to go south, to the forks of the Republican, then north again up to Sedgwick."

"He's not going to find Indians at the forks of the Republican," Barnitz said. "They're all here."

"I agree with you, but those were Sherman's orders." Gregory suspected the Indians knew Custer and his men were well to the north and would take advantage of this to hit western targets, like Pond

Creek Station and Fort Wallace, along the Smoky Hill.

"In the morning I'm moving my horses to the south fork," Barnitz said. "There's good grass there and my animals need it. I want you and another man to go ahead, scout both sides of the valley. Stay while the horses are grazing and sound the alarm if you see anything, or if you sense trouble. I want to be sure my boys have plenty of time to get the horses back here if something happens. As I said, you'll need another man. Take Fall Leaf with you."

"Fall Leaf is dead."

"Is that right? I hadn't heard." Barnitz was not sufficiently curious to ask what had happened to him, Gregory noticed. "Well, take Wyllyams then. He's been wanting a chance to do some pioneering."

"Fine by me," Gregory said with a shrug, "but my mother is Irish. Hope working with a mick won't be a problem for him."

Gregory was in the stables before dawn when Wyllyams came in bleary-eyed and smelling of alcohol.

"It's early this morning," he said with a yawn.

"It's same as it always is this time of day." Gregory pulled on the latigo, tightening the saddle's front cinch.

"Um, I say, Grover, I'm sorry if I said anything to offend you last night," Wyllyams said. "That micks and dagos comment . . . Well, I was rather in my cups and I'm sorry I said it. Barnitz told me . . . well, I certainly meant no disrespect to you or your mother."

Gregory nodded, said nothing. His mother wasn't Irish, she was from a German family, maiden name Schroeder. He said that only to watch the Englishman twist. Gregory had no patience with people who hated because of skin color or country of origin. There were good reasons to hate, but those weren't on the list.

"Your horse is ready," Gregory said, pointing to a bay mare munching hay in a stall. "I got her saddled for you."

"Good of you. And I thank you again for letting me ride along."

"I'm happy to have you, Wyllyams, as long as you do your job and look sharp. I suspect we'll need to be keen this morning and you're looking pretty rough. Are you up to it, limey?"

Wyllyams winced. "I guess I deserved that. Yes, Grover, I'm up to it."

In a few minutes they were riding south, past the long picket line of G Company horses. Barnitz was right, they needed rich forage. Even in the low morning light, Gregory could see they were thin and ribby, a hard-used lot.

"Looks like you boys have done a lot of riding," Gregory said.

"Yes, we were escorting a party of railroad surveyors across the plains, and a very tedious business it was too, with a great many pointless side trips. I am keen to do some actual Indian fighting. That's why I signed on, after all."

"I was wondering about that, Wyllyams. So it's our

Indians that made an educated Englishman like you cross the pond?"

Wyllyams smiled. "Yes, at least in part. And you're right, I am far from home, in every sense of the word. My family is rather well established in England, if I do say it myself, and I was expected to carry on in the family tradition. I graduated Eton and so forth, but then, well, as you Americans say, things hit a snag. I thought if I could, perhaps, come over here and distinguish myself as an officer, as an Indian-fighter, I might be welcomed back into the fold. That was my intention anyway."

"What did you do, if you don't mind me asking?"

"No, no, that's fine. Yes, well, I planted my seed in a kitchen maid. Not ours, mind, the girl worked at a neighbor's manor. When she told me I thought she wanted money, but no, the silly cow actually expected me to marry her. When I informed her that was not in the cards, she went to my father and demanded support. She brought the child along, little fellow looks just like me, so there was no denying paternity. Needless to say, Sir Frederick was not pleased."

"I guess not."

"Odd thing is, I do have some feeling for the child. Handsome brute, he is. I do send money when I have it to send, not for the mother but the child. God only knows what she does with it, the cow."

Gregory didn't like hearing Wyllyams call his child's mother a cow, and thought the less of him for it. Even if he didn't care for the woman, it wasn't right to talk that way.

The sky was beginning to lighten when they reached

the valley of the south fork. Wyllyams took the high
ground on the west end, Gregory the east. They had
been in position for less than an hour when the
G Troop horses arrived driven by twenty mounted
men. Gregory and Wyllyams had a prearranged plan:
If either man saw Indians, he was to signal by turning
his horse in a tight circle. The other would signal the
troopers below, then both scouts would ride down
into the valley and help Barnitz's troopers drive the
horses back to the fort. Gregory knew it would be a
close thing, because of the poor condition of the
company's horses, but there was no other way. They'd
simply have to outrun the Indian ponies.

At about seven o'clock Gregory saw a dust cloud
rising in the west. He trained his field glasses on the
Smoky Hill Road to see four horses running at top
speed from the direction of Pond Creek Station. They
were stage horses, running two and two, as if still in
harness. Behind them came four Indians, whipping
their ponies in pursuit. He turned Jeff in tight circles, as arranged. Wyllyams caught the signal and did
likewise, notifying the men in the valley below. They
deserted their cook fires and coffeepots and began
to round up the horses.

"Do the Indians know we're here?" Wyllyams said
as he and Gregory met on the valley floor. He was
breathing hard, and his face was flushed with excitement.

"If they don't, they will soon enough," Gregory
said. "They just hit Pond Creek, and they're coming
this way." A black cloud of dust and smoke hung in
the west, over the stage station.

The horses were collected quickly and Gregory and Wyllyams helped the troopers drive them the two miles back to the post. To Gregory's surprise and relief, they made the journey without mishap, but they arrived to find the garrison in a panic. Barnitz, senior officer, stood in the middle of the parade ground, trying to organize offensive and defensive formations. Meanwhile, two large groups of Indians, numbering perhaps one hundred warriors, appeared on the hills in the west and the north. As Gregory looked on, a giant on a gray horse gave a signal and the Indians pulled back, out of view.

"Grover!" Barnitz said. "Thank God!" He had been interrupted at his breakfast and still wore a cloth napkin tucked into his shirt collar. "I'm riding out to that ridgeline." He pointed northwest. "I've got to know what we're up against." He noticed the napkin and threw it to the ground. Gregory thought he might want to hang onto it, in case he found himself needing a white flag.

"I wouldn't do that, captain," he said. "There's no need to go out there. You're up against two hundred fifty to three hundred Sioux and Cheyenne warriors, maybe more."

"Splendid!" Wyllyams said, red-faced with excitement.

"How do you know that, Grover?" Barnitz said.

"The trails I saw on the ride here. There were many of them and they were wide, one joining another. The Indians know Custer's in the north, so they're concentrating their forces along the Smoky Hill. You said it yourself. The Indians are here."

"Yes," Barnitz said, "but I think you overestimate their numbers. Anyhow, we'll soon find out." He ordered his troop, plus ten men from Company I, to mount up. "Come on, boys," he said, raising his saber over his head. "Let's show these red devils what the Seventh Cavalry is made of!"

They'll see what you're made of all right, Gregory thought as the men began to ride away from the fort. *They'll see that when they slice you open.* He had no choice but to ride with them. When they crested the ridgeline they saw seventy-five to one hundred warriors, in two groups, on a ridge about a mile distant. When the soldiers appeared, the Indians came together, in an obvious show of alarm. *Too obvious,* Gregory thought.

"See there, Grover," Barnitz said, clearly relieved. "As I suspected, you overestimated our red adversary. Two hundred fifty to three hundred you say? You were way off, man, and thank God. Bugler, sound a charge! G Troop will finish with these fellows in no time."

"Wait!" Gregory said. "Hold off!"

Bugler Charles Clark, a tiny Texan, raised his horn, but looked to Barnitz for guidance before putting it to his lips.

"All right, Clark," he said. "Let's hear what Grover has to say."

"Captain Barnitz," Gregory said, pointing across the valley, where the Indians were retreating over the ridge. "That's not all of them. There's more out there, plenty more, just on the other side of that ridgeline. You ride after them and you'll be playing right into their hands."

Barnitz wheeled his horse so he and Gregory were face-to-face. "I know what you're about, Grover, don't think I don't. You're Custer's man, one of his sycophantic toadies, like Weir and Cooke and little brother, Tom. I am about to lead the Seventh Cavalry in its first major action against the Indians, but you don't want that, do you? You want the famous Boy General to have that honor. You want Custer to get all the credit and acclaim. Well, not this time, my friend. Custer won't soak up all the glory out here as he did during the war. Not if Albert Barnitz has anything to say about it."

Gregory was speechless. What Barnitz said was so ridiculous, it had never occurred to him that he, or anyone, *anyone* might think this way. He looked across the valley; soon the Indians would disappear over the crest. Gregory knew only too well what would be waiting for Barnitz and his men when he went after them.

"Ha!" Barnitz laughed. "You pretend surprise very well, Grover, but I've found you out, sir."

Gregory knew he had only a minute to make his case. "Captain Barnitz, I don't give a fig about glory, yours or Custer's. I don't. But if you ride over that ridge, you're going to find those Indians and hundreds of their Sioux and Cheyenne friends, waiting for you with guns and lances. Glory means nothing to me—Barnitz, I'm trying to save you from becoming the next William J. Fetterman!"

He struck a nerve. Every man in the army—indeed,

every man in the country—knew what had happened
to Fetterman and his eighty men at Fort Phil Kearny.
No one wanted to be heir to that distinction. Barnitz
turned in the saddle to look across the valley where
the last Indian horseman crested the ridge. Wyllyams
saw his commanding officer start to waver.

"Captain," he said, "this is our opportunity to
distinguish ourselves. Finally, after a wasted summer,
this is my chance for a commission and yours for a
brevet. The Indians are running, you can see that.
They're skedaddling—again! Grover doesn't know
what's over that hill. It's as you suspect—he's trying
to frighten you, to make you back down so Custer
can be first to strike, so Custer can be the Seventh
Cavalry's Golden Boy once again. Attack, captain!
Attack now, I say!"

Gregory looked at Wyllyams. He wanted to hit him
smack in the middle of his fleshy red face. Instead he
said, "I'd like a word of prayer with you, Sergeant."

"I'm sorry, Grover, but that's how I see it,"
Wyllyams said. "You don't have to ride with us, if your
loyalty forbids it."

Barnitz turned to his corps, fifty men on worn-out
horses. Gregory turned to them also, seeing sunburned faces that showed excitement, bloodlust, and
fear. Fear, most of all. Barnitz made up his mind.

"Sound a charge, Clark!" he said. "Make it ring!"
When the bugler lowered his horn, Barnitz raised
his sabre over his head. "Follow me, boys! Let the
savages taste our steel!"

The men of G Troop responded with a cheer and
Barnitz and Wyllyams led them forward at the gallop.

Only one mile separated the cavalrymen from the ridge where the Indians were last seen. They would reach them in a matter of minutes.

Gregory stayed back, a coldness in the pit of his stomach. He knew what was coming. Many of these men would soon die hard, agonizing deaths. Part of him, the biggest part, wanted to return to Rose Creek, take a hot bath, let Maggie fix his dinner. Let these idiots get what they deserve. Yes, he could do this, but he couldn't live with himself. His gun would be needed. Not only that, but he'd be branded a coward. He'd never work for the army again, and probably lose his hay contract to boot. No, there was only one thing to do.

"Sorry, Jeff," he said. With a heavy sigh, he urged the horse forward.

Chapter Twenty-eight

Jeff was stronger than the G Troop horses and Gregory caught up with Barnitz's company just as the first riders topped the ridge. The horse directly in front of him stepped in a prairie dog hole and stumbled, throwing its rider, a sergeant named Hodges. The horse did not fall, but continued running at top speed. Gregory stopped by the fallen man.

"Are you hurt?" he said, dismounting. Hodges lay on his back, blinking at the sun. Blood ran from his mouth. At first Gregory suspected internal injury of some kind, but then he saw Hodges had bitten his lower lip. As he pushed himself to a seated position, they began to hear the first sounds of battle: the rapid fire of repeating rifles, screams of men and horses, eagle bone whistles, the Indians' cries of *hi-hi-hi* and the chilling war whoop.

"I think I'm all right," Hodges said, getting shakily to his feet. His lips and teeth were red with blood. "My horse is gone though."

Gregory remounted and gave Hodges his hand.

"Climb up behind me," he said. "Jeff can carry both of us till we find your ride." Hodges swung up behind him and together they rode forward, cresting the hill to find themselves looking down on a sea of horror. Barnitz's fifty desperate men were up against no fewer than three hundred Cheyenne warriors in full battle regalia. The air was thick was dust and gun smoke, the whistle of Indian arrows and screams of fear and rage and pain.

Barnitz was in the middle of the action, wielding his sabre against a Cheyenne warrior. Gregory raised his carbine and shot Barnitz's opponent from the saddle. The captain turned to identify his savior and lifted his sword in salute. Beside him, Clark was using his bugle to fight off a stout warrior. It was not going to end well for the bugler, and Gregory rode to Clark's aid, with Hodges still behind him. Before they reached him, an arrow struck Clark in the shoulder, knocking him off his horse. No sooner did he get to his feet than the warrior rode down on him, leaned down, and with one powerful arm swept the tiny bugler up onto his pony and galloped away, with Clark screaming and struggling all the while. Before he could give chase, Gregory found himself in his own hand-to-hand fight with a Cheyenne warrior on a gray American horse. The Indian swung a stone war club, a blow Gregory deflected with the stock of his carbine though the blow shattered the walnut. Gregory threw the gun to the ground and prepared to defend himself best he could when a soldier on foot leapt forward and ran the warrior through with his sword, killing him instantly.

"I got him, I killed Roman Nose!" the soldier shouted gleefully, just before a bullet entered his brain, exploding his head like a melon. It was true, the warrior Gregory had been battling did resemble the famed Cheyenne war leader, but it was not he. Gregory knew Roman Nose, or Woqini, as his people called him. They had shared a meal of dog in Woqini's lodge in happier times. Then, Gregory considered him a friend.

By now, Barnitz's line was beginning to falter. The captain was at the front, fighting bravely—Wyllyams too—but the Cheyenne also fought with courage and determination and the cavalrymen were badly outnumbered. Sergeant Hamlin, he who had showed the yellow feather in action against the Indians days before, did the same again, turning his horse and making for the fort at top speed, calling for others to join him. Barnitz caught sight of this and managed to staunch an all-out rout by vowing to shoot any man who followed the coward Hamlin.

This prolonged the fight but, in the end, the outcome was unavoidable. The cavalry troops were forced to fall back to Fort Wallace, fighting every step of the way. Gregory saw Wyllyams fall from his horse, but was unable to reach him. The Indians surrounded the Englishman, who continued to battle though it was clear the end had come. Gregory could not see his final moments, so thick were the warriors around him. Once the fort was gained, the Indians retreated, taking up their dead and wounded. It was late afternoon; the fight had lasted three hours.

Seven troopers were killed, including Wyllyams and Clark, and six wounded. At sundown, Gregory rode with Barnitz and the so-called rescue detail, when no rescue was possible, only the collecting of bodies. In the red light of evening, the battle scene was hellish and starkly reminiscent of that night on Lodge Trail Ridge, a haunted place that was now called Massacre Ridge, when Gregory last rode with such a misnamed detail. The mutilation of these dead was no less inventive. Gregory found Clark's body stripped naked, his head pounded to a bloody jelly, his corpse broken and bruised, as if the bugler's killer had danced his horse over the remains.

But the worst savagery was reserved for Wyllyams. He had fought till the end, as evidenced by the scored and bloodstained ground around his body. The Englishman lay beside his butchered horse, which was stripped of tack and trappings. Wyllyams had been scalped and his skull fractured, exposing his brain above his left eye. His nose was slit and mostly removed, his throat cut, his chest cavity opened to expose his heart, his right arm cut to the bone, his legs scored from knee to hip.

"Jesus, Joseph, and Mary," Barnitz said. "Poor Wyllyams. I've never seen a thing like this, not in all my experience of war. What could inspire this . . ." He searched for a word. "This butchery?"

"The wounds have meaning," Gregory said. "Each one is a kind of calling card." He pointed to Wyllyams's arm. "That cut, that slash, is Cheyenne, means the Cut-Arm People. The nose, it shows the

Arapaho or Smeller People. And the throat, that signifies the Lakota, the Cut-Throat People." Of most interest to Gregory were the five arrows penetrating Wyllyams's body, each shot with terrific force, each striped with bands of red and yellow.

Chapter Twenty-nine

When Gregory failed to return to the camp on the Republican River, Custer sent a wagon train to Wallace for supplies and, he hoped, his wife. The wagons rolled into the fort the day after the fight, when the regiment was licking its wounds and burying its dead. Train commander Lieutenant W. W. Cooke went looking for Gregory and found him in his cabin, stretched out on his cot.

"Hello, Grover," Cooke said with a grin. He was a tall Canadian with full side whiskers that Ambrose Burnside himself would have envied. "I hear you boys had quite a fight yesterday. I'm sorry I missed it."

"Don't be," Gregory said. "I wish I'd missed it myself."

Cooke fished an envelope out of his pocket and held it out for Gregory. When he didn't take it, Cooke tossed it onto the cot. "General Custer told me to give this to you if you were still here at Wallace and Mrs. Custer wasn't. I'm afraid it won't bring you much happiness. General Custer hasn't been too happy himself lately, and I have the feeling he's been counting on you to change that."

Reluctantly, Gregory opened the envelope and read. As he expected, Custer rebuked him for not pursuing Elizabeth across the state. "If this finds you at Wallace, and Mrs. Custer is elsewhere, I now remind you of the assignment I entrusted to you. Obviously, I don't know the circumstances, but whatever they are, I expect you to complete the job you agreed to. That is: Find Mrs. Custer, wherever she is, and bring her to me. If this proves beyond your capabilities, Lieutenant Cooke is authorized to detach five men and charge them with completing your mission. Should this be necessary, your services will never again be required by me, or by any officer of the Seventh Cavalry. Also, I will instruct Captain Keogh to find another source of hay for his animals, no matter the cost."

Half smiling, Cooke pulled on his whiskers as Gregory read. "So, Grover," he said. "What's it going to be?"

Gregory looked at the peaked ceiling, at a spider at work in a corner. Custer was strong-arming him, but he did not know about Barnitz's battle with the Cheyenne and allies. If he knew how many Indians were in the area and their warlike frame of mind, surely he wouldn't want his wife traveling through their midst with only a few men to protect her. He put this to Cooke.

"I agree with you, Grover, I do, but my orders are clear," he said. "Custer is firm on this matter and I'm inclined to think he wouldn't change his mind, even if he knew what happened here yesterday. If you won't go, I'm going to cut five men loose and send them instead, all the way to Riley if that's what it takes. You need to decide and in a hurry because I'm starting back first thing tomorrow."

If he didn't agree to do Custer's demand, Gregory would lose his job at Fort Wallace and, eventually, his ranch. But Custer's orders made no sense. What if he found Elizabeth and she, knowing the danger, refused to return with him? She might, if she was as smart as he thought she was. It was what he, Jack Gregory, would advise her to do. But again, as the day before, he was not in a position to say no.

"All right, Lieutenant, I'll go. But I want those five men. Six of us might stand a chance."

Cooke considered. "That makes sense to me, Grover. And there's something else. I assume the general has already discussed this with you. At least, I hope he has. . . ." Cooke reddened and looked at the floor. Gregory thought he knew what was coming, but he wasn't about to help the tall Canuck out. "Well," Cooke said, "if you run into trouble, that is, if it should appear the savages will carry the day, that is, if Mrs. Custer is about to fall into their hands, well, if that should appear likely, General Custer expects you to . . ." Cooke hesitated, hoping Gregory would nod or otherwise show he understood. Instead, Gregory sat on the edge of his cot, regarding Cooke with a blank face.

Cooke continued in a rush, "Dammit, man, he expects you to kill her. Christ, Grover, you know how it is—shoot her in the head, make it fast, but whatever you do don't let the Indians get her."

Gregory cocked his head and looked up at Cooke. "What if Mrs. Custer doesn't want to be shot in the head? What if she'd rather take her chances with the red men? What then?"

Cooke glared at him. "Are you trying to be funny, Grover?"

Gregory shook his head. "No. She strikes me as a woman of strong opinions, and I reckon she'd have an opinion on this."

"I don't think the choice is hers, do you?"

"It should be."

"Never mind, dammit. You understand me. And there's one last thing. General Custer prefers no one else know about your mission. He has enemies, people who might try to make trouble for him. Again, you understand."

That's the only part of all this I do understand, Gregory thought.

Cooke asked for volunteers to accompany Gregory on his mystery mission and only one man came forward, a freckled Kentuckian named Reggie Simpson. When he stepped up, his mates did too, and Gregory had his crew. These included Simpson's fellow Kentuckians Jim Sprague and Tom Prince; Jacob Goldberg, the son of a New York businessman; and a Scotchman called Purves. Gregory called them to his cabin that evening, where he served coffee and store-bought gingersnaps.

"So, what's this about, Mr. Grover?" Simpson said. "Lieutenant Cooke didn't say much."

I bet he didn't, Gregory thought. "General Custer wants us to secure a valuable, uh, commodity, and bring it to him in the field. This commodity may be at Fort Hays or Harker, it may be at Fort Riley, it may be somewhere in between. Wherever it is, we're to find it and deliver it to him."

"You mean her, don't you?" Purves said. "We're talking about Mrs. Custer, right?" He spoke with a thick burr that Gregory found pleasing but could hardly understand. "Aren't we going for Goldilocks's wife?" Purves continued. "And what if she has that other woman with her—that Anna? Are we to deliver her as well?"

When Gregory did not respond, Simpson shrugged. "Custer and Cooke might think they've been cagey," he said, "but everybody knows old Cinnamon is pining for his wife. It's no secret."

"All right," Gregory said. "I won't lie to you. Yes, we're going for Mrs. Custer but her only; Miss Darrah stays where she is. This will be a dangerous job, and I thank you, each one of you, for taking it on. If we stay sharp, all six of us, and keep a keen eye out, we'll be all right. Still, maybe you'll write home tonight."

Cooke's wagons left at dawn, heading north to Custer's camp at the forks of the Republican. Gregory and his five men rode out at the same time, going east. Each carried a Spencer carbine and one hundred rounds of ammunition. In addition, the quartermaster provided rations for six days and two mules to carry the load.

They rode single file, with Gregory in the lead, traveling over hard, dry ground devoid of vegetation other than prickly pear and yucca, buffalo and grama grass. The late June sun was punishing, a white blister in the cloudless sky. Despite the heat, there was no complaining. Gregory was happy with his companions. To a man, they appeared a game lot.

After about ten miles they came to a dry stream bed and this they followed for another eight hot, dry miles when the bed began to widen and the soil underfoot grew dark and moist. Eventually they came to a small pool of cold spring water and a shady patch of good grass, where they stopped for a meal and to graze the animals.

"Any signs of Indians, Mr. Grover?" Simpson said as he bit off a piece of jerky.

Gregory shrugged. "Not much, but they're around—you can count on that."

Soon after they moved out, Gregory spotted an object on the trail ahead. He told the others to stop and rode out alone to investigate. It was a dead army horse, bearing the brand G7C, meaning it belonged to G Company, Seventh Cavalry. One of Barnitz's horses, probably stolen during the action two days before, shot in the head and stripped of all gear. Gregory examined the ground around the body, but it was hard and dry and told him nothing. He signaled to the others to join him.

"What's it mean?" Goldberg said.

Gregory wasn't sure. There were Indians ahead of

them, but he didn't know how many. He thought they were traveling fast and this horse, though she showed no obvious signs of injury, was unable to keep up. If so, why were they hurrying and where were they going? "I don't know," he said.

They camped by the Smoky Hill River, without a fire, taking turns standing guard. Goldberg, Sprague, and Prince threw down their bedrolls and fell asleep right away, but Purves and Simpson were edgy and sat up with Gregory, who took first watch. He was glad of their company. The night was bright with moonlight and all the shadows that come with it. An owl called from the cottonwoods, and Gregory felt a prickle on the back of his neck. Owls at night gave him jitters, a remnant of his time with the Indians. If you see an owl in the daytime, an aged Sioux man once told him, you or someone close to you will soon die. Many tribes thought them harbingers of death.

"Simpson," he said to the man sitting next to him, "why'd you volunteer for this job? I can't think of anything in it for you."

"Oh, there is," Simpson said. "It gets me away from Custer, for a time anyhow. I hate that son of a bitch. I've never hated an officer much as him."

"How about you, Purves?" Gregory said. "Why are you here?"

"I go where he goes," the Scotchman said with a nod toward Simpson. "Me and Reggie, we stay together."

"I see," Gregory said.

"Nothing unnatural, mind you," Purves added

quickly. "We're just mates, is all. Not like Sergeant Wyllyams, may he rest in peace."

"Wyllyams?" Gregory said. "What do you mean?"

"Well," Purves looked at Simpson, "not to speak ill of the dead, but he was a bugger, you know, a sodomite. That's why he came to America. The family found out what he was about, up in London, unnatural things with some actor fellow. The old sir was not pleased, and that's putting it mild, so Fred crossed the pond and hitched himself to the Seventh Cavalry. He thought if he could be a hero Indian-fighter and win a commission, well, maybe the old man would forgive, welcome him back into the fold. Sad, when you think about it."

"He told me something different," Gregory said, "about a kitchen maid and a baby looked just like him."

Purves shook his head. "No, I suppose he told me the truth of it, don't you? I mean, it's not the kind of story a man would tell on himself if it weren't so. It's the kind of thing that comes out when a fellow's having a come-to-Jesus moment with a mate, a fellow British Islander."

Yes, Gregory thought Purves was probably right. It explained Wyllyams's eagerness to fight the Indians.

"But me and Reg, we're not like that," Purves said again. "Just mates, us."

The owl hooted again, closer this time, and Gregory got to his feet. "Stay here," he said. "I'm going to have a look around. Keep your guns handy."

Simpson's freckled face paled in the moonlight. "Should we wake the others?" he said.

"If I'm not back in ten minutes, wake them."

Gregory took up his carbine and trotted to the rope line where the horses and the mules were alert, ears forward. He slipped the hackamore over Jeff's head, hopped up onto his back without a saddle, and kicked him forward out of the cottonwood thicket and onto the moonlit prairie. He would make a wide circle around their camp. He wasn't sure, but there was something—

He opened his eyes, blinking up at an already hot sun, rising in the east. He tried to sit, but the world slid sideways and he fell back. His head throbbed and his dry mouth tasted of metal, of copper pennies. He put his hand to his forehead and found a hot, pounding knot above his right eye. His hand came away sticky with blood. Again he tried to sit, this time rolling onto his right side and using both hands to push himself onto his hands and knees. His head swam and he vomited beef jerky and sour coffee. This continued until his stomach was empty and still he retched, so his insides felt raw and twisted. Finally he raised his head and wiped his mouth with the back of his hand. He felt like death until he saw Jeff, uninjured, cropping grass nearby and then he felt a little better. At the same time he wondered, *Why didn't they kill me, and why would they leave my horse?*

He crawled to his hat and got to his feet. The ground rocked like a boat on the ocean and it took some time to get his bearings. What had happened? The last thing he remembered was riding out of the trees and after that, nothing. He looked around, turning a complete circle, and saw nothing to provide any answers. He examined the earth, walking in the direction from which he had come, finding only Jeff's tracks. Then he broadened the search area, and yes, there they were, difficult to see, but the marks of unshod ponies, perhaps as many as six. He whistled for Jeff and he came right away, as he always did. Gregory mounted gingerly, feeling his head to be twice its normal size and heavy as a blacksmith's anvil. He rode for camp, dreading what he would find.

They had put up a good fight, this was clear from the number of spent carbine casings scattered on the ground, but Purves, Prince, Sprague, and Goldberg were dead. All had been scalped and each body shot with numerous arrows, some marked with the now-familiar bands of red and yellow. Purves seemed to have been singled out for special treatment, showing the cut throat of the Lakota people. His head had been pounded into a pudding of splintered bone and brains. He and Goldberg fought the most ferociously, as evidenced by the exploded metallic cartridges beside their bodies. Goldberg used the stock of his carbine as a club at the end, and to good effect, for the wood was bloodstained.

He found Simpson still alive, barely, sitting and leaning against a tree. His shirt front was soaked in blood. Gregory saw a wound in his throat and an arrow in his stomach. He asked for water and Gregory had to hold the canteen for him. As he drank, bloody water ran from the hole in his neck.

"They hit us maybe twenty minutes after you left." Simpson's voice was barely audible. Gregory had to lean in close to hear. "Me and Purves, we woke up Goldberg and them, but even with all of us watching and listening, we never heard them coming. Water . . ." Gregory gave him what was left in his canteen. Simpson would not live much longer.

"There was a white man with them," he said. "Dressed like the Indians, but he was white. I got a good look. He had a purple stain on his face and he was missing an ear. He was bad as the others, a right devil. I'm pretty sure I shot the son of a bitch, I think I got him."

So, Gregory thought, Cheney was riding with Pawnee Killer now. The choice may not have been voluntary, if one of his ears was off it likely wasn't, but even so he was doing the Sioux's bidding, killing his own people like a "right devil."

"The big Indian, he left me alive for you to find," Simpson said, his voice weakening. "He called you the rabbit. He said your time is soon."

* * *

Gregory stayed with the dying man, holding his hand, listening to his delirious ranting as he slipped away. Simpson regretted abandoning a woman named Hazel, and he hoped the child, a boy, brought her happiness. He called for his mother in Lexington and told her he loved her. Gregory asked for her name and how to reach her, but Simpson was too far gone to answer. He was in great pain and Gregory thought he would have to end his misery when Simpson heaved a final sigh and died.

After, Gregory sat beside the corpse and considered his next move. He tried to think coldly, dispassionately, but he burned with hatred for Pawnee Killer and Cheney, who killed these good men for no reason, and, most of all, for George Custer. It was Custer's fault these fellows were dead. Custer knew there was every chance this trek across Kansas would end in grief, and he did not care. Gregory's life, and the lives of anyone foolish enough to ride with him, meant nothing to him. He was a complete tyrant, a man who cared for nothing and no one but himself. At the moment Custer was consumed by thoughts of his wife—a woman who was far too good for him—but even that was driven by personal desire and with no concern for her welfare. George Armstrong Custer was a monster, a monster in charge of an army. How many more men and women, red and white, would die because of his hubris?

Gregory got to his feet. He went from body to body, checking each man's supplies. Goldberg's canteen was nearly full. He took this and as much food as he could carry. He would not bury these men; he didn't have time and he didn't have a shovel. Instead he saddled Jeff and rode east, toward Fort Hays. He would find Elizabeth, just as Custer wanted, but when he did the outcome would not be what Custer anticipated.

Chapter Thirty

He rode at night and lay low in the daytime,
keeping to the tree-lined streambeds and sleeping
when possible. The weather was cool and the nights
unseasonably cold. One blanket and the hate inside
him were sufficient, however, to keep him warm.
Many times he sensed that he was being watched. If
Pawnee Killer wanted to take him, what was he
waiting for?

It took five nights to cover the roughly two hundred miles that separated forts Wallace and Hays.
Though he had heard of the flood that demolished
Fort Hays, he was unprepared for the desolation
he found there. The ruins were a fantastic sight in
the darkness, a ghostly remnant of the busy garrison
he had last seen just weeks before. The frame buildings that weren't washed away had been dismantled
for use at the new post, now under construction to
the north, at the place where the railroad would
cross Big Creek. A few stone buildings remained, but
even these were uninhabitable, their earthen floors

pushed into muddy slopes against the walls. Only the flagpole, made of two long, planed pieces of wood joined together, stood fast.

He planned to ride on but something compelled him to dismount. He looped Jeff's reins loosely round the flagpole and began a solitary, moonlight tour of the ruins. It was a place he knew well, since before it was Fort Hays. Then it had been called Fort Fletcher in honor of the governor of Missouri—though he doubted the Thomas Fletcher he knew briefly during the war would be pleased that anything in Kansas bore his name—and consisted of nothing more than tents and a few dugouts. The men stationed here were charged with protecting more than one hundred miles of the Smoky Hill Trail, from Fossil Creek Station to Monument Station, but they were too few in number and too poorly supplied to do the job. The Indians attacked at will, burning stage stations, killing their keepers and stealing their livestock. The soldiers consigned to Fort Fletcher—those who did not fall victim themselves—sank into such a state of collapse and depravity, the post was abandoned and later reborn as Hays.

As Gregory passed a stone hut, maybe the remains of a warehouse, he heard a sound coming from within. He walked to the blackness where a door had been and peered in. He heard it again, an animal sound of pain. "Who is it?" he said, pulling his revolver from his belt. "Who's there?"

This time there was no doubt, a human cry responded to his call. Gregory entered, flattening himself against the wall. The hut's interior smelled of rot. There was a man sitting in a patch of moonlight, slumped against the stones. He was emaciated, and held a blood-soaked rag to his face. Gregory crossed the room to stand before the living skeleton. The man looked up at Gregory and lowered the rag. It was Louis Cheney, or what was left of him, half of his jaw shot away.

He said something, but his words were unintelligible. Gregory could see he was unarmed. Again, he tried to speak, his tone pleading. Though he couldn't make out his words, Gregory thought he knew what Cheney wanted.

"I suppose your friend Pawnee Killer left you here," Gregory said. "I'm surprised you lived this long, wound like that. Simpson thought he got you, and I guess he did."

Cheney made a guttural sound.

"Where's that God you were always gassing on about, Cheney? Maybe you two didn't have such a close connection after all. Otherwise, you wouldn't be in this pickle now, would you?"

Cheney groaned again. He was begging Gregory to kill him.

"Funny how things work out, isn't it? You didn't show any mercy to my friend Milo, did you? Or Fall Leaf or Simpson and those boys you and Pawnee Killer laid into out by Fort Wallace? And now you want me to show you mercy? Well, I'm sorry, Cheney, that's not how this ends." He shook his head. "Yes, funny, I've been planning to kill you, and now that the time's come, that's the last thing I'd do." Cheney cried out as Gregory tucked his revolver in his belt and walked to the door. Before leaving, he stopped and turned back. Cheney was trying to crawl after him, a skeletal arm raised in supplication.

"Truth is, you don't need me anyhow," Gregory said. "There's been a pack of wolves following me since Lookout Station. They'll be on you in no time. They'll show you all the mercy you deserve."

Gregory followed the well-marked trail leading to the new Fort Hays site, fourteen miles up the south fork of Big Creek. Arriving at one o'clock, he asked for and was immediately escorted to the commanding officer's quarters. Major Gibbs was wakened from a deep sleep.

"Grover?" Gibbs said thickly, tying the sash of his dressing gown. "What the hell are you doing here?"

"I'm on assignment for Custer," Gregory said. "Is Mrs. Custer here?"

"Mrs. Custer? God, no. No, I sent her and Miss Darrah to Harker. From there they were to go on to Riley. They may be there by now. I hope so anyway." He frowned as the whiskey-sleep fog began to lift. "Are you alone?"

"I am. Five men started with me, from Wallace, but they were killed by Indians and by a white man named Cheney."

"The hell. You're working for Custer? What's your mission? Was it worth the lives of five men?"

"I'm not at liberty to say, Major. I am going on, but I'd appreciate food and grain for my horse."

Gibbs regarded Gregory with bloodshot eyes. "I

don't know if I should let you pass. It's not safe. You're likely to go the way of those others. I could prevent it, you know. There are rules about such things."

"I know."

"Tell me your business."

"I can't, sir."

"Can't? Or won't?"

Gregory shrugged. "Same thing, either way."

Gibbs's eyes narrowed. "I could order your arrest, Grover. I could put you under guard and probably save your life." He waved his hand wearily. "Oh well, what the hell. Go find the quartermaster, tell him what you need." He lumbered across the room to a desk, scribbled a note, and gave it to Gregory. "Give him this. Good luck to you, Grover. You're going to need it. I'm going back to bed."

After a meal and a two-hour rest at Fort Hays, Gregory prepared to move on. He could cover another ten or fifteen miles before daylight forced him to find a place to hide. As he saddled Jeff, the quartermaster advised him to avoid Fort Harker. "They've got the cholera," he said. "Bad, what I hear. If I was you, I'd steer clear of there."

"Thanks for the warning," Gregory said. Cholera or no, he would have to put in there, to make sure Elizabeth had indeed moved on. Even so, he wasn't happy about it. Not much in this world was worse than cholera; he'd seen it before and knew what the disease could do. A stout man could be on top of the world at breakfast and dead by dinner.

He covered the sixty miles separating forts Hays

and Harker in two nights, arriving just before dawn on the morning of July 2. The post was eerily quiet, with no sentry to challenge him. The corral was empty, as was the forage yard. Gregory rode by workshops, commissary, and stables without seeing a living soul, without hearing a sound other than the *clop clop* of Jeff's hooves and the snapping of the garrison flag in the predawn wind.

The first body was by the guardhouse. It was a civilian in range clothing, facedown in the dirt, a tin cup in his hand. The second and third bodies were those of enlisted men, in various stages of undress, lying on the ground in front of a barracks. These were in a more advanced stage of decomposition. Gregory rode the length of the parade, counting seven bodies in all. These included two women, laundresses judging by their worn dresses and full-length aprons, and two children, a boy and a girl. The children's bodies had been covered with sheets weighted with bricks, but the wind had uncovered two blond heads. Birds or dogs had been feeding on the face of one of the women.

He heard a weak voice calling for help. He followed the sound the length of the parade to find a man lying on the porch of the commanding officers' quarters. This appeared to be a kind of makeshift hospital, with cots lined up in rows under the veranda. Only one bed was occupied. A man raised a bony arm as Gregory approached.

"Water," he croaked. "Please, mister, bring me some water." There was a barrel by the door. Gregory dismounted, looped Jeff's reins around the porch rail, and climbed onto the porch, his boots loud on the wooden steps. He filled a cup that lay beside the barrel and crossed the porch to the invalid, who reached for it eagerly.

"No! Don't let him drink that!" A tall man in an officer's uniform ran toward them, waving an arm. He closed the distance in four long strides, took the cup from Gregory's hand and threw its contents on the ground. Then he went to the barrel and tipped it on its side, wetting the green-painted floorboards.

"That water wasn't boiled," he said. "It was supposed to be boiled but I just discovered that was not done." He filled the cup with water from his own canteen and gave it to the man on the cot. "Here, drink this instead." He drained it and asked for more, which the officer—a surgeon, Gregory saw from his laurel wreath insignia—supplied.

"It's the cholera," he said, "people are dying by the score. It's a horror, like something from Dante. Dr. Sterner and I are trying to contain it with sanitation, but, my God, I've never seen anything kill so quickly. Poor Sterner, he lost his wife and unborn child to it." The physician looked at Gregory with weary eyes. "Who are you? Where did you come from?"

"My name is Joe Grover, I'm a scout for the Seventh Cavalry. I just arrived from Fort Hays. I'm looking for—"

"Hays, you say? How is it there? Are they afflicted?"

"Not that I saw."

"Thank God, but I fear they will be. This thing spreads like the devil. I've seen it before, during the war. It will be there and everywhere along the Smoky Hill Trail, unless we can get people to take precautions." He rubbed his eyes, then extended his hand. "Sorry. John Brewer, assistant surgeon. Hope you can stick around a bit. Grover, was it? We could use a healthy man's help."

"I'm sorry. I'm on a job. Is Mrs. Custer here?"

"No, she and that other woman, Miss Darrah, they left days ago, just as the contagion was breaking out. Poor Alice Sterner was supposed to leave with them, God rest her soul. Are you sure you can't stay just a day or two, Grover? We need help"—he extended his arm—"as you can plainly see."

Gregory looked about. "Where is everybody?"

"Dead, deserted, or evacuated, to Zarah or Larned," Brewer said. "Did you come through Ellsworth, that little town north of here? No? It's practically empty, or so I hear. There's no one around to help us, Sterner and me, and we can't keep up with care for the living, forget about burying the dead. In this heat, we need to get them in the ground fast. If you stay, Grover, I will see to it personally that you are well paid."

Gregory rubbed his jaw. "I could stick around today, I guess. But no more."

"Thank you, sir. While you're here, do not—under any circumstances—drink water that hasn't been boiled first, even if it's directly from the well. This is important, the boiling seems to purify it. Your horse can drink the water as it comes, the animals are unaffected. Now, help me carry Porter, here, to the hospital. I've finally got a bed for him. If you get any of his mess on you, wash yourself immediately with strong soap."

The dead house was a frame building just east of the hospital. It had two rooms of equal size; in normal times, one was used to hold the bodies and the other to prepare them for burial. Now both rooms were filled with corpses. Gregory counted twenty in the first and twenty-three in the second, and these numbers did not include the bodies still in the streets. The stench was powerful, and Gregory covered his nose and mouth with his neck kerchief, but it didn't help.

"I can't bury all these people, Brewer," he said. "I'd be here a week."

"A trench," the surgeon said. "Dig a trench. I'll find someone to help you."

Gregory, the hospital steward, Jenkins, and two of the few able-bodied enlisted men spent the day sweating under a hot sun, digging a pit that was twenty-five feet long, seven feet wide, and seven feet deep. The ground was hard and Gregory regretted his offer to stay. As they worked, Jenkins asked his business.

"I'm looking for a woman."

"Who isn't?"

"One particular woman. She was here. Mrs. Custer, the general's wife."

"Sure, I met her. A looker, she is, much better than

that other one, that friend of hers with the big teeth. Yeah, they got out of here just in time, just before Mrs. Sterner died. I hope they didn't get it too. I guess we would've heard."

"They left by train?"

"Yes, for Riley. Should be there by now."

Gregory leaned on his shovel. "Jenkins, if I leave my horse, will you take care of him? I mean, you personally? I'll pay you when I come back, in a few days."

Jenkins agreed eagerly. "Sure. You can count on me, Grover, I'll be here. I ain't running from no cholera."

They buried fifty bodies that day, grim work, with the corpses tumbled in, one on top of the other and covered with lime. The post chaplain read over the grave from the Seventy-ninth Psalm, and Gregory thought it a strange choice:

> *O God, the heathen are come into thine inheritance.*
> *The dead bodies of thy servants*
> *they have given to be meat unto the fowls of heaven,*
> *the flesh of thy saints unto the beasts of the earth.*
> *Their blood have they shed like water around*
>   *Jerusalem;*
> *and there was none to bury them.*

In the morning, Gregory collected his pay from Lieutenant Brewer and boarded the train for Fort Riley.

Chapter Thirty-one

"You should come with me, Liz." Anna and Elizabeth sat on the shaded platform, waiting for the train that would take Anna to St. Louis and, eventually, back to Michigan. "After all, what's keeping you here? General Sherman said it himself, you probably won't see Armstrong again this summer. Please, come with me. It's not too late."

Elizabeth looked out on the dusty, sunbaked streets of the little town that had grown up around the post. Most of the structures were only crude frames, covered with canvas. Some were made of logs scavenged from the flood-damaged ruins of old Fort Hays, with roofs of tin fashioned from fruit or vegetable cans, hammered flat and nailed to the wood. Dismal, dreary, Elizabeth was heartily sick of the scenery, heat, dust, and tedium, and tempted to do as Anna suggested. But she couldn't. God only knew what a mess Armstrong would make of things here in Kansas if left to his own devices. Done right, this war on the plains against the savages could save his career and pay dividends for the rest of their lives. Done wrong, it could be ruinous.

"I can't, Anna." Elizabeth put her arm around the other woman's shoulders, feeling the bones beneath the cloth. Anna had lost weight this summer. She had grown almost frail during her western sojourn. The experience had been a difficult one for her, and hard on their friendship too, although this had recovered somewhat once Anna announced her plans to return to the Wolverine State. She had finally given up on Tom, and this also was a relief to Elizabeth. Her brother-in-law had lost interest in Anna, it was quite clear, and Elizabeth feared her friend would embarrass herself by hanging on. "Part of me would like to go with you, Anna," she said, "but it really is impossible."

"I don't see why."

Elizabeth wasn't sure she could make Anna understand, but she wanted to try. "This is a very important time for Armstrong. If he is ever again to be a general officer, this is the time to make it happen. He's fearless, no one doubts that, and he has the potential to become a fine officer, but he has a tin ear when it comes to dealing with people, including his superiors. Sometimes his judgment is, well, flawed. He needs me."

Anna turned her head. "Maybe you give yourself too much credit, dear. You weren't with Armstrong during the war, not much anyhow, and he did quite well."

"True, but he had others looking out for him. Phil Sheridan, particularly. And beyond that, Armstrong has changed. He's had a taste of fame, and now he craves it. This is dangerous, it could make him even more reckless than he naturally is. Especially if brother Tom is there, egging him on."

"More reckless?" Anna said. "Is that even possible?"

Elizabeth smiled ruefully. "Do you know what I fear most of all?"

"That he'll be killed?"

"No. I worry that he'll do something rash or stupid that will cause the deaths of others, innocent women and children, maybe his own men. For me, that would be worse than an honorable death in battle. Far worse."

They heard a whistle, and a white plume of smoke rose in the blue sky.

"You're afraid he'll end up like Captain Fetterman?" Anna said.

"Fetterman really had no choice, from what I understand. He had to risk his troop to save those men who'd gone before him. I know some disagree, but I consider Fetterman's actions heroic. No, my fear is that Armstrong will put his men at risk for a less admirable reason."

Anna lowered her eyes. "Yes, I understand. He is capable of . . . well, he is selfish. He is, it's true. In many ways, Liz, I think you deserve better. Maybe I shouldn't say it, but that's how I feel."

Elizabeth was surprised, but chose to let it go. "Yes, well, ambition can be poison without good judgment to temper it," she said. "That's what I provide. And once an officer's reputation is tarnished, it cannot be restored. Just look at Colonel Carrington. People blame him, even more than Fetterman, for the disaster on Massacre Ridge. They say he was weak, a poor leader, that his officers did not respect him and wouldn't follow his command. His career is over. His wife, Margaret, is a fine, kind-hearted woman who is tethered for the rest of her life to a pariah. How I pity her."

The train chuffed into view and men in uniform began carrying baggage from the station house onto the platform. The two women sat silently, waiting for the inevitable parting. Elizabeth sensed that Anna was wrestling with a decision.

"Is there something, Anna?" she said. "Something you wish to tell me?"

Anna hesitated, then smiled and shook her head. "No, Liz, there's nothing."

They embraced when it came time for Anna to board, and Elizabeth was surprised to find her eyes filling with tears. Anna annoyed her, but maybe her friendship meant more than she realized.

"Well, good-bye," Anna said. "Write to me, Liz. I want to know how things are for you and Armstrong— and Tom too. It didn't work out for us, but I still care for him, you know."

"I do," Elizabeth said. "Maybe Tom will grow up some day and the two of you can try again."

Anna laughed. "Maybe, but I wouldn't bet money on it."

Elizabeth felt a crushing loneliness as the train

pulled away. With Anna gone, she was more alone than ever. There was no one she could talk to.

"Mrs. Custer."

She jumped, startled by the male voice at her shoulder. Turning, she saw Jack Gregory, hat in hand. He was freshly shaven and wore new store-bought clothes. Elizabeth had never seen him look so handsome.

"I've come a long way to find you," he said.

"Jack! Why, what a surprise—did Armstrong send you?"

"You could say that. But first things first. Have you eaten?"

"No."

"Good. Let's go to that restaurant. I'll buy you a steak."

"Oh, please. I couldn't possibly eat a steak in this heat."

"Well, you can watch me eat one." He offered his arm and together they stepped out onto the dusty street.

She had never seen a man eat so much. Gregory devoured a giant piece of beef, two wedges of corn-bread, three ears of buttered corn, potato salad with onions, green beans with bacon, a bowl of peach crumble floating in cream, and black coffee. She watched with amusement, sipping a glass of lemonade.

"Are you sure you've had enough?" she said as he dropped his napkin on the table. "Maybe another ear of corn?"

"No, I'm full up." When he realized she was teasing him, he smiled. "I guess it seems like a lot, but I've been eating nothing but elk jerky, beans, and crackers for weeks. A man builds up a hunger."

Something about the way he looked at her suggested hunger for things other than food and Elizabeth felt herself go warm. Why did this uneducated, disfigured man turn her into a blushing idiot? It was ridiculous.

"Say, do you have my wedding ring?" She had not thought of the ring for weeks, but was glad it came to her now. It offered a chance to control the conversation.

"I'm afraid I lost it," he said. "Sorry." Elizabeth thought he did not look the least bit sorry. He continued, "I'll pay to replace it, when I have the money. It didn't look like it was real expensive." Was this an insult? She frowned. "Has your husband asked about it?"

Armstrong had not asked. Indeed, as far as Elizabeth could tell, he hadn't noticed it was missing. "Yes," she said. "Yes, he has. I told him it was getting loose because I've lost weight, so I've been keeping it in my sewing basket." Why had she lied about it? Could he tell? To her annoyance, Elizabeth found herself blushing again.

Gregory stood and pulled out her chair. "I'll walk you back to the post." Again, she took his arm. It was late afternoon and shadows were growing long. The evening breeze was starting and, after the heat of the restaurant, it felt good on her perspiring skin. As they walked toward the post, he told her of all that had happened since last they saw each other. She was sad to learn of Romeo's death; not sad and unsurprised to hear of the demise of the Kemper twins. Those two, she said, were bound to come to grief. Then he told her of what had befallen Simpson, Purves, Goldberg, Sprague, and Prince.

"Your husband is responsible for their deaths," he said, feeling her stiffen beside him. "He sent us to find you and bring you to him in his camp, even though the Indians were thick in the area and had just attacked Fort Wallace in force. He knew the assignment was dangerous, and of no military value whatsoever—and I said as much—but he insisted. I blame him for the deaths of those five men, and the next time I see him I'll tell him so. Custer is a reckless, incompetent officer, and I'll say so to anyone who will listen."

He stopped and turned Elizabeth toward him, holding her by the arms. They were drawing curious stares from passersby, but he didn't care who saw them. "Elizabeth, your husband is a very dangerous man. There's something missing in him. He doesn't care about anyone but himself. There's plenty of men like him, I know that, but he commands a regiment. I see disaster ahead for him and everyone connected to him, and that includes you."

He was expressing the very fears Elizabeth had just confessed to Anna. Still, the words sounded treasonous coming from a man in Armstrong's employ. She stepped back, out of his embrace. "You're very bold to say these things to me, Mr. Gregory, and it is a mistake to do so. Armstrong is your commanding officer. It's highly inappropriate."

"I don't care, Elizabeth. I'm done with him. I won't spend one more day in his service. I'm here to warn you. That's the only reason I've come. He can court-martial me—he probably will. It doesn't matter. I'm here because I care about you. You must know that. You should leave him."

His eyes held hers and Elizabeth realized she was trembling. "I appreciate your concern," she said, turning her head, "but Armstrong Custer is my husband. I won't hear these things said of him."

"There's more." Gregory had been unsure whether to reveal this last bit, but now it seemed important she hear it. "He is unfaithful to you."

Her heart was pounding so she could barely hear her own voice. "That's ridiculous," she said at last. "You've heard stupid rumors. I've heard them too, of course I've heard them, and I don't believe a word—and neither should you. Idle gossip, spread by vicious, jealous little people. That's all it is."

Elizabeth was horrified to see pity in Gregory's pale eyes.

"No, it's more than that. I've seen things. I'm sorry, I didn't want to hurt you but you should know."

"Seen what things? You've gone this far, you must tell me."

"They say he's been with Indian women. They are brought to his tent in the evening. I haven't seen this, but I believe it's true. But this I do know: He's been with Anna."

Elizabeth thought her knees would buckle. "Oh, now I know you're lying!" She forced a laugh. "That's not possible."

"I saw them together, on Big Creek, not long after you and she arrived. Tom was with me, he saw them too. We agreed to keep quiet about it, but now I'm telling you. You deserve better. You should leave."

Elizabeth felt gut shot. The earth shifted below her feet. Those were Anna's words at the train station. She thought of Anna's strange demeanor at their parting. Was this what she was about to confess? "Why are you telling me this?" she said, and realized she was shouting. People were watching, and she managed, with great effort, to compose herself. "What do you want of me?"

"I want you to know the truth," Gregory said. "If you stay, he will continue to hurt you. I know men like him. If you were mine, I would protect you with all my soul. I would give you the respect and devotion you deserve."

She laughed, pretending a scorn she did not feel. "Well, that's something we'll never know the truth of."

He looked down at his boots, but not before she saw the damage she had done him.

Elizabeth was aware of the looks they were drawing from familiar faces. "I am finished with this conversation," she said. "I can walk myself back to my quarters. Your assistance, Mr. Gregory, is no longer needed—or wanted. Good-bye."

She turned and walked on alone. Hot tears ran down her face, and they were not only because she knew what Gregory had told her was true.

Chapter Thirty-two

He boarded the train the next day. Jack Gregory did not truly expect Elizabeth to leave Custer, but he had nourished a secret hope. He was angry with himself. Of course a woman like Elizabeth Custer would never cast her lot with a range rider like him, a harelip to boot, and he had been a fool to indulge in a dream. Even so, he thought he had been right to tell her of Custer's betrayal. He, Gregory, would never have her, but he hoped she would start again, while she was still young and beautiful.

At Fort Harker, the cholera was still in full bloom. More than one hundred soldiers and civilians had died, and every bed in the hospital was occupied. Gregory was relieved to find Jenkins in good health.

"Me and Jeff got along good," he said. "Got a soft mouth though, don't he, for a cavalry horse?"

Gregory stroked Jeff's muscular neck. "He won't take a bit, but I never needed one with him. Him and me, we understand each other." *He may be the only living creature I do understand,* he thought. "So, how much I owe you?" Jenkins gave him a price, which he paid, lightening his wallet.

"If you're getting low, Lieutenant Brewster could give you more shovel work," Jenkins said. "We got plenty of that."

Gregory had seen enough of death. He wanted only to get back to his ranch. He was away from Harker within the hour, anxious to put distance between himself and that charnel house. Jeff was happy to leave too—there was a new spring in his step.

He rode all through the night and made camp at dawn by the river. The morning was hot and sleep eluded him. Gregory's brain churned like a white-water river. There'd be trouble waiting for him at Wallace, Custer would have seen to that, but he had to go back. The army owed him money, plus he needed to get right with Keogh, he had to make sure his contract was still good. Without that, Rose Creek Ranch was finished. No, he'd go to Wallace and take his medicine. With that decided, he finally slept.

Fort Wallace was free of cholera when he arrived, but Gregory found the men there keenly aware of what was happening at Harker and anxious to avoid a similar fate. Most of the soldiers wore handkerchiefs over their noses and mouths, like an army of highwaymen. Gregory told Keogh the surgeons at Harker were ordering the men to boil water before drinking it. "They think that keeps it from spreading," he said.

"Boil the water?" Keogh said. "Who has time for that, and in this heat? No, the contagion is in the air, everyone knows that. Masks, that's the answer. You should be wearing one, Grover. So, Custer cut you loose? You all done there?"

Gregory stood before Keogh's desk with his hat in his hands. His adjutant, Captain Barnitz, sat at a desk by the open window, writing in a ledger.

"I'm not working for Custer anymore," Gregory said. "I've had my fill of him. He's dishonest. He has no regard for his men. He gets people killed."

Barnitz put down his pen and Keogh leaned back in his chair, tenting his fingers before his mouth. "I smell trouble," he said. "Did you desert? Tell me you didn't."

Gregory shrugged. "Custer might see it that way."

"How do you see it?"

"He gave me a job that was personal in nature. It was dangerous and served no military purpose. I asked five others to join me, and I wish I had not done that. They were killed by Indians, good men who died for no good reason other than to serve Custer's whim. I won't work for Custer again. He can have me court-martialed, I don't care. What I do want, Captain, is my old scouting job back and to work my ranch. I know this country better than any man and I will never duck a legitimate assignment. You know me. What do you say, Captain?"

Keogh and Barnitz exchanged a glance, then Keogh turned back to Gregory. "Does Custer know this?"

"I haven't seen him since I left his camp by McPherson."

The room went quiet. The only sounds were the *tick-tock-tick* of the Federal clock on Barnitz's desk and the rattle of weaponry from the open window as soldiers drilling on the parade shouldered their carbines.

Barnitz cleared his throat and stood. "May I speak candidly, Captain?" Keogh nodded. "I am familiar with the assignment Grover is talking about. Those men were dispatched from here at Wallace. Lieutenant Cooke carried the orders from Custer; it was while you were escorting General Hancock. I believe I told you about it, perhaps you don't remember. It was just after our fight with the Cheyenne."

Keogh, a heavy drinker, nodded. "Perhaps."

"I agree with everything Grover said. Custer's orders were inappropriate, though Cooke was cagey and I didn't learn the particulars until after Grover and his men left. Had I known, I would have intervened. Their mission was to find Mrs. Custer and bring her to Custer in his camp, even if they had to ride clean across Kansas to do it. They were to keep the assignment secret. As Grover said, it served no military objective, its only purpose was to satisfy General Custer's, uh, ardor. It's true, those men died for no reason. Custer is a perfect tyrant, a martinet. It must be said."

"Is that how it was, Grover?"

"Yes, sir."

"Did you find Mrs. Custer?"

"Yes, sir."

"And?"

"I advised her not to join her husband in the field, that it was too dangerous. I don't know what she plans to do."

Keogh released a long, low whistle. "You've kicked a tar baby, my friend, and no mistake. I wouldn't want to be the man to come between Custer and his lovely Libbie." He closed his eyes and rocked in his chair, considering. "Go to your ranch, Grover. Lie low for a bit. I won't make any promises, but I'll do what I can for you."

Chapter Thirty-three

Maggie was washing the cabin floor when Gregory arrived. She stood, wiping her hands on her apron, when he walked in.

"I didn't hear you," she said, pushing her hair away from her face. "Are you hungry? I have corn-bread and pie."

She was flushed from her exertions and the blue cotton dress she wore favored her complexion. Sometimes, at night, in the soft lamplight, with her black hair fanning her face on the pillow, Gregory could look at Maggie and still see vestiges of her loveliness. But years of hard work and one angry man had taken most of that from her. She was a good woman who deserved a man who treated her well. He was not that man, though he might have been once. Now it was over. *Why did she stay with him?* He often wondered. Her own people were done with her, and she with them. Maybe she thought no one else would have her.

"I'm not hungry," he said. "Where's Willis?"

She turned away. "The barn."

Gregory led Jeff to a rough, two-story frame building, where he found Sharp Willis sitting on a low stool, muttering to himself as he wrapped a mule's rear leg. He had his back to the door and didn't hear Gregory come in.

"Hello, Sharp."

Willis jumped to his feet, knocking over the stool. When he turned, Gregory saw an angry red mark high on his cheek. Someone had hit him, Gregory thought, and recently too.

"Joe. I didn't expect you." Willis was unshaven and tired looking.

"I'm going to be around for a while. How are things here?"

"All right. I'm getting ready to start cutting the south meadow, soon's I get this mule's foot right."

"What's wrong with her?" Gregory looked around the barn, not liking what he saw. The straw on the floor of the stalls was soiled and damp and tack that should have been cleaned, oiled, and put away was piled on the floor.

"Scratches, not real bad. I'm taking care of it."

"She wouldn't have grease-heel if you kept the straw dry. Looks like you let things get away from you, Sharp."

Willis's face reddened. "Well, it's not like I've had much help, is it? I told you we needed another man, I said it more than once. Not only that, but I was called over to the fort for scout work, what with you gone so long. A man can't be two places at once."

"Maybe you've had too much on your plate, Sharp. I reckon you have, but I'm here now and things will be different. And something else is going to be different. You're going to leave Maggie alone. That's not a suggestion."

Chapter Thirty-four

Elizabeth woke from a troubled sleep to the sound of boots on the stairs, running toward her darkened bedroom. Heart racing, she threw back the blanket and reached for the robe at the foot of the bed, but before she could put it on the door flew open and a man—Armstrong—bounded into the room. He took her in his arms, pushed her back onto the bed, and lay on top of her, kissing her and holding her so tight she could barely breathe.

"Libbie," he said, moving his mouth to her ear. "I've missed you terribly, desperately, I was a fool to let you out of my sight. When I think of what might have happened to you, alone in this country without me there to take care of you! Please, my darling girl, forgive me. Don't be angry with your foolish Bo."

She lay stiff and motionless, aware of his unwashed body and animal smell. "Armstrong, please," she said, trying to push him away, "let me breathe. You're crushing me."

He rolled to one side and she got out of bed, lighting the candle on the nightstand. She gasped at Custer's appearance in the flickering light. His clothing was dirty and he was unshaven, with at least three days' growth of beard. The skin beneath his sunken, bloodshot eyes was so dark as to appear bruised.

"My God," she said. "What has happened to you? How did you get here, to Fort Riley? I don't understand."

He leapt off the bed and began pacing. She had seen her husband in a manic state before, but never this agitated. She wrapped herself in her robe and sat in the rocking chair by the window. She would not make anything easy for him.

"I went to Wallace hoping to find you," he said. "My orders were to resupply at Sedgwick, but I went to Wallace instead, because I thought you were there." He did not look at her and did not slow his pacing. "Of course, I didn't find you, but instead a letter addressed to me, a filthy, evil letter, sent anonymously, naturally, cowards are always anonymous. The snake, whoever he is, made foul allegations about you and—I cannot bring myself to say his name, the thought of the two of you together is simply too disgusting."

"What did the letter say?" She would show him no mercy.

"It was about you and Joe Grover. The writer said he saw the two of you together here, that he had his hands on you, that you were making a public demonstration of your feelings."

He stopped before her chair. "Well? Is this true? Have you been unfaithful to me with a harelip scout?"

Elizabeth turned to the window and pushed open the curtains, admitting the blue predawn light. The morning gun boomed, overloaded with powder, shaking the walls and rattling the windows. From downstairs came the sound of breaking glass as a piece of china or pottery fell to the floor. She turned to face her husband and saw a flash of something— fear?—in his tired eyes.

"I have never been unfaithful to you," she said, "not with Joe Grover or anyone else. You, however, cannot say the same to me, can you?"

"I can. Of course I can." He dropped to one knee and reached for her hands. "Don't tell me you've started listening to those rumors about me and Indian women. It's all nonsense, you know that. We've talked about this before."

"Have you been with Anna?" she said. He started; obviously this he was not expecting. "You may as well tell me the truth."

Custer got up and resumed his pacing. "I see my friendly correspondent has been in touch with you too."

"Answer me."

Custer turned to her. "I have never been with a squaw. Never. The idea disgusts me, you must believe that."

"That's not what I asked you."

He was about to deny it, Elizabeth saw his eyes shifting as he prepared the lie, but then thought better of it. His jaw muscle tightened and he looked at her directly. "Yes. I was with Anna once, one time only, shortly after you arrived at Big Creek. Not that it matters, but it was she who pursued me, not the other way around. I was angry with you at the time. I honestly don't remember why. Libbie, it was a mistake, a terrible mistake, and we both knew it. Anna means nothing to me—I still can't believe it happened. Please, forgive me, Libbie. I will never, never do anything like that again, I promise."

Elizabeth turned her back to him to look out the window. The post was beginning to stir. The horses were being led from their stalls to the picket line for morning stable call, the blacksmith was already at his forge. At that moment she realized that despite the tedium, the harsh elements, her husband's frequent absence, the lack of female companionship, she loved her cavalry life in the West. She loved the prairie mornings, and the red evenings even more. She even loved the tension, the promise of excitement and danger that gave life to every waking moment. Elizabeth knew she could never return to Michigan, to the sewing circles, porcelain painting, and the reading groups that filled the lives of the women she knew there. No, she was an officer's wife. She had cast her lot with General George Armstrong Custer, and even though he was not, and would never be, the man she hoped him to be, this was the life she had chosen and she would make the best of it. She returned to her chair.

"Tell me how you came to be here," she said. "Do you have orders to be at Fort Riley? Did you bring the company?"

He shifted his weight from one foot to the other.
"I may have some trouble with this," he said, "but I
was in a frenzy to see you. I wouldn't let anything
stop me. Do you still love me, Libbie? Am I still your
darling boy?"

He is a child, Elizabeth thought. He is a fearless soldier, an athlete, an excellent horseman, a tireless
campaigner, but he is an infant who will never make
his way among adult men without her guidance.
"First, tell me what you've done. Tell me everything
so I can figure out a way to make it right."

It was worse than she thought. He had bolted his
command at Fort Wallace, leaving Major Joel Elliott
in charge, taking seventy-five men and the regiment's best horses. They first stopped at Fort Hays,
then moved on to Fort Harker, in all covering a
distance of one hundred fifty miles in fifty-five
hours. Along the way, Custer stopped a wagon train
commanded by Captain Frederick Benteen and
helped himself, over Benteen's objections, to supplies. This, Elizabeth knew, would be a problem.
Benteen was her husband's sworn enemy and hers as
well, once telling a mutual acquaintance, who passed
it along to Elizabeth, that "Mrs. Custer was a shrill
harridan whose heart would get lost in a thimble." At
Castle Rock Station, Custer stopped and searched
two mail coaches—an illegal act—looking for a letter
from her.

We'll say he was looking for orders, Elizabeth thought.
"Go on."

By the second day, Custer's men were tiring and
some were falling behind. He sent a sergeant and six

men back to bring up stragglers, and they were struck by a party of fifty or sixty Cheyenne warriors. The survivors found Custer at Downer's Station, where he was having a meal. They told him two men had been killed.

"What did you do?" Elizabeth said.

Custer shrugged. "I finished my meal and went on."

Of course, Elizabeth thought. "Were there troops at Downer's Station?"

"A detachment of infantry."

Good, she thought. *We'll say you left them to recover the stragglers, who stopped without authority.* "Continue."

Custer arrived at Harker at two a.m. and woke Colonel Smith, commanding officer, and told him he was taking the train to Riley to see his wife. "He was half asleep," Custer said. "And here I am. He sends you his regards, by the way."

Again, he dropped to his knees and took her hands. "Do you still love me, Libbie? Am I still your beloved Bo? Your Autie?" He gave her his boyish smile.

She waited a full minute before answering. She wanted to be sure her meaning was absolutely clear. "I will remain with you as your wife," she said, "and aid your career—our career—in any way I can. I promise to maintain the appearance of a doting and dutiful wife. In return, you must agree to let me guide your political and professional decision-making. This will be our private arrangement, no one need know of it. But I will never share your bed or lie with you again. I will take my pleasure as I wish, with whomever I wish, and you are free to do the same, as long as you are discreet. If you ever humiliate me again, I will leave you in a heartbeat."

His mouth fell open and he rocked back on his heels. "You can't mean this," he said.

She smiled sweetly. "Defy me and find out."

Chapter Thirty-five

The fall of 1867 was unusually wet, as the spring had been. For weeks on end, the sun hid behind dark, lowering clouds and it rained most every day. The Smoky Hill River ran high, and even tributaries that were normally dry filled with water that reached knee-deep. Roads turned to mud slicks and structures finished with sod roofs became so saturated they dripped water even when it wasn't raining. The first snow of the season came early, in late October, and the long winter that followed was marked by a series of blizzards. Everyone said that the winter of 1867–68 was the worst in memory. Gregory, though, thought it less than the winter before, the time of his long, murderously cold ride from Fort Phil Kearny to Horseshoe Station.

He and Willis struggled to complete the harvest. They took advantage of the few dry days and started cutting early in the morning, soon as the dew was off, and continued until it was too dark to see. They worked together long hours, cutting and drying and stacking, day after day, seldom speaking. When it came time to deliver the hay to the fort, Willis went alone because Keogh had advised Gregory to keep his head down. As he expected, Custer had asked for his arrest.

"He was angry, no doubt, but Custer's got his own troubles now," Keogh said. He had ridden out to Rose Creek one August morning to deliver the news. "He's been court-martialed, charged with abandoning his command, mistreating deserters, and other things. The way I hear it, it was all about his wife. You know what this was about?"

So, Gregory thought, the letter he left for Custer at Fort Wallace had had the desired effect. "No idea," he said.

"He'll be tried next month at Leavenworth," Keogh said. "I'm going to forget about that arrest business. He will too, with all the trouble he's got. Even so, I'd lay low a while longer if I was you. Anyhow, Grover, there won't be much scouting work, now that winter's coming. Stay here at Rose Creek. I'll vouch for you when the time comes."

Gregory spent the fall painting the cabin and weatherproofing it before the cold descended. The two-room house was not well made to begin with, with just single board walls that he'd planned to improve before Custer called him away. Now he saw the house was in even worse condition than he thought. It must have been miserable during the hot, windy summer, though Maggie had not complained. In some places the boards had been sprung, forced apart by the dry wind. He covered these openings with tar paper on the outside and building paper on the inside. These fixes weren't pretty, but they would keep the weather out till he had time to do better. When it wasn't raining, he and Willis worked outside, repairing fencing and leaks in the roof of the barn.

After the first snowfall in October, Gregory had plenty of time for thinking and he thought often of Elizabeth. He tried to forget her but it was her face he saw in the evenings as he and Maggie sat by the fire, waiting out the storms. During one of his trips to Wallace, Willis learned that Custer had been found guilty on all charges—the two most serious being abandonment of his command and ordering the execution of deserters on the spot, without trial—and sentenced to a year's suspension of rank, command, and pay. He and Elizabeth had retreated to Fort Leavenworth after the court-martial and eventually would return to Michigan. The charges against Custer were serious indeed, and while courts-martial were fairly routine, even for officers, it was unusual for one of Custer's standing and reputation to actually be tried. *How did Elizabeth feel about her husband's fall from grace?* Gregory wondered. *Would this, on top of his betrayal, convince her to break free of him, or did she still feel obliged to honor her commitment?* Throughout the dark, brutal winter, Gregory found it difficult to think of anything else.

On the coldest nights Willis stayed with them. They did not have enough fuel to warm the cabin and his shanty too. On these occasions, they passed the hours sleeping, repairing tack, or playing cards. Maggie sewed, cooked, and cleaned. Always, Willis's eyes followed her about the room, hungrily, furtively. For her part, Maggie seemed oblivious to him. On Christmas Eve, tensions spilled into the open.

Ten inches of snow fell that day and the thermometer hanging outside the cabin door dropped to twenty degrees below zero. Despite the cold, Maggie ventured to the barn that morning and killed two chickens, even though that left her with only three laying hens to last until spring. After cleaning and quartering them, she stewed the meat in a slow pot with onions, carrots, and flour dumplings. A savory aroma filled the cabin, reminding Gregory of warm, happy holidays on the Cass County farm, with his parents and sisters, when he and the girls would find an orange in their stocking on Christmas morning. No fruit had ever tasted so sweet, not before and not after.

For dessert, Maggie made a mince pie, a treat she had not made before, using a recipe of beef hearts, dried apples, raisins, and sweetened vinegar. She served the pastry warm, in bowls of thick, sweetened cream. Gregory was impressed.

"Where'd you learn to make this, Maggie?" he said, lifting a dripping spoonful to his mouth.

She responded with a smile. Because of the damage to the left side of her face, Maggie's smile was a sneer. She knew this, and did not smile often. "Last fall, when I was at the soldier fort, I asked the lady at the store what her man ate for Christmas. I told her I wanted to make it for you, and she told me. She was not afraid to be kind to a Sioux woman."

After dinner Gregory opened a bottle of whiskey. He and Willis drank most of it as they sat by the fire. Willis watched Maggie as she cleaned plates and pots in a tub of soapy water.

"I wish it was me instead of you," he said.

"What?" Gregory was nodding in his chair.

"I said I wish it was me Maggie cared about instead of you. Why do women always want the man who doesn't give a damn and not the one who does? Why is that?"

Across the room, Maggie froze, then continued her washing.

"I don't know, Willis, and I don't want to talk about it either." In fact, Gregory had often asked himself the same thing, first about Rose Reynolds and lately about Elizabeth Custer. "Now isn't a good time."

"It never will be a good time." He slurred his words. "I keep waiting for things to change, but I don't think they're going to. She goes to all this trouble for you, and what do you care? Maggie's just a whore to you, an Injun whore with an ugly scar on her face who cooks your meals and cleans your house and washes your clothes. She's more to me, Maggie is—or she would be, if she'd have me."

He kept his eyes on Maggie as he said this but she gave no sign of hearing.

"Shut up, Willis," Gregory said. "You're drunk."

Willis belched. "I'm done with this, Grover," he said. "Done with you, done with scouting for the army, done with all this shit. I'm leaving soon's the weather warms up. Come spring, you'll see the last of ole Sharp Willis. Maybe then she'll be sorry. Maybe then . . ." He drifted into mumbling and was soon asleep, with his head back and his mouth open.

Maggie kept her back to Gregory and did not look up from the tub. Uncomfortable, not knowing what to say, he got unsteadily to his feet, walked to the wall peg where his heavy buffalo overcoat was hanging and put it on, along with his muffler and gloves.

"I'm going to check on the animals," he said. Maggie did not respond.

The wind was blowing snow and Gregory had to fight his way to the barn. He could not see far and he'd had enough to drink that he was glad of the rope Maggie had strung from the house to the barn. A man could lose his life making the short journey in the midst of a Dakota blizzard. Inside, Jeff greeted him with a nicker. The barn was warm and free of drafts, a sounder structure than the house. The horses, mules and chickens were comfortable. Not for the first time, Gregory thought if construction quality was the indicator, Rose Creek's previous owner valued animals more than people. He put a match to the lamp, walked to Jeff's stall and gave him a carrot from his pocket. "Merry Christmas," he said. Gregory settled on a pile of sweet-smelling hay, pulled one of Jeff's blankets over him and dozed. He'd stay with the creatures till the trouble at the house blew over.

When he returned, Willis was still snoring in the chair, a line of drool running from his mouth to his shoulder. In the room where they slept, Maggie was in her bed, her face to the wall. He could not tell if she was awake. Gregory undressed, climbed into his bed with his face to the window and dreamed he had lost his way in a blinding blizzard.

Chapter Thirty-six

As it turned out, Willis did not leave in the spring. There was plenty of work at the ranch, and Gregory bumped his pay to thirty-five dollars a week. No mention was ever made of his drunken Christmas Eve declaration.

The Indian season promised to be another hot one. One sunny April morning, Captain Henry Bankhead, Fifth Infantry, Myles Keogh's successor as commander at Fort Wallace, rode out to Rose Creek to ask Gregory to return as chief scout. Bankhead was accompanied by Quartermaster Lieutenant Frederick Beecher.

"I need you, Grover," Bankhead said. "Oh, I know you're worried about that Custer business." He waved his hand dismissively. "Keogh told me about it and I say forget it. I don't see Custer coming back here anytime soon, and anyhow with all his problems he's probably forgotten all about you. Custer, they went easy on him, in my opinion. Anyone else would have been dishonorably discharged."

Gregory wanted to know if Elizabeth was still with him but he was unsure how to put the question. "Any idea when, that is, if he returns, will he have his usual troop with him? His brother, Mrs. Custer, so on?"

"I don't know," Bankhead said, "and I don't care. What I do care about is getting you back to Fort Wallace. We're going to have big trouble with the Sioux and Cheyenne this spring and summer. It's already started. Oh, I know the Indians signed those treaties last fall, but like Sherman says, that's just senseless twaddle. The redskins aren't going to do the things they agreed to. The Cheyenne aren't going to live on the reservation and become Christian farmers, and the Sioux aren't going to stop fighting the railroads and wagon roads and military and do all their hunting south of the Arkansas River. Everybody knows that. Grover, I need you, I need to know where they are and what they're up to. Keogh says you're the best there is."

Gregory looked around at his place. The winter had been hard on it. The west-facing side of his cabin showed more tarpaper than board and the outbuildings had suffered too. Even the sturdy barn could use a new roof. Gregory wanted to spend more time here this summer, he wanted to rebuild the house and maybe plant some trees, even flowers. Someday, Rose Creek Ranch would be the kind of place a cultivated woman, a woman like Elizabeth or Rose, could call home, a place to raise children. Jack Gregory had always had his dreams, and lately, during this last long, cold winter, these had taken on a different flavor. Never before had they included flowers and children.

Bankhead saw him waver. "Grover, I'll pay you one hundred dollars a week."

This was more than Gregory could turn away. He'd need the cash to improve the ranch, and it had been some time since he'd sent money to his mother and the girls.

The two men shook hands. "When do you want me?" Gregory said.

"Now. Just last week they attacked a railroad camp east of here, burned some cars, tore down telegraph poles, rode down on the boys and scared the crap out of everybody. The next day they stole sixteen mules from one of our contractors. So, like I said, it's starting. Come to the fort tomorrow, get with Beecher here. He'll set you up."

Beecher said, "I've already got some men lined up to work with you. A team of ace scouts, you might say."

Gregory shook his head. "I pick my own team. Otherwise, I won't take the job." He didn't want to be saddled with a West Point shavetail or moon-faced mollycoddle looking to make a name for himself. Those were the kind got you killed.

"Yes, yes, I understand," Beecher said with a smile. "Just come meet these fellows, that's all I ask. Will you?"

"All right," Gregory said. "I'll meet them. But if I don't like them, they're gone."

As Gregory and Willis watched the two men ride back to the fort, Gregory felt the hair lift on the back of his neck. Suddenly, unexpectedly, he had a bad feeling.

"Looks like you'll be busy again this summer," Willis said. "Don't worry. I'll take care of things here." He looked at Maggie, hanging wash on a line. "You can count on me, Joe."

Inside the quartermaster's office, two men were waiting. It was high noon and the windowless room was hot and airless. "Come in, Grover, come in," Beecher said. "Meet the boys. This is Cephas Parr and that long drink of water is Frank Espey."

Gregory offered his hand to Parr, a short, stocky man with lively blue eyes and skin burned dark as an African by the sun. "Hello, Black Bill," Gregory said. "It's been a long time. How've you been keeping?"

Parr winked as they shook hands. "Hanging on, like a hair on a biscuit."

Then Gregory turned to Espey, tall and razor-thin. "Frank. You and Bill been working together all this time?"

"We have, ever since that job we all did together up north, at Fort Halleck," Espey said. "What was that fellow's name? The half-breed they sent us out for? The one whose head came off?"

"Stubbs," Gregory said. "The woman-killer John Stubbs. The hangman misjudged his weight."

"You aren't lying," Parr said with a deep, rumbling laugh. "Stubbs. Oh well, son of a bitch got what was coming to him. And Fall Leaf, what's that old redskin up to?"

"Fall Leaf is dead. Last summer, we were working together at the time."

"I am truly sorry to hear it. He was a good man."

Beecher walked around his desk and took a seat. For the first time, Gregory noticed the lieutenant had a bad limp. "That went well," he said. "Now that you boys are reacquainted, let's get down to business." He motioned for Gregory to take the empty chair next to Parr's. "General Philip Sheridan has made me coordinator of Indian intelligence and mediation. It is a distinct honor and I am eager to reward his confidence in me." Beecher rubbed his hands together and smiled at his guests. "This will be my first chance to work with scouts in the field, and I don't mind telling you, I am ready for it. A man gets his fill of sitting behind a desk pushing papers around. God knows, I have."

Beecher was of medium size, with short dark hair, large blue eyes and a sweet smile that would have looked more natural on a woman. Gregory hoped the young lieutenant was up to the work. Enthusiasm and naiveté were a bad combination in an officer. He and Parr exchanged glances.

"So, you men are to keep tabs on the Indians," Beecher said, "spy on them, if you will. Also, we are authorized to negotiate with them, if necessary. As you know, there's already been trouble east of here, just last week, and the general anticipates another hot summer. He's impatient. General Sheridan wants an end to this nonsense, an end to their continuing interference with the railroad's progress. You men were chosen for your scouting abilities, obviously, and because you know the Indians' languages. Grover, you have Sioux and Cheyenne, correct? Espey and Parr, you have those and Arapahoe as well, yes? Good. You—that is, we—will visit the chiefs in their lodges, eat with them, trade with them, win their trust. We—that is, I—will report directly to Sheridan himself. I'm sure I don't have to tell you what a golden opportunity this is to advance ourselves in our chosen careers."

Beecher beamed at the three weathered men sitting before him. "Well?" he said, looking from one to the next, "any questions? Grover, what about your man, Sharp Willis? Would he be able to join us, if needed?"

"I need him at the ranch just now, but I might free him up in a couple weeks."

Parr cleared his throat. "Lieutenant, I think you should know this may not be easy as you think. That is, we won't be riding into a Sioux village and asking the head man what his intentions are. I mean to say, feelings have soured, what with that Hancock business last summer. We used to be on good terms with the chiefs, me and Espey, but that string is pretty well played out."

Beecher regarded Parr with raised eyebrows. "Well, you'll just have to restring it. As I said, we've been given an opportunity and we damn well will make the best of it! Meet me here tomorrow morning at six o'clock. Be ready to ride."

Outside, the three scouts stood at the rope line where their horses were tethered. "Well, Jack," Espey said with a grin, "or do I call you Joe? No matter. Me, you, and Black Bill, we've been in more tight corners than a feather duster and this looks to be another. I only hope it ends better than last time." He held up his left hand, with two fingers ending in shiny knobs at the middle knuckle.

"I told you not to go in there, Frank," Gregory said. "I told you she was crazy. You should've listened to me."

Parr and Espey took the northern route, exploring the country to the north and west, along the North, Arikaree, and south forks of the Republican River. Gregory and Beecher started south, riding Walnut Creek to the west of Fort Zarah. This would not yield any result, as Gregory told Beecher from the get-go. "The Indians are north and east of here," he said. "We'll find their villages on Beaver Creek, and if not there, then along the Solomon."

But Beecher insisted they begin their scout on the southerly route. "General Sheridan suggested we search there first and that's what we'll do."

Gregory knew Sheridan's suggestion was just that, and that a man of Sheridan's experience would yield to a scout's superior knowledge, but Beecher was adamant. It was clear to Gregory that pleasing the general was Beecher's main purpose. Despite his obvious ambition, as they went deeper into the field, and more days passed, Gregory began to suspect that Beecher was more than a little afraid of actually finding what they were looking for. One morning, after ten days of hot, dry riding through the sandy soil of the Arkansas River lowlands, Gregory decided it was time for word of prayer with the young officer.

"So, how is it our paths never crossed before this, Lieutenant?" he said, warming to his subject. "How long have you been at Wallace?" They were sitting on the ground drinking coffee. Gregory was so confident there were no Indians about, he built a fire.

"I arrived in October of sixty-six," Beecher said. "We've traveled in different circles, you and I. While you were out scouting, I was planning and supervising the construction of the post, parts of it anyhow. I laid out the cemetery."

Gregory was unsurprised. Beecher had the chill of the grave about him.

"How'd you get that hitch in your step, if you don't mind me asking?"

"No, I don't mind." Beecher touched his right knee. "Chancellorsville. A shell shattered my kneecap, the pain was incredible. They sent me home to heal, and then, when I was almost recovered, I had more bad luck. Broke it again in a carriage accident. That was pretty much the end of my war. I don't suppose the leg will ever be much good, but at least I've still got it. Plenty of men can't say that."

"You're not lying. So, what's your experience been here in Kansas? Much truck with Indians so far?"

Beecher fixed his blue eyes on Gregory. "You think I haven't? Why do you ask?"

Gregory smiled. "No reason, Lieutenant. I'm just talking, no need to get your back up." Beecher was a good man, Gregory could see that, and he was intelligent too, but Lieutenant Frederick Beecher was not lucky. He had an air, a kind of pall, hanging over him that told Gregory the young officer would not live long. It was the kind of thing a man came to recognize when he'd seen it often enough, and Beecher had it in spades. Gregory saw it that first day in the quartermaster's office and he reckoned Parr and Espey saw it too. No doubt that was the reason Gregory got stuck riding with him.

"No, you're right, Grover." Beecher looked down at his coffee. "I don't have any real experience. Well, I saw some action last summer, fifty or sixty Sioux attacked us when we were quarrying stone for the hospital. Two of my men were killed. I haven't been back to the quarry since." He swallowed a mouthful of coffee. "I'll be honest with you, Grover, the sight of those painted savages riding down on us, the war whoops and the eagle bone whistles, well . . . I was more frightened that day than at any time during the war, including the day my knee was ruined. That's the reason I asked to work with you scouts, though I didn't think General Sheridan would approve it. I need to overcome this fear. I must conquer it before it becomes paralyzing."

Gregory suspected something like this, and he admired Beecher for admitting to it. "It's nothing to be ashamed of," Gregory said. "The Sioux and Cheyenne are worth being scared of. Only an idiot would think different."

"Thank you, Grover, but you know what I mean."

Gregory threw his unfinished coffee into the fire. It was time to move on. "One thing that might help is to get to know the Indians better, Lieutenant. They aren't all bloodthirsty killers. Not all of them. It might help to remember that most of the time, Indians are just as scared of us as we are of them."

Beecher nodded. "That's probably true."

"And if it's Indians we're looking for," Gregory continued, "we're in the wrong place. We need to go north to Beaver Creek. The Cheyenne will be there, an old chief I used to know called Turkey Leg. I used to live with his people during my trading days. He's there every year at this time, there or a bit south, at the head of the Solomon River. We're wasting our time here."

Beecher also threw his coffee into the fire, sending up a thin line of white smoke. "All right, Grover. We'll go into Fort Zarah today and I'll send a telegram to Wallace. I'll let General Sheridan know where we're headed."

"And while you're at it, Lieutenant, ask them to send a man to Rose Creek. I want Willis along when we go into that village. Tell him to meet me at Turkey Leg's camp on Beaver Creek in three days. He'll know the place."

Chapter Thirty-seven

"Are you sure about this?" Sharp Willis trained his field glasses on the peaceful camp of Turkey Leg's Ohmeseheso Cheyenne. "We haven't seen Old Leg for years, no telling how he's feeling about white men these days. And there's Sioux in Leg's camp." Willis handed the glasses to Gregory. "Look down to the west end. Those are Sioux lodges. Are you sure you want to go in there?"

It was dusk. They could smell the smoke from the squaws' cook fires, hear the cries of their children and the barking of the dogs. The scouts had waited for the cover of darkness to approach the camp. Looking through the glasses Gregory saw the Sioux lodges, and a number of small wickiups too. These were troubling, indicating the presence of young, single men.

"Want has nothing to do with it," he said. "It's our job. We'll wait till it's full dark and quiet"—although both knew an Indian camp was never truly quiet—"and go in from that end." He pointed to the north part of the village, which was closest to Turkey Leg's lodge, recognizable because it was brightly painted. Gregory was counting on a Cheyenne custom that held any man who was once a friend was safe in another man's lodge, even if the friendship had gone sour. He hoped Turkey Leg was old-fashioned enough to cling to that tradition. Their lives depended on it.

"Tell me again, what is it Beecher wants us to do?" Willis said.

"Talk Leg into moving his people to the reservation. When he won't do that, and we know he won't, then we need to get him to rein in his bucks, make them stop killing settlers." In recent weeks Indians had launched a series of raids through the Saline and Solomon valleys, attacking stagecoaches, killing woodcutters and hay contractors, stealing livestock and killing and scalping civilians.

"General Sheridan is at the end of his patience," Beecher told Gregory and Sharp that morning. "He will tolerate no more interference." The officer had planned to enter the Cheyenne village with his scouts, but had fallen ill the night before. He would remain in their camp, too weak to ride. Gregory thought that was just as well. "Tell Turkey Leg if he agrees to move to the reservation, he will be saving the lives of many of his people," Beecher said. "Make sure he understands that."

Gregory and Willis had tethered their horses in a stand of trees by the water and hunkered down in the tall grass, waiting for the darkest part of the night. At about three o'clock, clouds covered the moon. A pirate moon. Gregory smiled, remembering nights on the Cass County farm when he would scare America Alice and Sarah with stories of violent, treasure-hunting buccaneers who sailed under a pirate moon, looking for little girls to steal and hold for ransom on their filthy vessels.

The two scouts crept around to the north side of the sleeping village, trying to stay downwind of the horses. They were lucky that three teenage boys were guarding the pony herd. Gregory thought they looked to be about the same age as Little Wolf, the boy from Turkey Leg's camp that Higgins tortured and killed. These boys had no doubt been his friends. Watching them wrestling and skylarking, Gregory remembered something his granddaddy used to say: one boy would give you good help, two boys were fair help and three boys were no help at all. This was true of Indian boys too. They were ignoring the ponies they were supposed to be watching. Gregory slipped up behind one, grabbed him by the arm, and put a knife to his throat. Willis did the same with another, leaving one youth free to run. He froze, poised to take flight.

"Listen to me." Gregory spoke to the boy in Cheyenne. "We are here to talk to Turkey Leg. Nothing more. If the three of you stay quiet, we won't hurt you. We won't hurt anyone. Sound the alarm, and all of you will die, these first and then you."

"Let's just kill 'em now," Willis said, also in Cheyenne. "Let's not risk it."

"There, do you see what you're up against? What is your name, son?"

"Tall Bull."

"Tall Bull, this is a fine name for a boy. Do you want to live to be a mighty warrior, worthy of that name?"

The lad nodded.

"Then take us to Old Leg's lodge and you shall. I promise, no one will be hurt. All right, Tall Bull?"

Again, he nodded.

"Start walking. We'll keep your friends close, just for good measure."

They moved through the village and the dogs that crowded around did not snarl and bark, for they knew the boys. When they came to the chief's lodge, Gregory and Willis entered through the door, boldly. The young men ran on silent feet back to the pony herd, keen to avoid censure.

The interior of the tepee was hot and dark, other than a silver circle of moonlight shining through the smoke hole, and smelled like an old man. Turkey Leg did not wake when they entered, but his aged woman did. She sat up, holding a robe to her bony chest, and shook her sleeping husband.

"Why do you wake me?" the chief said, rolling onto his back. "I was having a sweet dream." When he saw Gregory and Willis, he sat up in his robes. "What is this? Medicine Jack and Willis, my old friends? What brings you to my lodge in the dead of the night?"

"Thank you, Turkey Leg," Gregory said. The Cheyenne thought he had special medicine because he once cured a girl's fever by giving her quinine he happened to have in his kit, left over from his own bout with breakbone fever. "We have come with a message from the Long Knives. May we sit?"

"Yes, yes, sit. Woman, make peppermint tea. We will smoke."

With a complaint, the old woman crawled from her bed while Turkey Leg took up his sandstone pipe and filled the bowl with tobacco. Gregory would have preferred to dispense with this time-consuming business, to deliver Beecher's message and leave before the village began to stir, but a smoke was required. Finally, Old Leg was ready to hear their business.

"The trouble along the Saline and Solomon rivers must stop," Gregory said. "White men have been killed, railroad cars burned, women violated, horses stolen. The bluecoat soldiers sent us here to ask the great chief Turkey Leg to control his young men, to make them stop their raids on the white people. If he does not do this, his people will come to harm. The bluecoat soldiers are out of patience."

The lodge was filling with smoke, from the tobacco and from the old woman's fire. Turkey Leg pulled on his pipe, regarding Gregory through narrowed eyes. "My young men did not do these things you speak of. My young men have been hunting to feed the people. They do not violate women."

Gregory believed warriors from Turkey Leg's village had participated in these raids. They and some Lakota fighters had been recognized. Whether Old Leg sent them, or even knew of their involvement, was another question. Either way, he had to rein them in or his people would suffer. Generals Sheridan and Sherman would put an end to the Indian problem, even if it meant mass extermination. Gregory knew this.

"My friend," he said, "this is a desperate time. Many lives, including those of your women and children, hang in the balance. The best thing is to move your people to the reservation. If you won't do that, talk to your young fighting men. Tell them if they don't stop, they will bring death to their women and children and old people. It brings me no happiness to say these things, my friend, but they are true. Please do the right thing to save your people."

Turkey Leg nodded, his eyes on the fire. "I appreciate the courage of my friends Medicine Jack and Willis to come here and say this. The truth is, I do not control the young men as I once did. They are angry and not always respectful as they should be. I will do what I can, but I do not promise. Now let us drink our peppermint tea."

As the old woman served them they heard the sound of riders entering the village on running horses and voices raised in excitement. Turkey Leg put his tea aside and got to his feet. "I must find out what has happened. My friends will stay here."

Gregory and Willis looked at each other as the old man left the lodge. His woman followed.

"This is bad," Willis said. His face was wet with sweat. "We need to get out of here." He crawled to the rear of the lodge and lifted the hide from the ground. "We need to go now, while we still can."

"We won't make it out of the village without Old Leg's protection," Gregory said. "We'll wait till he comes back."

Realizing the truth of this, Willis crawled back to sit with Gregory on the floor of the lodge. They heard many excited male voices, but could not understand what was being said. Finally Turkey Leg and his woman returned. The chief's face was grim.

"Warriors from my village have had a fight with the Long Knives on the Saline River. Six of our men were killed and feelings are high. Also, it is known that you are here. The boys told their fathers." The angry voices grew louder, a sound like the buzzing of thousands of blueflies. Turkey Leg looked anxiously to the door. "My friends must leave at once. I will protect you, but you leave now."

They had no choice but to follow the old chief out of the lodge where they were met with jeers and scores of angry faces. Turkey Leg shouted them down.

"These two men are my friends. They had nothing to do with the fighting on the Saline River. I gave them my word they could leave the village unharmed. Do not bring dishonor on me. Let them leave."

Gregory's eyes met those of Tall Bull in the crowd. The boy smiled and drew his finger across his throat. "Start walking," Gregory said to Willis, "and don't stop, no matter what happens. Don't look back."

They walked shoulder-to-shoulder through the crowd, which was growing larger and louder in the dawn light. Snarling dogs snapped at their legs. Willis drew back his leg and kicked one in the stomach, sending it flying. At the same time, some object, perhaps a thrown stone, struck Gregory in the back. He heard Turkey Leg cry out—"Stop! None of that!"—and kept walking. His heart boomed and blood roared in his ears. He looked at Willis and saw his face shining with sweat. Gregory balled his fists. At any moment, he expected the feel the thud of an arrow in his back, or the hot explosion of a bullet. But these did not come. He and Willis kept walking, unmolested, and the voices grew less, the dogs running alongside them fell away. They broke into a run. At last, after what seemed like hours, they saw their horses, still tethered where they left them. Never had Jack Gregory been so glad to hear Jeff's welcoming nicker. Gregory laughed with relief as he and Willis mounted and kicked the horses into a gallop, anxious to put distance between themselves and the village. After about a mile they slowed to a walk.

"Damn, I thought sure we were dead men," Willis said. "I won't be doing any more work for Lieutenant Beecher, if you don't mind."

Gregory turned in the saddle and looked behind them. He didn't see any followers, but he wasn't sure they were out of the woods. They rode in silence for another two miles. Gregory did not blame Willis for quitting Beecher; in fact, he was thinking he'd had enough too. The money was good, but keeping his hair on was more important. They rode for an hour, then riders appeared on the trail ahead, silhouetted against the rising sun. Gregory and Willis reined in and the horsemen came forward. Sioux, by the look of them. Gregory counted seven, four men and three boys.

There was no mistaking the tallest rider. He had broad, powerful shoulders, and he wore a white man's hat with a single feather affixed at the crown.

He rode the fine black stallion. The Sioux and his companions stopped, blocking the trail.

"Hello, Rabbit," Pawnee Killer said. "I thought it was you, back in the village, but I wasn't sure. You left in such a hurry." He smiled. "Tall Bull, are these the white men you told me about?"

The boy rode at his side. "Yes, father."

"So now it comes to an end," Pawnee Killer said. "It has been a long time coming. Before I kill you, I want to know, how is Mapiya? Does she please you, Rabbit?"

Gregory did not answer.

"I said, does she please you?" Pawnee Killer stopped smiling. "Her face is not so beautiful now, is it? It's your fault, you know that, Rabbit? It's because of you I held the glowing ember to her cheek, even though it hurt me to do so. Mapiya spat on my devotion. You should not have laid with her, but you did, and then you were stuck with her, when her beauty was gone. And now I will punish you, Rabbit, as I punished her."

Willis looked at Gregory. "Maggie? Is he talking about Maggie?"

Gregory did not respond, did not take his eyes from Pawnee Killer's face. The Sioux drew a long gun from a sheath attached to his saddle and pointed it at Gregory's chest. They were no more than twenty feet apart. Gregory knew he was about to die, but there was a chance he could finish Pawnee Killer first. A slim chance. His hand moved toward the revolver he wore in his belt.

"Do you think you can shoot me, Rabbit?" The

Indian smiled. "Go ahead, try it." His companions had their weapons drawn and pointed at Gregory.

"I'm going to go for him," Gregory said in English to Willis. "Do what you can to save yourself."

"We're dead," Willis said. "Both of us."

Gregory made his move, but not fast enough. Pawnee Killer fired first, striking Gregory in the chest. The impact knocked him from the saddle and onto his back, where he lay staring at the sky. There was pain, a burning, crushing pain like nothing he had known before, but he fought it down, using his mind to trick his body, as he had first done as a friendless boy. He was oblivious of things around him as gradually the pain receded, until he felt no hurt, no fear, only the deepest calm and relaxation. Every worry, every fear, he had ever carried flowed out of his body, like warm water, into the soil beneath him. He was completely at peace, for the first time in his life.

Closing his eyes, he saw faces floating up through the darkness: his mother, America Alice, and Sarah. He saw ghosts: his father, surrounded by flames. William Quantrill, with his watchful, hooded eyes. Milo Mendoza, with his lazy smile like butter sliding off a hot biscuit. Fall Leaf, small and capable. He saw the women he had loved: the blue eyes and freckled nose of Rose Reynolds. Elizabeth Custer's intelligent face and bright smile. He saw Mapiya, achingly beautiful as she was when he so recklessly pursued her, not as she was after Pawnee Killer was finished with her. Even so, he kept her and protected her and therefore did not castigate himself. If he was the cause of Mapiya's disfigurement, he had paid his debt to her also. He provided for her, as he had provided for his mother and sisters. He had done his duty, as his father had told him to do, and he had no regrets.

A shadow blocked the warmth of the sun and Gregory opened his eyes. Jeff stood over him, his head lowered so it was just inches above Gregory's. He tried to touch the familiar face, but his arms would not move. Jeff leaned in closer, his breath hot on Jack's face. Jack Gregory's last view of this world was his own image reflected in the horse's bottomless brown eyes.

Chapter Thirty-eight

Sharp Willis's account of Gregory's death was met with disbelief. Captain Bankhead, in particular, was suspicious that the Indians would kill Jack Gregory then ride away, leaving Willis unharmed. He and Beecher questioned Willis on his return to Fort Wallace.

"It's strange, I know it, but that's how it happened," Willis said. Bankhead listened, rubbing his chin whiskers. "Joe knew the Indian that shot him—a big Sioux, with a white man's hat, he called Joe a rabbit. I don't know what it was between them, but when he was done with Joe, he was done with me too. He, that Indian, said he wanted me to take a message to Maggie, the woman Joe lived with."

"Well, you're a lucky man, Willis, I'll say that for you. Guess you'll be taking over that hay ranch too, now Joe's gone."

"Yes, sir, I plan to. I believe that's what Joe would want."

Lieutenant Beecher said, "Actually, Willis, I know

something about that. I thought I'd ride out to Rose Creek later today."

"What for?"

"It's a business matter. Something Joe asked me to see to before this last scout."

Willis shrugged. "Suit yourself."

When he arrived at the ranch, Maggie was sitting in a rocker on the porch, peeling potatoes from a pot she held in her lap. He dismounted and stood in the yard. "You hear about Joe?" he said.

"I heard."

"I wanted to tell you myself, but Bankhead kept me at the fort, asking questions. He seems to think Joe's death was peculiar."

"I think it too."

"Well, maybe it was, but that's how it happened." He smiled and walked toward her. "It's just us now, Maggie. You and me. Or should I call you Mapiya? That Indian who killed Joe, he knew you."

She set the pot down on the floor and put one hand in the pocket she wore at her waist. "Don't come closer," she said.

Willis stopped and extended his arm. "Don't be like that. We're a team, Maggie. We'll be good together. I don't know what it was between you and Joe, but I'll treat you better than he ever did. You'll see. I'll treat you right. I've wanted you for a long time. You know that."

Maggie stood. "Yes, I know that. That's why you killed him. You think with Jack gone you can have me and his ranch, but it's not going to be that way. It will never be that way."

"What?" Willis's smile evaporated. "No, Maggie, no. I never, I swear it. I didn't kill him, it was that Indian, like I said, the big Sioux with the hat. He had a message for—"

Maggie pulled a revolver from the pocket and put a bullet in Willis's left eye. She stood over him and watched him die, then took him by the heels and dragged his body to a hole that was waiting in her vegetable garden behind the house. She buried him beneath the place she had cleared for corn.

Later that day, Lieutenant Beecher rode out to the ranch with a deed, a document he had witnessed and signed, in which Jack Gregory left Rose Creek and all his holdings to the Indian woman, Maggie. Beecher found her sitting in a rocker in a patch of late afternoon sun, peeling potatoes for her dinner.

The first book in the trailblazing trilogy of the brave men and women who risked their lives to build a future in the untamed heart of the American frontier . . .

FRONTIER

Fort Kearny, Nebraska, is the gateway to the west for a new breed of pioneers. Civil War veterans and widows, card sharps and Indian agents, felonious bankers, dreamers, and drifters—they arrive every day hoping to forge their destiny. Colonel Henry B. Carrington, commander of the Eighteenth U.S. Infantry, is assigned the unenviable task of securing a trio of forts in the dangerous Dakota Territory.

At his command is a rising young officer Mark Reynolds and his spirited bride, Rose, who longs for danger and excitement. Her wish comes true when army scout Jack Gregory learns that three native tribes are preparing to defend their land against Carrington's troops. As the drums of war intensify, Gregory takes off on a deadly mission of his own, Rose risks temptation in the arms of an army surgeon, and Carrington faces the greatest foe he has ever known . . .

Now, four days before Christmas, at a lonely outpost in the foothills of the Bighorn Mountains, they must make one final stand. The fate of a nation—and the history of America— will be written in blood.

FRONTIER

by S. K. Salzer

On sale now, wherever Pinnacle Books are sold.

Prologue

Fort Phil Kearny, Dakota Territory
December 21, 1866

Rose heard the wagons before she saw them. She began to shiver as the rattle and clang of the iron wheels grew louder. Sounds moved with deceptive clarity through the thin mountain air, especially after sundown, but the wagons were close, only minutes away.

The other women gathered with their children in one of the officers' cabins but Rose waited with the men by the quartermaster's gate, its heavy plank doors open wide to receive the approaching train. They stood without speaking, eyes fixed on the ribbon of road that trailed off into the gathering darkness. The last of the light clung to the snowfields atop the Bighorn Mountains, a gleam in the distance.

"Riders on the Bighorn Road!"

The sentry's voice boomed from the blockhouse moments before Captain Tenodor Ten Eyck and his advance guard emerged on horseback from the gloom followed by foot soldiers lumbering like bears in their heavy greatcoats. As the first wagon rolled through the gate, Rose saw that its bed was filled with naked corpses, stacked head to heel like firewood. Here a stiffened arm protruded, there a leg, white as Italian marble. A second wagon, bearing the same cargo, was close behind.

Colonel Carrington stepped forward, stopping the wagons. "How many, Captain?" he said.

"Forty-nine, sir." Ten Eyck dismounted and walked to Carrington's side. "Including Fetterman and Brown."

"And Grummond? What of him?"

Ten Eyck shook his head. "I don't know, Colonel. It was too dark to continue the search. I fear they've all gone up."

Carrington turned on him, his face contorted with rage. "Dammit, man, you should have taken the road. You might have been there in time, you might have saved them!"

Ten Eyck's one good eye opened wide. "Colonel, I needed the higher ground—surely you see that. My men were on foot, most of them, naturally I was concerned that if I marched them through that defile—"

Carrington raised his hand. "We'll discuss this later. Now is not the time." He pulled himself to his full height of five feet four inches, though in Rose's eyes he had never looked smaller. "Take these men to the hospital. If there isn't enough room, use one of the unfinished buildings. It doesn't matter which."

Ten Eyck gave the order and slowly men came forward to unload the bodies of fellows they had laughed and worked with just hours before in the unusually warm December sun. Rose gasped when she recognized the seal-gray head of Private Thomas Burke sticking from the pile of corpses in the second wagon. Just that morning he had repaired a leak in her cabin roof. Now his eyes were bloody cavities and a stick protruded from his open mouth.

She turned her head and wrapped her woolen shawl more tightly around her shoulders. At that moment there was only one place she wanted to be, only one person she wanted to be with. She ran to the stables where the men who rode with Ten Eyck were tending to the mules and horses. Immediately she saw him, Daniel Dixon, taller than the others, unsaddling his horse in the flickering lamplight.

"Daniel!"

He turned when she called and walked forward to meet her, taking her hands in his. They were warm, despite the frigid night air.

"What happened out there?" she said. "What did you see?"

The surgeon's angular face was half in shadow. "They're dead," he said. "Fetterman and every man who rode with him. Eighty-one men, dead."

Rose shook her head, unwilling to believe this, fearing what it meant for her, for each one of them. She saw her dream of a free, unbound life in the West, a life big as a man's, go all to smash.

"You can't be sure of that," she said. "Grummond and his troop are still out—they might come in yet."

The scout, Gregory, joined them, his cigarette glowing orange in the darkness. "Don't kid yourself, Mrs. Reynolds," he said. "They're dead all right— that or worse." To be taken alive was the greatest fear of every man, woman, and child at the post, the stuff of nightmares. "I'll warrant Red Cloud and his warriors intend to finish us off too, at first light most likely. We'd best be ready."

"How could this happen?" Rose said. Tears stung her windburned face. "How could things go so wrong?"

Dixon laughed bitterly. "It's been nothing but wrong, from the very beginning. Fetterman, Grummond, all those men were doomed from the start, from the day the U.S. Army sent us up here. The army used them, used Carrington, used all of us. Sure, the colonel will take the blame for what happened today, but the die was cast long ago. Tecumseh Sherman and his friends sacrificed those men to the god of railroads and commerce. The world will see that someday."

Gregory grunted and ground his cigarette into the frozen mud with his boot. "Well, I pray you live to see that day, Doc," he said. "But right now I wouldn't lay odds on it."

Chapter One

Fort Stephen Watts Kearney, Nebraska
May 16, 1866

Lieutenant General William Tecumseh Sherman arrived in the middle of a windstorm that unsettled the animals, dirtied the freshly cleaned clothes hanging along laundresses' row, and sent the giant garrison flag to snapping like pistol shots. Women in poke bonnets, children in homemade clothing, shopkeepers in aprons, Mexican teamsters, blanket-wrapped Indians, all gathered shoulder to shoulder on the boardwalk to catch a glimpse of the great national hero and commander of all western armies. Sherman's visit was a major event for the soldiers of the Eighteenth U.S. Infantry, many of whom had soldiered with "Uncle Billy'" in Georgia, the Carolinas, and earlier, at Kennesaw Mountain, Peach Tree Creek, and Jonesboro. They loved him as one of their own. No matter how big he got, Bill Sherman never would be too big to sit down with a private and eat a plate of beans at his campfire.

Rose Reynolds tried to find a place in the crowd. Colonel Henry B. Carrington and the post's commanding officer, Lieutenant Colonel Henry Wessells, stood before rows of sweating soldiers under the hard blue sky as Sherman's custom-made Dougherty ambulance rolled through the gate at the head of a column that included an overdue supply train. When it stopped the men shouldered their muskets with a rattling clatter.

A gust of gritty wind grabbed Sherman's hat as he stepped from the vehicle and sent it bouncing along the ground. A junior officer bolted after it.

"Welcome to Fort Stephen Watts Kearney, General," Wessells said, stepping forward. "It's good to see you again."

Sherman returned Wessells's salute without enthusiasm and surveyed his surroundings. A bustling and important place during the gold rush years, Fort Kearney by 1866 had taken on an aspect of decay. The original sod structures listed to one side like drunkards and even the newer wooden buildings were poorly constructed and in need of paint. The surrounding landscape, in all directions and far as the eye could see, was brown and sere, bare of any hint of green other than the rows of transplanted cottonwoods bordering the parade lawn.

"My God, Wessells," Sherman said. "This place hasn't improved any. What a country." He accepted his hat from the breathless junior officer and slapped it against his leg, releasing a cloud of dust.

"It has potential, sir," Wessells said. He was a small

man with bushy white hair and a well-trimmed beard. "All it needs is more water and good society."

Sherman laughed without humor. "That's all Hell needs," he said. "Damn place is rotting away. I'm inclined to let it go to the prairie dogs."

Rose could not believe her ears. To her Fort Kearney was a magic place, far better than her native St. Louis with its dirty streets and foul smells. Kearney was the gateway to an exotic new world of beauty and strangeness and danger. New characters arrived every afternoon at two o'clock, when the heavy Concords of the Western Stage Company rumbled in for a team of fresh horses and to discharge passengers connecting with the Holladay lines out of Missouri. Rose entertained herself by inventing histories for weary, rumpled travelers from faraway places like Denver and Salt Lake City as they climbed down from the carriage and stood blinking in the white sun. Men in suits with waistcoats and top hats were card sharps, Indian agents, or felonious bankers absconding with suitcases full of cash; ladies in fitted traveling suits were heiresses fleeing abusive husbands, actresses bound for San Francisco, or women of opportunity returning to their families for a chance at redemption. The fort's dusty streets teemed with Indians, scouts, and malodorous mountain men with hair-raising stories of wild red warriors, giant flesh-eating bears, and arctic cold. Let all this go to the prairie dogs? Surely not.

Sherman moved up the line of men standing at attention, pausing occasionally to greet one he recognized, before he and the high-ranking officers retreated to headquarters for a cool drink and cigars. The ladies of the post hurried back to their quarters to make themselves beautiful for the soiree Wessells would host that evening. It would be a gala occasion, one of the few the families of the Eighteenth Infantry had enjoyed since arriving at Fort Kearney the winter before. The air was charged with excitement, not only because tonight there would be dancing and good food—thanks to an uncharacteristic spasm of generosity from the post sutler—but because Sherman's presence meant the long weeks of waiting finally were coming to an end. Soon their great adventure would get under way.

Officers blacked their boots and unpacked epaulettes, plumed hats, and dress coats while their wives pressed the wrinkles from their finest gowns. Rose took extra care, choosing first an Irish poplin of London smoke, with a mandarin collar and leg-o'-mutton sleeves, then putting it aside in favor of a Nile green silk that she knew showed her blue eyes to advantage. Her auburn hair she carefully arranged in a braided coil at the nape of her neck covered with a snood of sparkling silver thread. She was pleased with the effect despite the dusting of freckles across the bridge of her nose. She hoped Mark would not notice. He was critical of women who "used a hardship posting as an excuse to let themselves go," as he put it, but try as she might there was no escaping the Nebraska sun.

"Our mission must be very important," she said, admiring her husband standing shirtless at his shaving stand. "Why else would General Sherman come all this way from St. Louis?"

Mark turned his head to shave his clean jawline. "It's probably to do with Carrington," he said. "Maybe he's changed his mind about giving Carrington the command. One can only hope. Why couldn't he have chosen Custer? Or Hancock even?"

"You should be careful what you say, Mark. Someone may hear you." Rose could not judge Carrington's military competence but he seemed to be a kind and intelligent man, and she liked his wife, Margaret, very much. You could tell a lot about a man by the woman he chose.

"Carrington's in completely over his head and everyone knows it," Mark said, wiping traces of lather from his face with a hand towel on which Rose had embroidered his initials. "Someone should have the courage to say it."

As he finished dressing, Rose sat on their bed and watched Sam Curry and the regimental band cross the parade ground to Wessells's quarters, the shining brasses reflecting the last of the golden light. Carrington had insisted the band accompany the regiment on its march up the Bozeman to the Powder River country, despite the disapproval of his officers, who called it frivolous and an unnecessary complication. Carrington said music was good for morale and would not change his mind.

Only officers and their wives were invited to the reception. Sherman stood in the parlor greeting them as they passed by in a line. Rose was a little disappointed at his appearance. Rail thin with uncombed red hair, a rumpled suit, and dusty shoes, Sherman looked more like a farmer than one of history's giants.

By the time Rose and Mark neared him, Sherman was showing signs of impatience, shifting his weight from one foot to the other. But when Rose reached him his hawk-like face brightened. He took her hand and raised it to his lips, giving her a roguish smile. Rose was surprised. The Savior of the Union was a flirt.

"General Sherman," Carrington said, "may I present Lieutenant Mark Reynolds? He's with us on detached service from the Second Cavalry. He'll have our boys riding like Tartars before we reach Laramie."

Sherman pulled his eyes away from Rose and returned Mark's salute. "Yes, Reynolds, I've heard good things about you from my brother-in-law, General Ewing. Tom says you were a great help to him in Kansas City with that border business. He says you've got a good head on your shoulders, studied law at the University of Michigan, I understand."

They were interrupted by a howl. Carrington's striker, Seamus O'Reilly, pulled two boys by their ears from their hiding place under the stairs and hotfooted them out the kitchen door. One of the boys was Carrington's older son, Harry, the other his friend Bill Kellogg. The two had stolen into Wessells's house to get a glimpse of Sherman.

Later there was dancing, and Sherman repeatedly sought Rose as a partner. He was not a good dancer and smelled of cigars but Mark was proud of the general's attentions to his young wife and encouraged her to accept his offers. At midnight when the party ended Mark escorted her back to their quarters, then left to join the other officers for cards.

Rose lay in bed, anticipating the grand adventure that lay ahead, too excited to sleep. A bar of silver moonlight fell across the foot of her bed, and a cool night wind played with the calico curtains at the open window. Bored with life in St. Louis, sick to death of needlework, painting flowers on porcelain vases, and other polite ladies' pastimes, she had long dreamed of this. What was waiting for them in the Powder River country? What would a truly wild Indian look like? She had never seen one, only the hang-around-the-forts who struck her as sad and ashamed. How would the mountains be, and the rivers of snowmelt that ran so fast and cold your hands froze when you held the giant fish that swam in them? She had long heard of these things and soon she would know them firsthand. Finally, she thought, her life would truly begin. She was still awake when Mark, smelling of whiskey and cigar smoke, climbed into bed beside her and, to her disappointment, immediately fell asleep. She was still awake when the sentry called the hour at three. At last she drifted off only to be jolted awake by the boom of the morning gun and the sound of breaking glass. Overloaded with powder, it shook the walls and broke her parlor window.

Chapter Two

Rose's head pounded like a blacksmith's hammer and she burned with fever. She tried to hide her illness from Mark, hoping it would pass. Many officers had disagreed with Sherman's decision to let wives and children accompany the regiment on campaign. A sick wife, she knew, would be a nuisance to her husband, so she stayed in the wagon—an army ambulance refitted and made comfortable for long-distance travel—all morning with a wet cloth over her eyes. When they stopped at midday she told her black serving woman to make her excuses.

"Tell them I'm resting, Jerusha. Tell them I couldn't sleep because of all the noise."

A week had passed since they left Fort Kearney. A pack of wolves had shadowed the column since the Old California Crossing, galloping alongside at a distance by day and fighting ferociously among themselves at night. Then at midnight they were startled by a new sound, a deep, rumbling thunder that seemed to flow from the very earth, rocking the wagons and frightening the horses. Women clutched their children and wide-eyed soldiers stumbled from their tents asking each other what was happening and getting no answers. All was confusion until chief scout Jim Bridger climbed up on a wagon tongue to announce the rumble and thunder were not caused by an earthquake but by stampeding buffalo, miles away. The campers returned to an uneasy sleep.

Rose's misery worsened as the day progressed. Every jolt of the wheels along the washboard road sent a rocket of pain up her spine. In her desperation she discovered the pain was less if she traveled on her hands and knees and Mark found her in this position during a rest stop. He went looking for Sam Horton, the regiment's chief surgeon, and found him eating gingersnaps with Margaret Carrington and her two sons, twelve-year-old Harry and Jimmy, age six.

"Excuse me, Doctor," Mark said, tipping his hat to Margaret, "but I wonder if you might look in on Rose? I think she has a fever."

The plump surgeon got to his feet, brushing crumbs from his immaculate serge trousers. "Of course, Reynolds. I'll fetch my bag."

By the time he got there Margaret was already inside the ambulance sitting by the younger woman's side. Rose lay on her back, a patchwork quilt drawn up to her chin. Despite the day's heat, she was shivering.

"It's nothing," she said, looking at Horton with red-rimmed eyes. "I told Mark not to bother you."

"Shush now." The physician sat on the bed, measured her pulse at the wrist, then placed the smaller end of a belled, wooden stethoscope against her chest and leaned forward, listening with closed eyes.

"Too fast," he said. "When did this start, my dear?"

"This morning."

"Do you have pain? Headache? Stomach? Any bowel complaint?"

"I do have a headache."

Horton took from his bag two glass vials—one blue, the other green—and gave them to Jerusha.

"This is quinine," he said, raising the blue vial. "Give her a teaspoonful every hour. This"—he raised the green—"is laudanum. Of this, four drops every three hours. No more, no less. Keep her comfortable and make sure she takes plenty of water. Do you understand?"

Jerusha nodded and Horton turned back to his patient. "We'll be at Fort Sedgwick this evening," he said. "I can do more for you there."

Margaret insisted on traveling in Rose's ambulance the rest of the afternoon. Despite the difference in their ages, the two women had grown close during the long weeks at Fort Kearney. Rose was intelligent and, like Margaret, fond of reading novels. Most important, she did not try to impress or curry favor with her the way some of the other officers' wives did.

At sundown the column pulled into Fort Sedgwick, a run-down collection of sod buildings on the South Platte River. Mark carried Rose to the blockhouse, hastily converted by the post quartermaster into a lady's sickroom. Harry Carrington watched the effortless way he carried her, even as he climbed the steps of the blockhouse, as if she weighed no more than a box of groceries. Harry wished he was strong enough to carry her like that.

Semiconscious, Rose was only vaguely aware of being moved, of being placed on a mattress that smelled of fresh hay and pipe tobacco. Her bones ached and her clothes were wet with sweat. She drifted into a troubled sleep, at times struggling for consciousness like a drowning swimmer fighting for the surface. Always she failed, sinking back into the dark and suffocating depths. The fever burned inside her, taking her to a different time and place. She saw her favorite brother, Tim, killed in '61 at Wilson's Creek, Missouri, standing alone on a hillside of glowing autumn colors. She tried to call out to him, to warn him of the Rebel sharpshooter in the tree, but could not make a sound. He jumped when the bullet hit him, then lay crumpled and still on the ground. As his spirit left his body, floating heavenward, she heard the faint and distant sound of a string orchestra, a soothing melody of violins and violoncello, clarinets and flute, French horns and tuba, alternating with a chorus of booming male voices, then the crunch of wheels on gravel.

A gentle hand lifted her head and pressed a cool

cup of water, sweet as wine, to her lips. She opened her eyes expecting to see Mark but instead found herself looking into the eyes of a stranger. They were alone in the red twilight.

"Who are you?" Her voice was raspy and hardly recognizable as her own. "Where is Doctor Horton? Where is my husband?"

She tried to sit, but the stranger pushed her back on the pillow. The room spun and she thought she would be sick.

"You're a strong woman, Mrs. Reynolds," he said. "Stronger than most. I believe you've turned the corner today. You had me worried."

Exhausted, Rose closed her eyes and dreamed of water. She woke to a sunlit room and ravenous hunger. As if on cue, Jerusha appeared carrying an ironstone mug.

"Beef broth," she said, setting the mug on a table beside the bed. "Can you take it?"

Rose nodded and Jerusha helped her sit, packing pillows behind her back. Dizzy and light-headed, Rose sipped the broth slowly till the mug was half-empty. Feeling better, she took stock of her surroundings.

The room was small, with a canvas roof and log walls chinked with plaster. A cannon stood in the center, its muzzle pointed toward a small square window. The wall on either side was pierced with a double row of loopholes, one high and the other low, for standing and kneeling gunmen. Jerusha's straw-tick mattress was on the floor.

The broth was hot and salty and sat heavily in her empty stomach. Still, she forced herself to finish it. Outside, the soldiers began to drill. Rose heard an officer's staccato commands, the rattle of muskets, the rhythmic pounding of boots on the ground.

"Good morning, ladies." A tall man appeared at the open door wearing a surgeon's linen jacket over civilian clothing. "May I come in?"

The door was low and he had to stoop to enter. His face was familiar and strange at the same time, like someone she had met in a dream. He smiled as he walked to her bedside.

"It's good to see you eating," he said. "You're feeling better then?"

"Yes, much better, though there's a dreadful ringing in my ears."

"An effect of the quinine. It will pass."

He had a pleasing voice, deep and resonant, with a barely discernable Southern drawl. Rose found it relaxing and wanted him to keep on talking. Instead he gave her his hand. "We haven't met properly. My name is Daniel Dixon. I'm the post surgeon. I've been looking after you the last few days—with Jerusha's most competent help."

Rose understood he wanted her to know any delicate issues had been addressed by another female.

"You've had dengue fever. Breakbone fever, the men call it. You had an additional complication"—he paused—"which resulted in some blood loss, but this resolved naturally. You shouldn't have any future problems."

Again, she understood what he was saying. "I'm afraid I've been a burden to you," she said. "I'm sorry. Why did Sam Horton fob me off on you? Where is he?"

Dixon dropped his eyes and sat in the chair by her bed. "First things first," he said. "I need to check your pulse." He held a finger to her wrist. "A bit fast yet, but steady and strong. Much better than before."

"Where is Doctor Horton?" she said. "Where is my husband?"

He looked uncomfortable and Rose knew something was wrong. "Lieutenant Reynolds asked me to give you this before he left." Dixon removed an envelope from his jacket pocket and, when she did not take it, put it on the table beside the mug. A fat fly crawled along the mug's lip.

"What do you mean, before he left?" Rose said. "What are you talking about?"

"Your husband's regiment moved out two days ago," he said. The words struck her like a blow to the stomach. She closed her eyes, remembering the music she heard at the height of her fever—the strings and the brasses—and realized it was no dream but the regiment's musical farewell to Fort Sedgwick. Mark was gone. He had abandoned her in this savage place.

She could not look at Dixon. She did not want to see the pity in his eyes.

"You need rest," he said. "I'll look in on you later."

Only after he left did Rose reach for Mark's letter, opening it with a shaking hand.

June 3, 1866
Fort Sedgwick, Dakota Territory

My dearest Rose,

It pains me to leave you in this hole but the regiment moves in the morning and I must go with it. Carrington depends on me and I cannot hang back. Sam Horton assures me you will recover soon, otherwise I would not go.

Of course you must come on soon as you can. I've left Spicer behind to assist you. Carrington says a supply train bound for Fort Laramie will arrive at Sedgwick within the week. If you're strong enough— and I trust you will be—you and Spicer must join it. Naturally your little outfit will travel much faster than ours. We should be reunited at Laramie, if not before, as you may well overtake us.

Be brave, my darling, and know that I await you with anxious arms.

Your loving husband, Mark

P.S. The Indians have been quiet this spring between Sedgwick and Laramie so you need have no concerns on that score.

She looked up to see Jerusha in the doorway. Rose thought she saw a smile, unpleasant, like a sneer, but immediately Jerusha's face became the usual mask, revealing nothing.

"Please heat some water, Jerusha," Rose said. "I want to wash my hair."

When she was gone Rose gave way to tears. How

could he do this? Surely Colonel Carrington would
have allowed Mark to stay if he had requested it.
Doubt, like a rat, nibbled a tunnel into her thoughts.
She remembered her oldest brother's words on the
night she and Mark announced their engagement.
"What's the hurry, Rose?" Joe had said. "Get to know
him better. If he loves you, he'll wait."

Joe disliked—or distrusted—Mark for some reason
Rose did not understand. She sensed it. But nothing Joe could say would have made a difference, for
she was determined to marry Mark Reynolds and she
would not wait. No man had ever affected her as
Mark did. From the moment he walked through the
doors of the Blair house that warm June night he
had occupied her every thought. Her love for him
was like a cavalry guidon, flying full in the wind, or
a church bell ringing clear and true. He felt the
same—she was sure of it. A woman knows these
things. So why had he left her? She must have been
disgusting in her illness; sweaty, foul-smelling, not
feminine. She should never have let him see her that
way. It was her own fault; she should have kept him
away.

Jerusha returned with a porcelain basin and a
steaming bucket of water. On shaking legs Rose
climbed from the bed to the chair, took the empty
basin in her lap, and leaned over it as Jerusha
poured the hot water over her head. Though her
scalp was tender from fever, she did not complain as
Jerusha vigorously lathered her hair with a lemon-
scented soap, the fragrance Mark liked. Yes, she had

been disgusting. The suds floating in the basin were brown in color, as if they had just bathed an animal.

That night Rose lay sleepless in her bed, thoughts churning and boiling inside her skull. She imagined the challenges ahead and knew she had to make herself strong to survive them. The frontier was no place for womanly softness.

At midnight, with the moon shining through the square cannon portal and Jerusha asleep on her straw mattress, Rose pulled a pair of scissors from her sewing basket. Then, without a mirror and without lighting a candle, she took the scissors to her hair, so thick it was still damp from washing, and cropped it till it was short as a boy's, watching her hair fall like long satin ribbons to the puncheon floor.